THE BREAKING POINT

The eighth in the Mayflower
series of *Denise Robins* Romances

The Breaking Point

Denise Robins

Mayflower

Granada Publishing Limited
Published in 1973 by Mayflower Books Ltd
Frogmore, St Albans, Herts AL2 2NF
Reprinted 1973, 1975

First published in Great Britain by
Hutchinson & Co Ltd 1956
Made and printed in Great Britain by
Cox & Wyman Ltd
London, Reading and Fakenham
Set in Intertype Times

THE first rays of the rising sun touched the leaves of the walnut tree which stood in the middle of the lawn facing the old farmhouse, and turned them to gold.

The birds sang, life on the farm stirred and became suddenly noisy. Tranquillity no longer brooded over Queen's Lacey. There was a violent clucking and scurrying of hens as they were let out of their houses; a lowing of the cows in the big clean cattle sheds which had the white starkness and brightness of hospital wards. The owners of Queen's Lacey – one of the most progressive and prosperous farms in the district – and one of the oldest, for it dated back to 1658 – were never behind the times. Mrs. Chalford and her three sons had recently added another hundred head to an already big herd of Friesian cattle, making two hundred and fifty in all. And the latest system of keeping poultry had been installed over a year ago. They were justifiably proud of their chickens – one thousand of them, being the special joy and concern of the youngest brother, Pip.

Now a short stocky Estonian boy – one of the ten farm hands who were employed by the Chalfords – came out of his cottage and made his way to the milking shed. He had married an English girl and settled in Buckinghamshire. They occupied one of the cottages on the estate. Another Estonian looked after the chickens; the rest of the staff were English. The Estonians were popular. They worked hard and were polite, charming boys.

The farmhouse looked its best at this early hour with the first rays of the sun slanting on the fine old roof and mellowed bricks. It was a long low building with character and must have been built originally for a nobleman of the Stuart period, later given over to farmers. It had a certain importance and dignity. Over the stone portico there grew a mature and lovely wistaria which was not yet in bloom. In June the flowers hung like great branches of pale violet grapes interspersed with feathery fronds of green.

As a rule nobody in the family stirred before seven o'clock

when Mrs. Chalford had her tea. But she and her sons rarely failed to meet for eight o'clock breakfast in the big dining-room which contained some of the best walnut panelling in the county.

But this morning, Anthony Chalford, who was twenty-eight and the eldest of the sons, had already bathed and dressed before the Austrian cook, Mitza, started to make tea.

Tony had had a bad night. He, who as a rule slept the clock round, had found himself waking up, looking at his watch to see what time it was; hearing the distant chimes of a church clock; putting his light on, reading last night's paper, trying to sleep again. Always with his thoughts returning to Christa – and what he was going to tell his mother about her in the morning.

At a quarter to seven, wearing corduroy slacks and a blue fisherman's jersey, with silk scarf tucked into the neck, he walked next door into the room where his brother Richard slept.

Richard was twenty-six. He shared the family passion for Queen's Lacey and for farming, but he was less of a materialist than the rest of them. He liked literature and music and was the only one who ever opened any of the books in the small library which had belonged to their father. Old Chalford had died when the three boys were still at Shrewsbury.

Mrs. Chalford was the farmer. She had neither time nor taste for the arts, although when she was not busying herself with the farm she did some beautiful tapestry work.

Each of the boys had known that it was her wish that they should make farming their career. Tony had taken his degree in law. Having got his degree, however, he decided to use his brains and knowledge entirely on his mother's behalf and had become the business manager and financier of the family; the one to whom they all turned in problems of stocks and shares. Tony believed that the present prosperity was due to his brains and management. He did little, really, on the farm itself and left it to Richard who had taken a degree in agriculture at Cambridge like Francis – the younger brother – more generally known in the family as 'Pip'.

All three boys, once they left the Varsity, returned to Queen's Lacey; each to take his part in the running of the farm, without question.

Julia Chalford had brought them up with this sole idea. She had taken it for granted that it was what they would do. She was a dominant, strong-minded woman and her control had always been absolute. Quite apart from the fact that they adored the place and wanted to return to it, there was the money angle. Their father had left them little except Queen's Lacey and the land that went with it. Every penny was in the hands of their mother. She, herself, had been the daughter of rich landowners in Kent and come to Queen's Lacey as a bride forty years ago.

She was generous to her sons within limits. She saw to it that the money never went out of her control. The boys received a generous income, but it was an income that could be stopped at any moment that Julia Chalford liked to raise a finger.

So far everything had worked well and peacefully. Richard, at one time, had hankered slightly after a more artistic life, but two years of National Service in the Army had done a lot towards changing his attitude. He had loathed soldiering, and returned to the peace and beauty of Queen's Lacey, thankful to be a farmer again.

Now young Pip had just finished his two years in the Army and was taking his particular place on the farm. He seemed to enjoy it and if he had no particular talents, he plodded on and played his small part.

Anthony, with no respect for his brother's feelings, pulled back the curtains and flooded the room with sunlight.

'Do you mind – I want a word with you.'

Richard sat up. He scowled and ran hard brown fingers through a thick mop of chestnut hair. He never wore a pyjama top, summer or winter. His fine muscular body looked golden brown against the whiteness of the sheet. He very often went around the farm like that without a shirt, which offended his mother's susceptibilities.

'Really, Richard,' she would protest, 'you *are* a gentleman – I do think you oughtn't to *look* like one of the farm hands.'

Richard always laughed which annoyed her. She was a woman of cold dignity and pride and disliked any form of joke being directed against herself or her family.

Now Richard frowned at his brother, and blinked at the wristwatch he had forgotten to unstrap last night. He then flung a pillow at Tony's head.

'For the love of Mike – it's not *seven* yet!'

Anthony picked up the pillow and returned it to the bed.

'Sorry, but I've something on my mind.'

'Well, that's new. You haven't got much in it,' said Richard and yawned loudly.

7

Anthony looked at him darkly, a slight colour had risen to his cheeks.

'Well, if you're going to be so unpleasant—' he began.

'Oh, come on – I'm only pulling your leg, Tony – what is it?' asked Richard, and sat up and reached for a cigarette and lit it. Folding his arms, he smoked, regarding his brother less angrily. He was really quite fond of Tony, although in Richard's opinion he had inherited their mother's worst qualities. That awful lack of humour – that pompous touch. If there was one thing Richard could not abide it was pomposity. Greatly though Richard respected his mother, he had never quite understood her. Tony was equally difficult to understand. They were both curiously cold and aloof; never gave anything away; so good–so honest and integral – yet, somehow, in Richard's estimation, so inhuman. Funny that you could grow up with people like your mother and brother, know them all your life, and yet not know them at all.

Richard's own nature was warm and open and even inclined to be emotional. He could not remember ever having seen his mother betray emotion except on the day that her favourite dog – a golden retriever – had been run over by a car belonging to a neighbour. Then and then only Julia Chalford's cool dignity had broken. She had knelt beside the dying dog which was pinned under one of the wheels, looked with terrible eyes at the driver (poor chap! how the boys had pitied him) and said:

'*You careless fool!*'

Then she had burst into tears and run into the house. The boys had buried the retriever. When they met their mother at supper, she seemed quite composed and herself again. She had never spoken of the dog from that day to this, which was seven years ago. And she never did speak to the man who had run over him. She could be an implacable enemy.

Richard imagined that Tony might be equally implacable if crossed. On the other hand, Tony had a surface charm that he could use at times with great success. It was Richard's opinion that Tony enjoyed exercising this charm and that he liked being popular, even if such popularity was short-lived. Richard had known one or two people who had started by enthusing over the charming Anthony Chalford when first they met him. Tony would be delightful and show great interest in them, then suddenly cool off and for no reason except that he was bored – treat them like dirt. He was a disappointing character.

Of his two brothers, Richard preferred Pip who was a quiet

rather shy youth, completely dominated by his mother and bullied at times by Tony. He adored Richard who championed his lost causes.

There were long periods when Richard and Tony worked here at the farm, but saw little of each other apart from it. For they had their own friends, and seldom liked each other's. Richard had learnt that it was whenever Tony wanted something that he 'turned on the charm'. He was producing it now. Ordinarily he would have been furious at having a pillow thrown at his dignified head. Now he approached Richard with an ingratiating smile.

Richard grinned back at him; puffing at his early morning cigarette which he always felt to be the best of the day.

'Really, Tony, you manage to look the belle of the ball even at this hour,' he said, 'I don't know how you do it.'

Tony who was inordinately conceited, did not object to this remark despite its unfortunate phraseology. He knew that he had a good figure. Even at work on the farm he never failed to look debonair. He was as fair as Richard was dark. He wore his hair brushed back smoothly from the temples. He had the kind of skin that burns in the summer and was very pale in winter. His eyes were a cool blue. He had thin aristocratic features. Richard always said that Tony ought to have gone into the Diplomatic Service or stood for Parliament, but curiously enough, of the three boys, Tony was the one who most sincerely loved Queen's Lacey. He was immensely proud of the magnificence and prosperity of the farm. He had been delighted when the other day an expensive magazine had sent journalist and photographers down and Queen's Lacey had appeared in print – occupying two prominent pages.

The paragraph about himself had especially pleased Tony.

> *Mr. Anthony Chalford is a tall, good-looking young man – eldest of the three sons in one of the most remarkable Buckinghamshire families. He is seen here beside the latest type of tractor.*

The article had gone on to say that the Chalford family had occupied Queen's Lacey Farm for over a hundred years, and then touched on the remarkable qualities of Julia Chalford who had been left a widow while the boys were still at school; brought up her sons and run the farm during the war years and made such a success of it.

9

Tony sat down on the end of his brother's bed.

'I've got something to tell Mother this morning which isn't going to please her very much,' he said.

Now Richard's eyes opened more widely. They were very bright attractive eyes, greenish in colour, with thick black lashes. He had an impish curve to lips that were fine-cut and sensitive. He said:

'Hello, what have you been up to? Got yourself in debt? Don't answer, I know you haven't. You're far too careful with the £ s. d. Well – what *can* you possibly have done that won't please Mama?'

Tony Chalford's fair skin flushed up; it might almost be called a blush which somehow endeared him to Richard who thought it a regenerate sign. He had never known Tony to be ashamed of anything.

Then Tony blurted out:

'I – I'm going to be married.'

Richard, struck dumb, stared at his brother. Then he blinked his lashes very quickly.

'Crikey!' he said.

Tony coughed.

'I would have told you before but I hadn't quite made up my mind.'

Richard blinked again.

'What about the girl – when did she make up *hers*?'

'At the same time, I suppose,' said Tony haughtily.

'You – going to get married – ye gods and little fishes, this will certainly shake our dear mother to the core!' exclaimed Richard.

'That's what I'm afraid of.'

'All the same,' said Richard. 'You're twenty-eight. I suppose it's time you got married. If it comes to a matter of that it's time I did, too. But I won't. I've never met a girl I'd like to tie myself up to for the rest of my life.'

Tony only half listened to this. He was deep in his own thoughts and the anxieties that had pursued him all night.

Yes – he knew that it was time he got married. But Mrs. Chalford had never encouraged the idea of matrimony with any of her sons. Tony was, as he knew, the one on whom she leaned – the vitally useful person who helped her control the financial side of the farm. Richard was essential so far as work on the farm was concerned, the buying and breeding of the cattle – the produce. Pip was a mere boy still and too young to think of

10

marriage. Anyhow, few marriageable girls were included among the friends who came to Queen's Lacey.

'You sly old dog, Tony,' said Richard suddenly, 'Who have you been seeing without any of us knowing? What is all this about?'

Tony began to tell him.

CHAPTER TWO

HER name was Christa. Christa Morley. Tony had only got as far as that statement when Richard began to look more interested. The name caught his fancy.

'It's unusual. I like it.'

Tony explained that Christa had a Scandinavian grandmother after whom she had been called. He also produced a photograph for Richard and remarked rather arrogantly, Richard thought, that she was 'damned good looking'. Richard smoked his cigarette and studied the snapshot of Christa which Tony said he had taken a couple of weeks ago standing outside the door of the tiny cottage in a small mews, off the King's Road, Chelsea, where Christa lived with her widowed mother.

'Damned good looking' Richard decided was an understatement, typical of Tony who lacked imagination. The girl was positively beautiful.

'Ravishing,' said Richard lightly and raised his brows as though surprised that anything as lovely should have fallen in love with Tony.

Certainly Mama was not going to be pleased. From what Tony was telling him, this girl Christa possessed none of the qualities which their mother would wish her daughter-in-law to have. She was well bred, which was something. But of course, Richard thought with one of his cynical turns of mind, old Tony would never have made 'that' mistake and married beneath him. Christa's father had been a doctor. And Tony with great pleasure had dug out the fact that Christa had an aunt with a title. Christa was a Londoner – knew nothing about country life and would be quite disinterested in farming. Her mother ran a florist's shop in Chelsea. The mother was charming, Tony said, and very plucky. She had been left with very small means on

11

which to educate Christa, but had done so to good effect. Tony had met Christa by one of those accidents of fate; on his way to a wedding in Chelsea, he had stopped at the Morley's little shop which they called *The Greenhouse* and bought a carnation. Rather sheepishly, he said to Richard:

'I think I fell for Christa the moment she put that flower in my buttonhole.' He added with his slight drawl, 'And she did for me.' He went on to say that he had seen Christa quite often during the last four months. He had decided at last to get engaged and bring her down to meet his mother tomorrow. If it could be arranged, Christa could spend the week-end at Queen's Lacey and get to know them all.

Richard raised his brows again.

He studied the snapshot which he was still holding in one hand. The girl had a nymph-like figure. Tony had caught her with one raised curved arm, her fingers touching the scarf which the wind was blowing away from her temples. Hers was a lovely classic pose. She looked very slender and had a wide sweet smile. The face was too small for Richard to see the features closely, but Tony described her as being in feature slightly like that enchanting actress, the late Gertrude Lawrence; tip-tilted nose, golden-hazel eyes, wide mouth, immense charm. Her colouring was fascinating. She had wheaten fair hair and a fine pale skin.

'I must say she seems "the tops",' said Richard, returning the snapshots to his brother, and yawning, 'Sorry I shan't be here to meet her.'

'Why – where will you be?' Tony put the snapshots back in his wallet.

'You've forgotten, old boy, it's my holiday. I leave this evening with Jimmy Oxley for the fair fields of France.'

Tony frowned.

'Oh, yes, of course. You and Jimmy are off. Oh, well, you'll be back for the wedding.'

'*The wedding*.' Richard blinked and slid out of bed. He was not quite as tall as his brother, but beautifully proportioned. He gave one the impression of vitality and an alertness of mind and vision which Tony lacked. Tony was no visionary.

'The *wedding*,' repeated Richard. 'So soon? Don't tell me you are going to rush the girl to the altar. Mama will have a fit.'

'That's the whole point,' scowled Tony. 'I see no object in waiting. As a matter of fact there are all kinds of issues at stake, and many reasons why I want to get married as soon as possible. Christa's mother isn't at all well. The shop's too much for her and, naturally, once Christa is my wife she wouldn't be there to help. At the same time the little place seems to make money and the idea is that it should be taken over by a niece of Mrs. Morley. Gradually Mrs. Morley will retire. The niece is looking for a job now and doesn't want to hang around, so the sooner we get it all settled the better. I know it sounds rapid to you but you must remember that Christa and I have been seeing each other for over four months.'

Richard, running a comb through thick hair which was the colour of dark chestnut bronzed by the sun, eyed his brother sceptically.

'You know your own business best, but I reckon Mama will need some time to get used to the idea of losing one of her little boys.'

'I think she will,' said the older brother gloomily. 'But I shall soften the blow by telling her that Christa and I mean to live in the district.'

Richard pulled a clean shirt out of the drawer, walked to his window and looked out. What a day, he thought. He liked this view of the long drive with its fringe of Dutch elms; the grass pearled with dew. He watched the handsome black and white Friesians which were now being led by Vorrow into the field beyond the lily pond and rock garden which were his mother's particular pride. He hoped that this good weather would persist and follow him to France on his tour of the wine country.

It was a little hard for him to concentrate on the thought of his brother's marriage. His mind was full of this precious two weeks ahead. For the last couple of years he had taken his holiday in the spring abroad with Jimmy Oxley who had been at Shrewsbury with him. Like himself, Jimmy enjoyed literature, music and good food and wines. Richard never cared to be away from Queen's Lacey for long. He loved every inch of this farm and enjoyed his work on it. But there were moments when the tie became irksome and more particularly the constant necessity to run things in the way his mother wanted. Greatly though Richard loved and respected her, this last year or so he had found his mother more difficult, and intolerant. The farm was run on the most modern and up-to-date lines but in paradox Mrs. Chalford herself was old fashioned, out of touch with the world. She disapproved of almost everything and everybody to such a degree that it had become tiresome.

He felt the need for independence of thought and action. That was one of the reasons that he upheld when arguing to himself against marriage, why he had become a sworn bachelor. He could not, would not, be dominated by a woman for the second time in his life. Mama was enough.

Tony, however, seemed anxious for further enslavement, Richard thought humorously. Well – let him get on with it. It might be quite nice to have a sister-in-law as attractive as Christa Morley. But he repeated to Richard that he thought their mother would be upset by 'an ugly rush'. Tony looked stubborn.

'Well, I'm afraid I'm going to be adamant. As you know Mother's word is law at Queen's Lacey but I must manage my own personal life in my own way.'

'You'll be lucky if you can,' said Richard and flung back his handsome head and laughed, then went off to the bathroom, whistling. His mind had reverted to the prospect of taking the car across the Channel this evening and getting away from the whole family.

His parting words followed Tony as he left Richard's bedroom and went downstairs. They made him feel distinctly uneasy.

He strolled into the kitchen and found Mitza stirring the tea she had just made in a huge family teapot. She was a short flaxen-haired woman on the stout side, with weak eyes. She half shut them when she spoke because the light hurt them. She had been told repeatedly that she must get glasses but rejected the idea. That slit-like glance gave one the impression that she was mean or sly, but in reality she was a good-tempered creature who had far too much to do but did it willingly. She genuinely loved her job and Queen's Lacey where she had served the Chalfords for the last six years. She had made this her home, and all her relatives in Austria being dead, she had no intention ever of returning there.

Like most of the employees at Queen's Lacey she respected Mrs. Chalford and adored Richard who was the one person privileged to tease her. Mr. Anthony, she was not so fond of. In her mind she called him 'Herr Chalford', and likened him to a certain haughty gentleman who owned a Schloss in the Tyrol where Mitza and her mother had once lived and worked before the war. She never found 'Herr Chalford' as friendly as the other two young gentlemen. But she bade him a pleasant good morning and offered him a cup of tea which Tony accepted.

14

He grimaced as he sipped it.

'Must you make this frightful strong stuff, Mitza? It's sheer poison.'

Mitza's half-shut eyes glared at him, but she answered politely. 'The whole house it complain if I make not strong tea.'

'I suppose you realize how the price has gone up lately?'

Mitza coloured and banged a saucepan as she took one down from the long row of shining copper pans which were her pride and joy. This big sunny room which led out into a courtyard, and beyond to the orchard and paddock, was her domain. She knew quite well that she was a splendid cook. Guests came from a long way to taste her *apfel strudel*. She knew also that no young modern girl would do as much work as she did, helped only by Betty the wife of the Estonian boy and Mrs. Akers the 'daily' woman from Coleshill. Mrs. Chalford trusted Mitza – left most of the management of food and meals in her care. Mitza had had many a fierce fight with tradesmen against rising food prices. Her loyalties were all for this family. She resented Mr. Anthony's suggestion that she was being extravagant with the tea. The resentment glowed in her but she made no comment. Tony was the only one of the family who disliked Mitza. He called her sulky and unco-operative. He moved off without further conversation.

Mitza's plump face was redder than usual and her lips tighter as she poured the criticized tea into a row of cups. The farm hands would all be coming in for a quick drink in a moment.

'*Ach*,' she muttered, 'he is careful with his money, *that* one,' and with a viciousness she rarely displayed, she seized the tea caddy, dug her spoon into it and put another portion into the teapot, then slammed down the lid.

That joke pleased her and creased her face into a more amiable expression. As she took a gulp from her own cup the small blinking eyes surveyed her kingdom with satisfaction. Mrs. Chalford had modernized the kitchen three years ago. It all delighted Mitza. The blue and white china; the stainless-steel sink, the great refrigerator which now and again broke into a gentle soothing hum.

There were red and white padded chairs and a big enamelled table. And in the adjoining pantry, all the butter and eggs and cream that any cook could use without stinting. The deep freeze was packed with meat and poultry. No one need go hungry at Queen's Lacey; nor ever did.

In the courtyard, Tony ran into Gomme who was the head

15

cowman and a good type. His father had been employed at Queen's Lacey before him. He touched his cap to Mr. Anthony and bade him good morning.

'Looks like a fine day,' said Tony.

'Grand to be alive, sir.'

'Everything all right, Gomme?'

Gomme pushed back his cap and scratched his head.

'Bit of trouble last night, sir. Young Tanner got full of beer as you might say, and had an accident with his motor bike down there by the Magpies.'

Anthony clicked his teeth.

'Was he hurt?'

'Bit bruised and shaken and buckled up his old machine. His wife said he wouldn't be able to work today.'

Tony's fair skin reddened.

'That makes two of them off, what with Philpots and his appendix. What a damn nuisance. You know we're expecting another fifty head of cattle on Monday. There'll be plenty to do.'

'As you say sir,' nodded Gomme.

Behind his hand, the man concealed a dry smile. He thought:

'It's the work he's worrying about – not Philpot's appendix or young Tanner's accident. Like his mother he is – not much sympathy! But I suppose it's the way to get on in the world.'

It was the way to get on in Gomme's world, too, for he came from a long line of farming folk and a hundred years ago his grandfather had been living in a hovel under unspeakable conditions, little more than an underpaid slave. The feudal spirit still lived in Alfred Gomme, and clashed with the outlook of the modern youths, half his age. For them the farm work was more a job whereby to earn money than a personal joy. Gomme derived much satisfaction from his labours and from any word of praise that fell from the lips of his employers. Young Tanner and one or two others among the ten men employed at Queen's Lacey were what Gomme called 'slackers'. The kind to do as little work for as much money as possible. And it was not that they didn't get coddled these days, he reflected, not only by the Government but the Chalford family. They even had an estate car which they were allowed to use. In Gomme's young days it was 'shanks's pony'.

'How's that new Estonion chap, Heino, working out, Gomme?' said Anthony.

'Not too badly at all sir, sticks at it.'

'It's a pity,' said Anthony with some bitterness, 'that we have to employ foreigners in order to get jobs well done. They do work, these chaps. The English labourers today are not at all like you, Gomme.'

The man coloured and wiped his mouth with the back of his hand, embarrassed but pleased. Compliments did not come often from Mr. Anthony. Yes, he was the spit of his mother – thought the cowman. And she was a proud difficult one; never made a mistake and expected those who worked for her to be the same. Generous in the broad sense but a bit cheeseparing over little things – the pair of them.

Anthony took a quick walk down the drive. The rooks were cawing noisily in the tall elms. With every moment the sun grew warmer. It was a May day such as Anthony rarely remembered at Queen's Lacey. He began to think about Christa and to wonder how she would like it down here. She was bound to be impressed by the magnificent farm. By the house, too; but she might find the interior a bit old fashioned. Except for the modernized kitchen and an occasional coat of paint and a few new curtains elsewhere, it was all the same indoors as it had been when Tony was born. Christa was young and had modern ideas. She and her mother were both town bred and with that difference that must always mark the Londoner as being apart from the country-born. That little mews cottage which Anthony found cramped and in which he would loathe to live, nevertheless had charm, and originality. Christa liked brilliant colours and unique designs. How would she fit in at Queen's Lacey? Tony asked himself the question a trifle wryly and with a quick vision of her. Rarely without a cigarette between her fingers, and she enjoyed a cocktail. *His* mother neither drank nor smoked. There were casks of sherries and good wines in the cellars. It was a custom for the Chalfords to drink wine with their dinner every night, and since the boys had grown up they were of course allowed to choose their own drinks. But they knew that their mother disapproved of gin and that she held cocktail parties only under sufferance.

How would Mother like Christa?

Full of self-possession and intensely vain, Tony had rarely experienced such lack of confidence as he had felt since falling in love with Christa Morley. With his extreme good looks and that charm which he knew so well how to manufacture, perhaps he had expected her to drop into his arms as quickly as other girls

17

had done. The others to whom he had been only temporarily attracted. Such affairs had never been serious or lasted for long. Tony by nature was a cool sensualist, too egotistical to make a good lover. He had been altogether surprised by the appeal which Christa had for him. Perhaps it was because she had been aloof and difficult to get – despite the warm friendliness with which she always welcomed him. But what he had at first imagined might develop into just 'an affair' with the girl from the florist's shop, had turned into something much deeper and more serious. He had fallen genuinely in love with Christa. He had been astonished to find himself wanting to spend both time and money on her. He even tried anxiously to conceal his faults – to be his very best in her company. He constantly invaded the Morley's small home. He was punctiliously polite and nice to Mrs. Morley – took her out with Christa – brought her flowers. He wanted them both to think that he was wonderful and to make quite certain that when he proposed to Christa she would accept him. To his immense surprise she turned down his first proposal.

He remembered now, that first evening when he had taken her back to the mews after a theatre; her mother was already in bed. It had been a good evening although the show had been Christa's choice, rather more serious and intellectual than Tony cared for. He preferred thrillers. She had thanked him warmly and he had suddenly taken her in his arms and kissed her. For a moment she had kissed him back. He had not known a woman's lips could be so soft yet so firm; so seductive, yet so cool. That kiss had shown him that behind the reserve that made Christa such a dignified person, she could be passionate and deeply responsive to physical love. But when he lost his head and asked her to marry him, she refused.

'We've only known each other a month – I do like you very much; I think you're marvellous, but I *must* be more sure. I take the idea of marriage seriously. I've seen one or two of my girl friends make such awful mistakes. It would hurt me too much to find myself married to the wrong man. I *feel* things so deeply. . . .' He could remember vividly the way in which she had pressed both her hands to her breast as she said those words. How big and brilliant her eyes had grown. The irises were light gold, but the pupils so large and black that they made her eyes look dark in emotional moments.

Of course he had tried to assure her that she would not be making a mistake in marrying him. Then she had said:

18

'You come from a big family and before you fell in love with me you used to tell me that your mother is dead against you boys marrying and leaving home. I think I'd be terrified of her.'

'You wouldn't,' he had argued (against his own convictions).

But Christa had been adamant. So, with renewed passion and vigour Tony continued his pursuit. He resorted to the kind of dishonesty so common to men and women in a like situation. He pretended to enjoy the serious plays or concerts that Christa favoured. He assured her that her taste was his in all things. He did everything except take her down to Queen's Lacey. He knew it was because he was afraid. Of his mother – of the effect the two women might have upon each other. So he concocted various excuses; either that 'everybody was down with flu', or 'everybody was away'; always some reason for putting off the evil day. If Christa seemed content, Tony was not at all sure that her mother was equally deceived. Tony was a little nervous of Sarah Morley. She had all the charm that she had bequeathed to her daughter and she was a courageous woman with modern ideas, and still quite attractive at forty-five. But he felt that he did not really *get on with her*; that she did not believe every word he said (as Christa did). When Mrs. Morley had, in fact, asked him one day when he was going to show Christa his famous farm, he had coughed and answered:

'To tell you the honest truth, Mrs. Morley, I have been waiting in the hope that Christa would change her mind and become engaged to me. I've got a sort of feeling I want to take her down to Queen's Lacey and tell the family that it's *fait accompli*, then marry Christa very quickly.'

Mrs. Morley had made no comment. For the next few weeks he pursued this course until the day came when Christa said 'yes'. His heart had leapt with triumph when she had finally locked her slim supple fingers around his neck and whispered:

'Darling Tony, I have begun to feel we really will be happy together. You shall see – Christa will turn into a good solid farmer's wife.'

They had laughed together and Tony had said:

'Nothing of the kind. I want you to stay as you are.' All in the fervour of the moment without meaning it.

Christa would *have* to become a farmer's wife. He had no intention ever of abandoning Queen's Lacey or the handsome income which his mother allowed him and his brothers. When Mrs. Chalford died, things might be different. Then he might sell his share to the other two boys, leave the district and travel a bit. But Julia Chalford was a healthy hearty fifty-five. Tony was quite sure she had another useful twenty years ahead of her, he would not wish it otherwise. There was a particularly strong link between him and his mother.

Well – here he was – about to break the news to her. Richard might be right when he hinted that he, Tony, would not find it easy to live his personal life as he wished. But he must have a shot at it. He could no longer shirk the issue. He must bring Christa down here tomorrow.

CHAPTER THREE

As Julia Chalford walked into the dining-room, the grandfather clock in the big oak-panelled hall, a feature of which was a fine Jacobean fireplace, struck eight o'clock. Mrs. Chalford adjusted the little enamelled watch which was pinned on the lapel of her tweeds.

'One minute slow,' she said.

'Which means you are one minute later for breakfast; shame on you, Mama!' said Richard.

She made no comment but gave him a somewhat supercilious glance.

'Good morning, dear boys,' she said.

Tony got up. With his habitual courtesy, he pushed her chair in for her, then returned to his place, wiping his lips with a table napkin.

Richard took one or two noisy gulps of his coffee. Pip who was reading a poultry paper glanced over the rim of it and said:

'Jolly nice morning, Mum.'

She smiled at him. She usually felt benevolent towards her youngest born. He was not very clever, poor Pip. None of them ever knew how he had got his degree; he had just scraped through. But he was a plodder and one could not help being attached to him. He was rather like an amiable puppy, with his fair thick hair; his faculty for breaking things, his blue shy eyes. She also felt kindly disposed towards him because he was so

20

completely under her thumb. He did exactly what she wanted, when she wanted it.

They were all different. As she helped herself to coffee and toast, Julia Chalford cast another almost hostile glance at Richard. She felt no pride because he was the brilliant one. He was a rebel – less subject to her domination – and recently she had found him growing more argumentative, more individual. She felt a hostility towards him for which she had her own dark secret reasons.

To a woman of her spirit, any form of rebellion was tedious. The one thing in the world that Julia Chalford most enjoyed was the complete enslavement of her family. She did not expect to be argued with. So far, Tony and Pip had been good sons and neither had given her real cause for alarm. Not so Richard who was growing further away from her every year. Yet he was in paradox an excellent farmer. Fourteen years after her husband's death, James no longer had power to irritate Julia. He had lain so long and peacefully in his grave at the church in Amersham which had been his favourite, and where most of the Chalfords were buried. But in his lifetime, he and she had been constantly at loggerheads. He had been a farmer, but a bad one, more interested in books and bird-watching. It was she, in fact, who had kept the farm going during the war years. She who was the dictator at Queen's Lacey. Well – she had proved herself both able and judicious. She prided herself on the fact.

She endured Richard's temperament only because of his love of the land and of Queen's Lacey. That was something in his favour. But she detested his sense of humour. He and he alone could make her flush with anger when he directed any of his jokes towards herself.

Her pale blue eyes, unbeautiful and hard under their short sandy lashes, then turned with real pride and pleasure to her first-born. Her dear Tony! So handsome, she thought; such a thorough *gentleman*, and so like her own father. Neither a poet nor a dreamer. She understood and appreciated Tony's logic, his sense of thrift, his legal mind – his business capabilities.

She tried to engage him in conversation about the meeting at which they were due at the Milk Marketing Board in Slough. He answered shortly, and seemed unlike himself. She said:

'Is there anything wrong, Tony?'

'Nothing. I'm fine, thanks,' said Tony, pushing back his chair and fumbling in his pocket for his cigarette case.

Richard looked up from his eggs and bacon and grinned. He began to sing in a theatrical voice:

> ' *"In delay there lies no plenty*
> *Then come kiss me sweet and twenty."* '

Pip sniggered.

Julia Chalford's lips tightened. She knew her sons well. Pip, of course, was weak and devoted to Richard who, his mother had always thought, had a bad influence on him. But there *was* something the matter with Tony; she could tell that.

Richard glanced at Tony's back. He was staring out of the dining-room window.

'I think Tony wants a doctor. He is a *very* sick man,' said Richard.

'Why do you say that?' asked Mrs. Chalford sharply. She was an excellent mother and fully believed that her sons returned the devotion which she lavished upon them.

Now Tony swung round and growled at his brother.

'I hate these saucy moods of yours, Richard, especially during breakfast. Do go out and get rid of some of your superfluous energy.'

Richard laughed.

'I shall soon be getting rid of it in France, *mon cher*. This time tomorrow I hope to be enjoying my coffee and *croissants* in Rouen.'

'Oh dear – yes – of course you're crossing over to France tonight,' said Mrs. Chalford.

Pip suddenly pushed back his chair.

'I must be off. I've got a date with Joe Thornton.'

'About the chickens?' asked Mrs. Chalford.

'Yes.'

'Remember me to him,' said Mrs. Chalford.

Joseph Thornton was an old friend. Only the green hedges marked the boundary line between their two estates. They had always got on very well. 'And also to Susan,' she added.

'Don't mention me—' cut in Richard.

Now Pip's round schoolboy face flushed and he looked at Richard with a scowl.

'I think you're being rotten to Susan. When I was with Mr. Thornton yesterday he kept asking why you never go over to see them at Hillside nowadays.'

It was Richard's turn to flush – a very faint colour rising

22

under his rich tan. Some of the humorous sparkle left his eyes. He said nothing but once out in the hall with his younger brother, he spoke in a soft voice that had a menacing ring to it.

'If I were you, Pip, I wouldn't meddle in these affairs. You don't know anything about Susan and myself. And please do *not* discuss me with old Joe.'

Pip, very red now, expostulated.

'Everyone knows that Sue is in love with you and you've been going round with her and—'

Richard interrupted. He still spoke softly but his eyes had narrowed and he gave Pip a very gentle shove from behind.

'That's quite enough. Just learn to keep your mouth shut. And if you'd like to know – I have *not* been philandering with Sue Thornton. I've known her ever since she was a kid with pigtails – just as you and Tony have. If she's gone and got herself all het up about me, just because I was mistaken enough to kiss her under the mistletoe last Christmas, that's *her* fault. But I haven't asked her to marry me, neither do I intend to play games with her in the cornfield. I don't happen to be that way inclined. Now do go and fold the chickens' wings and see that they say their prayers.'

'Silly ass,' muttered Pip and with burning ears slouched out of the house. He was no longer a schoolboy but Richard always seemed to be able to rub him up the wrong way.

'Well – was Rich only making one of his poor jokes – or *are* you ill, Tony?' Mrs. Chalford asked her son.

He flung himself into a chair beside her. He took a deep breath at his cigarette.

Queer, he was thinking, how a mature man of twenty-eight years could still feel like a foolish youth who had something to confess to a mother who was almost certain to want to administer chastisement.

'Well, go on dear,' said Mrs. Chalford, and gave him an encouraging smile.

Now that he was about to tell her of his love for Christa and his desire to marry, he felt strangely awkward. What could his mother know of passionate love? Yet she must have been fond of his father to have married him, and to have begotten three sons. But the old man had died at an age when schoolboys rarely notice or inquire into the love-lives of their parents. And only in later years had Julia Chalford given them to understand that she had found their father more of a hindrance than a help at Queen's Lacey.

23

She had never shown any desire to marry again; she was a type that Tony, when thinking of other women, would have called 'frigid'.

He coughed, frowned at the point of his cigarette, and remained silent until Julia Chalford grew really alarmed.

'Tony, something *is* wrong. Have you anything disastrous to tell me? If so, get on with it. I think you should know by now that I can take a blow without making a fuss.'

He gave a slight laugh but avoided her gaze.

'I wouldn't call it disastrous, Mother, it's just that – well – it may be a shock to you.'

Now her heart plunged, seemed to stop beating, then continued more rapidly. She took a clean handkerchief out of the bag which lay on her lap and put it against her lips; it smelt of eau-de-Cologne. She never used perfume.

'Ah!' she said. 'It's something to do with a woman.'

'You've hit it.'

'Have you got some girl into trouble?'

Now Tony burst out laughing. He felt the tension easing.

'Really, Mother, how supreme of you to jump to such a conclusion. I thought you had more respect for me. I am not given to running round the countryside getting girls into trouble.'

Mrs. Chalford allowed herself to join in the laughter.

'Well, dear, you're in such a state – what *have* you done?'

'I've become engaged,' he announced abruptly. 'I want you to know that I'm going to be married.'

There was a complete and utter silence. Mrs. Chalford looked straight ahead of her at the portrait of her grandfather. A shockingly arrogant bewhiskered face. She was remarkably like him. He had been a terrifying figure but she had been so small when he died that she could remember little except his icy voice and the patronizing manner in which he had patted her head and given her sixpence one Christmas just before his death.

What Tony had just said was a stunning blow. As she did not speak, he continued:

'Her name is Christa Morley.'

'I see,' said Julia Chalford, pushing away her plate and folding her hands on the table, biting a little at her lower lip. 'Well – go on.'

Tony went on. He told her all that he had told his brother Richard earlier this morning. He made the same excuse that he had made to Christa's own mother for not having introduced Christa to Queen's Lacey before now.

24

'I wanted to be quite sure, then bring her down here as my future wife,' he ended.

Julia Chalford moistened her lips with her tongue. Her clear mind had taken in very word that Tony uttered. She had not missed a single detail. He had gone into a florist's shop in the King's Road, Chelsea, and bought a buttonhole for a wedding (she could remember the very wedding because she, herself, had attended it). There he had met this girl whose mother kept the shop. Christa was, to use his own words, remarkably beautiful and intelligent; they had fallen in love with each other; he had proposed to her and had been accepted.

Frantically Julia sought to put this thing in its best aspect. Thank God, at least, the girl was *a lady*. Her father had been a doctor. And she had an aunt who was the widow of a baronet. Mrs. Chalford, by nature a snob, could not have borne it if one of her sons had decided to marry a cheap second-rate young woman. She did not relish the idea that Christa's widowed mother was running a shop and the girl, herself, served in it. Of course these days nobody thought badly about that sort of thing. Many a woman of distinction had gone into 'trade'. Julia, herself, could only be called a 'farmer'. But the Chalfords were and always had been wealthy owners of property. These Morleys seemed to be hard-up and 'nobodies'. Tony had disappointed her. She had expected him to choose quite a different sort of girl – one of the hunting set around here.

'I'm sorry, Tony,' suddenly Mrs. Chalford spoke. 'I always hoped it would be Ursula.'

Tony, hands in his pockets and a cigarette between his lips, scowled a little.

'I'm sorry if you had hopes there, Mother. Ursula and I are just good friends and I admire her. But that's all.'

That's all, the mother listened to the echo of those words and thought again; Tony is a fool. The one I thought so sensible. So cautions. If this had been Richard I would not have been at all surprised, but Tony – rushing into marriage with a girl like that – it really is incredible.

Ursula – Lady Corby – was a young widow (no family), the same age as Tony. Her husband, Sir Alan Corby, had been killed in a flying fatality during a tour of India. A brilliant young man attached to one of the big jet engine manufacturers. Three years ago they had bought a lovely old place near Forty Green and become friends with the County crowd down there. Ursula rode to hounds – was slim and good looking and came

25

of a Buckinghamshire family. She was even interested in farming. Always talking about taking it up now that she had been left a widow. She would have been the very wife for Tony.

The disappointed mother sat still and continued to listen while her eldest born enumerated the many virtues of his chosen wife. Then he produced the snapshot that he had shown Richard.

Julia Chalford put on her horn-rimmed glasses and examined Christa's lovely figure and face.

'I can't see much but she looks quite attractive,' she said grudgingly.

'She's wonderful,' said Tony with enthusiasm, 'I know you'll agree when you meet her.'

Mrs. Chalford returned the photograph.

'You think you really are in love this time – it isn't just an affair?'

'No, I know that I want to marry Christa.'

'And what about the differences in your temperaments – your environments. Do you think a girl who likes town life will ever fit in at Queen's Lacy?'

'Christa is very amenable and she doesn't dislike the country.'

'Doesn't dislike the country – huh!' Julia Chalford echoed those words quite angrily, rose, buttoned her jacket and putting her hands in her pockets, walked to the window and looked out of the garden. Cheam, their gardener, was busy taking half-dead wallflowers out of the bed that ran along the wall of the wing which had been built on to Queen's Lacey about two hundred years ago. A wing of the house that was not often used. There was more than enough space for the family in the old part which they preferred. She said:

'You've always loved Queen's Lacey – just as we all do – haven't you Tony?'

'Of course, Mother.'

'And your life lies here – your work.'

'Of course,' he repeated, 'my marriage to Christa won't alter those facts.'

Julia Chalford turned to him with an excess of emotion which she rarely displayed.

'You must think well before you bring a wife here, Tony. She must be the right one or you will destroy the whole peace and unity of our home.'

Tony gave a brief laugh.

'That's putting it a bit dramatically, Mother.'

'I'm not given to dramatics. I am merely telling you what I feel. And I can't believe that a beautiful girl whom you say is artistic and who likes London life and doesn't know anything about the country, is the right one for you. You must remember that when I am dead you will be the head of the family and the whole running of Queen's Lacey and the farm will rest on your shoulders.'

'I know that, Mother, but I tell you my marriage to Christa couldn't destroy either the peace or unity of our home, as you term it. She's quite willing to live down here and I know she'll soon love it as much as I do.'

'Where was she educated?'

'Oh, in some convent I believe,' repeated Tony vaguely.

'She isn't a *Catholic*'! broke out Mrs. Chalford in a tone of dismay.

Tony laughed again.

'No, Christa isn't a Catholic. She just went to a convent because her mother thought the education was good.'

Mrs. Chalford breathed a sigh of relief.

'Oh, well,' she said, 'you boys must make your own lives, I suppose.'

'Well, we've got to carry on the good name, haven't we? Which means we must marry,' Tony said with a touch of humour unusual for him. He had no great sense of humour. But his ideas of life and how it should be led were not cast in quite so stern and unbending a mould as his mother's.

Her expression softened.

'I suppose that's true,' she nodded. 'And I shall quite enjoy having a grandchild. But I wish—'

'That it had been Ursula Corby,' he finished for her. 'Sorry, Mother, I just happened to come across Christa.'

'Well, I must meet this paragon of beauty and virtue and we will celebrate your engagement,' Mrs. Chalford said, as though the words were torn from her lips.

Already in her mind she felt hostile towards Christa, and bitterly jealous. She could not bear the thought of sharing her eldest and best-loved son with this unknown young woman from a Chelsea florist shop. She said:

'You won't get married too quickly, will you? I believe in long engagements.'

'Well, I don't,' said Tony. The force of his present desire for Christa had lent him a new feeling of strength and superiority.

27

'I've known Christa for four months now and I did not ask her to marry me until I had made up my mind about it. And we don't want a splashy society wedding, neither of us do. I mean the whole countryside and county turning out. Christa's mother is not well off and they haven't the money for a big affair. I just want to marry Christa in a little church near her home by special licence, say in about a month's time.'

Now Mrs. Chalford looked at him in unrestrained dismay, a very decided colour mounting her bony face.

'You want a marriage as early as June? But Tony, *why*? What will everybody think? It's absurd! You just can't mean it!'

He sighed impatiently. He had known there would be strong opposition over this decision. At first when he had told Christa that it was what he wanted, even she had demurred, but finally she had fallen in with his views because she was more worried about her mother's health than she ever let Mrs. Morley know; besides there was Judy, her cousin, who was going to help run the shop. Tony tried now to explain all this to his mother. How Judy, for reasons he would not go into, would be coming to London in a couple of weeks' time and it would suit them all if she could go and live at the cottage with Mrs. Morley. Waiting would only complicate matters.

What Tony did not tell his mother was a truth that he barely admitted even to himself; the fact that he was rushing Christa into the marriage *because he feared losing her*; because he knew that if she had too much time and leisure in which to think about it she might change her mind. Once she had entertained doubts about their marriage being a success. He did not want there to be any lapse of time in case those doubts returned. For the first time in his life, Anthony Chalford was in the throes of a blind, almost crazy passion which could be assuaged only by possession.

It was not long before Julia Chalford realized this also. She viewed it with a sense of frustration. But it had been the same in her own life, she thought. Once and once only she had lost her sense of proportion and enough of her control to make a hasty marriage – with Tony's father. And what had happened? During the honeymoon she had realized how far removed her tastes really were from those of the too gentle and dreamy man whose good looks and charm had attracted her. Incapable, herself, of real passion, she had soon cooled and grown impatient of him. Was there not a grave danger that Tony would do the same?

But she was too intelligent a woman to risk alienating her son by exhibiting definite disapproval. If she wanted to keep him she knew that she must be more subtle in her treatment of him. She laid a hand on his shoulder with a rare gesture of tenderness.

'Well, my dear, it's a bit of a shock, as I've said, but I offer you my best wishes. You know of course that I only want you to be happy.'

His handsome face brightened. He stood up and touched her cheek with his lips.

'Thanks very much, Mother. I know you'll love Christa and so will Rich and Pip.'

'I'm sure we shall,' said Mrs. Chalford smoothly.

'I'll bring her down this afternoon for the week-end if I may. We can put her up, can't we?'

'Yes, of course.'

Then Julia Chalford added:

'Does your–your fiancée' – she stumbled over the word–'like this idea? I mean – only a month in which to get a trousseau. Doesn't she want to be a "white bride"?'

'Yes, but she can get it all done in a month; she has a great friend who runs a dress salon and they're going to make her wedding dress and so on.'

'I suppose you've even planned the honeymoon,' Mrs. Chalford said clenching her fingers.

'We rather think Paris and Rome,' said Tony. 'Christa's very artistic, you know, and loves music and pictures. Rome's her ideal.'

'She sounds more like Richard than you,' his mother remarked.

'Oh, yes, Rich and Christa ought to get on quite well together,' said Tony casually, 'but I don't think that husband and wife need necessarily have the same interests in order to hit it off.'

Mrs. Chalford felt that she was totally unable to discuss the matter further. She walked across the room glancing at her watch.

'I must go out and see Gomme. You know he doesn't think that new calf of Buttercup's is going to live. I've got an appointment with Mr. Golly.'

'If he doesn't do any good I hear there's a new first-rate vet at High Wycombe.'

Julia turned and walked back to her son. Her pale blue eyes held something of real feeling as she looked up at him.

29

'Tony dear – don't let this marriage rob you of your enthusiasm for the farm – remember how dear Queen's Lacey is to all of us.'

'But of course, Mother, I've never forgotten it. I tell you my marriage won't make any difference.'

Now Mrs. Chalford asked the big salient question.

'Where, then, are you going to live? You won't leave Queen's Lacey will you?'

'Well, Mother, I suppose Christa and I must find a home of our own.'

Silence for a moment, then Julia Chalford said:

'Where did you intend to live while you are looking for one?'

'Well, I thought maybe you wouldn't mind if we stayed at Queen's Lacey for a bit.'

Her spirits rose. Her eyes sparkled.

'I hoped you'd say that. Of course I shall want you to come here, and I see no reason why you shouldn't remain.'

'Not for good—' began Tony.

But she drew him to the window and pointed to the Queen Anne wing which jutted out from the house forming an L shape.

'Why buy another home when we have all this space? You can have the wing done up and make it your own small home. There is space for a sitting-room and two bedrooms. There is also a bathroom. You could have it all decorated to your choice.'

Tony looked doubtful for a moment, then felt a slight excitement rise within him. After all, he had lived his entire life at Queen's Lacey. He did not really want to leave it. He had got used to its spaciousness, its dignity, its age. He wouldn't like to exchange it for a cramped modern house or a little cottage. Besides which he knew there was nothing suitable for sale anywhere around here at the moment.

'It's a wonderful idea, Mother,' he said eagerly, 'but of course I'll have to ask Christa.'

'Of course,' said Mrs. Chalford with a tight-lipped smile.

CHAPTER FOUR

'THE funny thing is,' said Christa, 'that Tony doesn't really bear any resemblance to the sort of man I *meant* to marry.'

'That,' said her mother, 'worries me sometimes. I think that the sort of preconceived picture a girl gets of the man she would like to marry is often the right one.'

Christa Morley carefully put away between tissue paper the cobweb chiffon nightgown which she had been embroidering.

It was laid with the rest of the things that she and Mummy were making (when they had time) for Christa's trousseau.

Then with a light laugh Christa said:

'What a horrid thought, Mum. Do you seriously think Tony is a wrong choice?'

Mrs. Morley hesitated. She wanted to assure Christa that she had only been joking. But she couldn't. Mrs. Morley was a frank woman. She could never be accused of paying idle compliments. But how difficult it would be to say what she *really* wished to say now:

'I don't care at all for the man of your choice. He is charming, but not kindly. He may prove stubborn. So many weak people are. He is deceitful. You've got my nature – you like sincerity. You never told lies when you were small. But you're in love with Tony Chalford's charm, the wonderful prospect of a lovely home and a husband instead of earning your living working in a florist shop. Or is it that you are twenty-four and you think it is time you got married? Whatever it is, I cannot feel that Tony is your man.'

But no – she couldn't say anything like that. She just hoped that she might be wrong. Certainly Christa seemed happy enough.

Mrs. Morley watched Christa move across the sitting-room, find a cigarette and light it. Now the girl stood looking down out of the window into the mews. It promised to be a glorious May morning. The weather had been altogether wonderful for nearly a week. At any moment now Tony was due to arrive. He was taking Christa down to Queen's Lacey to stay for a night, and meet his family.

31

How beautiful she was, the mother thought, with the shining fairness of silver hair and the large eyes that could almost be called a golden hazel – darkly lashed. Her skin was exquisite. A tip-tilted nose and a wide mouth gave her face character. Her figure had all the slim grace, the clean-cut lines of youth.

She looked tranquil but the big mouth suggested passion and humour. Her friends found her amusing and she had both individuality and genuine charm.

Sarah Morley was the kind of mother who refused to keep a daughter chained to her side. When her husband had died, she had weakened and clung to Christa for a little while. But the weakness had passed. During these last two years, she had shared life with her daughter in this tiny mews cottage but encouraged her to get out and move in a circle of her own young friends.

Eighteen months ago, Christa had been practically engaged to a man older than herself. Mrs. Morley had been fond of Jack Martindale, and pleased because, like Christa's father, he was in the medical profession. Unfortunately after an operation he had suddenly contracted blood poisoning. He had died within a few days. It had been a terrible shock to Christa. For a long time the girl had been unlike herself. Then with the resilience of her years, she recovered.

Now *this*.

The man whom she was going to marry one month from today was a very different proposition from Jack Martindale. But in spite of Mrs. Morley's secret doubts, all seemed to be going well. The haggard look that had hollowed Christa's cheeks after Jack's death had disappeared. She went about now with that 'bloom' on her that so often seems to appear on a woman in love. *Why worry?*

Last night Tony had taken Christa to a theatre. The mother heard her come in, called her up to say good night and the two had chatted over a cup of tea. Christa had adored the play – *St. Joan*. She had said:

'It was absolutely splendid. But poor old Tony was bored stiff.'

Sarah had raised her brows and made no comment. She could imagine Tony being bored stiff by a Shaw play, or by anything that made him use his imagination or artistic perception. He lacked both.

Christa thought that Tony, who was a materialist in his way, would be good for her, but the mother did not agree. There was a softness – a romantic quality in Christa which demanded careful handling. Mrs. Morley could not imagine Tony being sensitive enough for Christa. This falling in love business was dangerous, she told herself, with a deep sigh. Some called it a hypnotic state. Well – one *could* wake up and find the hypnotic spell broken.

Mrs. Morley looked at her watch.

'Your young man should be here in half an hour,' she said.

Christa turned round and smiled.

'In a way I'm looking forward to seeing the great farm at last and meeting the family. In another way, I'm *terrified*!'

Once more Sarah Morley's inborn tact forbade her making any comments. But another thing that troubled her was Tony's obvious dependence upon his mother.

This morning, however, Mrs. Morley conquered her depression and returned Christa's smile encouragingly.

'Oh, I'm sure it'll be all right, darling. You get on with most people and I'm sure you will do so with – with Tony's Mama.'

Christa looked with deep affection at the small slight woman who, for all her petite figure and the fragile beauty which she had bequeathed to her daughter, had always been such a tower of strength. She was a darling. Christa dreaded leaving her – even for Tony.

The sound of car wheels and scraping of tyres sent Christa running to the window. With a pang of jealousy which Mrs. Morley could not quite control she now noted the radiance that transfigured Christa's face – the bright pink of her cheeks.

'It's Tony!' she exclaimed.

She is very much in love, the mother reflected. *I want it to be like this but I want it to stay so. Oh, God never let her be disillusioned!*

Out of the car stepped Tony; debonair in his well-tailored grey flannels. Mother and daughter watched him lift a huge bunch of yellow tulips out of the car. As he saw them at the open window, he waved and called out to them:

'Coals to Newcastle, but Queen's Lacey tulips are famous – and they're not for The Greenhouse but for my future mama-in-law.'

Sarah Morley thought:

'Sweet of him and he really is awfully nice. Why should I *worry?*'

She made herself scarce as the tall young man walked into the cottage and took Christa in his arms.

Christa, herself, felt that strange new thrill of pleasure which gave her all the happiness of a woman deeply in love. But she was still a little shy of her passion, and of expressing her feelings to Tony. She was somehow too conscious of what might be termed his truly English reticence. He kissed her lips with passion, but released her quickly, as though half afraid of his own ardour. With an arm around her, he walked with her into the sitting-room and began to apologize for not having come for her earlier. He had meant that they should lunch at Queen's Lacey, but Vorrow, one of the Estonian boys on the farm, had had a slight accident with the new tractor and Tony had had to stay and see to things.

'My brother Richard who generally deals with Vorrow has gone off to France on a holiday. There's only Pip at home and he's a bit of a youngster still and Mother had a date in Aylesbury.'

'Of course, darling, I quite understand,' said Christa.

'I can't tell you how much I'm looking forward to introducing you to my home,' added Tony.

'I've just told Mummy – I'm petrified,' laughed Christa.

Against his own convictions he laughed with her.

'Absolutely no need, my family will all love you. If you're ready, sweet, we'll get along at once and not waste any more of this lovely day. I can't tell you how glorious the country looked this morning.'

She knew that he did not strictly care much for London life, although he had made an excellent escort for her during the weeks they had been going out in town. He always did things well and had an impressive manner with head-waiters. They had enjoyed the best seats at the theatres – the best tables at Christa's favourite restaurants. But she was quite aware that life really began and ended for Tony on his mother's farm.

Christa, who loved her London and had never really lived out of it except when on holidays – hoped fervently that she would be able to share his enthusiasm for Queen's Lacey. Well – now at last she was going to see it and *know*.

She was in tremendously high spirits when at length they drove together in Tony's big blue saloon car down the Western Avenue towards Beaconsfield. Just before they had left Chelsea, she had presented herself to Tony and pointed to her feet.

'Correctly shod for Queen's Lacey?' she had asked with a provocative glance. Her eyes seemed to disappear in a tangle of lashes when she smiled like that.

'You look perfect,' he said, and was sure in his own mind that his mother would agree. Christa had forsaken her usually high heels for a more sensible type of leather walking shoe. She wore a grey flannel suit – as well cut as his own – with a crisp white piqué blouse; no jewellery except her big pearl earrings set in gilt, which were new favourites. No hat; fair hair shining, and a short camel-hair coat over her shoulders. She looked, Tony thought, from head to foot very right indeed for the country.

He decided not to mention for the moment his mother's suggestion that they should live at Queen's Lacey. Christa said:

'Do tell me what your mother said when you told her.'

'Oh, I must say she was a bit shaken,' he confessed and cleared his throat.

'I should have thought she might have been rather pleased at getting one of you three boys off her hands,' said Christa gaily.

'Oh, yes, of course,' said Tony vaguely and echoed her laugh.

'When will your brother, Richard, be back from France?'

'In a fortnight's time—'

'In time for our wedding,' said Christa softly.

'Yes,' said Tony and now his hand reached out and felt for hers and pressed it against her knee, making her heart jolt again with that sheer physical thrill of contact with him. He might not be at all like the man she had dreamed of. He was not in the least like Jack – poor Jack whom she had loved and lost before they even had a chance to buy the engagement ring. But she was in a state of warm contentment that made her feel relaxed and happy in Tony's company; and that she really had been waiting to find *him*. That all was well with her world.

'Oh, Tony!' she said suddenly. 'I love you very much.'

He slowed down and took his eyes off the road for a single instant to glance down at her and respond to the warmth in her eyes. Christa's eyes were really of a staggering beauty, he thought. He was immensely proud of her, and of his conquest. Just for the moment he was also ready and willing to respond to her romanticism. He would never have termed himself a romantic man, but he found it exceedingly pleasant to be the beginning and end of such a beautiful girl. It was flattering to hear her say those words: 'I love you very much' – without restraint.

'I love you, too,' he said. 'Enormously.' And put aside the

35

memory of his mother's face as it had looked when he had broken the news of his forthcoming marriage.

That same face was expressionless when at length the great moment came and Tony introduced his future wife to his mother.

The meeting took place half-way down the drive at Queen's Lacey. Christa had been admiring the famous Dutch elms. Just before that she had given a cry of pleasure at her first glimpse of the fine old farmhouse. Then she and Tony saw the two figures that appeared, walking across the paddock in which a grey mare stood frisking her tail at the flies beside a small grey donkey. The figures came nearer. Tony muttered: 'My mother and brother Pip.'

He added that the mare was an old favourite that Julia Chalford used to hunt. It had now grown old and was allowed to graze here in peace. The small donkey was the mare's inseparable comrade. The mare had a sore on one fetlock, and Mrs. Chalford who, Tony said proudly, was as good as any vet, had probably been treating it.

So Christa's first view of Tony's mother was of a Julia in her right setting; dressed as she liked to dress; in tweeds, with a beret set at an unbecoming angle on the faded auburn head and wearing long boots. Horn-rimmed spectacles in hand, and eyes narrowed to pin-points, she advanced towards the young couple in the car which Tony had stopped. He and Christa both got out. Christa felt suddenly nervous but Tony took hold of her hand encouragingly.

'Come along, darling.'

Shyly but with that charming smile which most people found disarming, Christa walked up to the older woman and held out her hand.

'Hullo – how do you do – I'm terribly pleased to meet you at last—' she began, stammering a little.

Julia Chalford stiffened in every limb, but her face was a mask. Quite graciously she replied to Christa's greeting, and pressed her hand. If Christa had expected to be embraced or kissed she was disappointed. Mrs. Chalford made no gesture of that sort. She said:

'I'm glad to meet you. You two must have done good time coming down. It doesn't seem long since Tony went up to town.'

'There was nothing much on the road,' said Tony.

'Well, well, let's all go in. I must wash my hands. I've been

36

treating Mabel, my old hunter.' She gave Christa this information, then turned and began to walk towards the house. She
waited for nobody but expected to be followed. That was
obvious to Christa who was perceptive of other people's actions
and sensitive to their moods. She knew at once that she and
Tony's mother were not going to make friends easily.

Christa turned now to the tall fair boy who looked a bit like a
very young Tony, with a chubby face. He was untidy and badly
dressed and he apologized sheepishly for his appearance.

'Oh, that's all right, Pip – a farmer must be a farmer when
he's at the job,' said Tony airily, rather conscious of his own
elegance. Christa held out a hand to Pip who took it for a
second in rather hot clammy fingers, then dropped it. She
thought he looked rather a pet. His eyes – which were the same
pale blue as Tony's and their mother's – stared at the pretty fair
girl with open admiration, then turned away as though embarrassed. He was painfully shy she thought. The boy was thinking:

'Gosh, what a glamour girl! Old Tony has found a winner.'

For the next few minutes Christa had no time in which to
think about the family which was so soon to become hers. She
was too busy absorbing her first glimpse of Queen's Lacey. All
that was artistic and beauty-loving in her responded to it. She
had already fallen in love with the countryside. The lovely
woods and villages as they drove through Buckinghamshire; the
golden broom and the bluebells, the fresh green fields; but this
place – Tony's home – was magnificent. She could understand
now why he loved it. Later, Tony said, he would take her round
the farm. Now he escorted her into the house. Once indoors, out
of the sun, it was quite cool, she needed her coat again. Her
quick eye noted at once the absence of radiators. Julia Chalford
abhorred central heating. She also liked plenty of fresh air and
Christa saw that most of the doors and windows were wide
open, Mrs. Chalford did not mind draughts, apparently.

In the excitement of the moment, these things did not particularly worry Christa. Although she was like a cat, who
needed warmth and sought it. The little mews cottage never
lacked a fire. But now she had eyes only for the splendid Jacobean house. Its magnificent timber, the carved panelling and polished floors. Great jars of tulips and beech leaves looked perfect
in hall and drawing-room.

'Oh, how adorable,' exclaimed Christa. 'And who arranges
the flowers? They are so artistic. Is it you, Mrs. Chalford?'

Mrs. Chalford took off her jacket. She was pleased to exhibit the fact that she did not feel the cold. She wore only a thin blouse. Christa's knowledgeable eye was quick to see that Mrs. Chalford's tweeds were good and expensive; and that the woman had a certain distinction; later Christa discovered that never a hair of that faded auburn hair was out of place. No matter what work Mrs. Chalford did, the freckled hands seemed always to be scrupulously clean, with short pared nails. She had paused in the hall to change her muddied boots for a pair of clean suede shoes. It made Christa feel that she ought to change her own. Looking over her shoulder, Mrs. Chalford then told Pip to go round by the kitchen and get rid of *his* dirty boots.

Christa, in her present happy mood, was amused by this. Mrs. Chalford seemed to treat her sons like small boys, and they accepted the fact. She even told Tony that his hair was ruffled and needed brushing. Whereupon Tony apologized hastily and smoothed down the offending hair.

'Gracious,' thought Christa, 'I shall have to be careful. There is none of the "do as you want and let your hair down girls", about *Tony's* Mama!'

They all gathered in the drawing-room. Here Mrs. Chalford motioned her guest to a chair and answered the questions Christa had asked about the flowers.

'You are interested in floral arrangements, of course, from a professional point of view,' she said with a smile which tried to be pleasant, but failed. 'Well, strange though it may seem, it is Richard who is so clever at doing the flowers. He arranged these before he went away. I am afraid I am not at all artistic.'

Christa glanced inquiringly at Tony who laughed.

'Yes – one of old Rich's foibles is his passion for arranging flowers. A bit pansy I call it.'

'Tony, *really*!' from Mrs. Chalford. Then she gave that tight-lipped smile at Christa.

'Young people today seem to say whatever comes into their heads. I know there are a lot of jokes about "pansies" and so on, but I dislike it intensely, don't you?'

Christa stammered a reply. She knew that Tony had only been joking. Another thing she was to learn rapidly was that her future mother-in-law had no sense of humour.

Tony said:

'I'll go and bring in Christa's case. Pip – I want a word with you – business. . . .' And the two brothers sauntered out.

Christa's gaze wandered around the room. It was long and L shaped looking out over a lawn fringed by a big bed of tulips against a wall that was covered with brilliant purple aubrietia.

Settling down now to her survey of things she could also see that Julia Chalford's taste in the home was by no means her's or Mummy's. This room was too much of a 'mess'; a few lovely bits of furniture, yes – but a jumble; a mixture of period pieces; too many poorish water-colours on walls which were painted cream and now fast becoming yellow. There were sensible chintz covers and curtains to match – but in a green and yellow pattern which was modern and wrong for this gracious old house. The rugs were old – and clashed with the chintzes. No taste here, and everything meticulously tidy (like the mistress of the house, thought Christa wryly). Even the magazines and papers were folded edge to edge, on the table. There was a piano at one end of the room but it was shut, and covered with photographs. Christa wondered if it was ever used.

Now Julia Chalford started to do the questioning: about Christa's family; her upbringing; her mother; her home. And finally about the engagement.

'It came as quite a surprise to me,' she finished. 'I never really thought of Tony as a marrying man.'

Christa gave her rich sweet laugh which was such a natural thing.

'Oh, but why not? Don't all men eventually want to marry?'

'I suppose so,' said Mrs. Chalford grudgingly.

'Of course you don't want to part with any of your boys – that I understand,' went on Christa, 'I'm sure I'd feel the same if I had three marvellous sons.'

Mrs. Chalford said nothing. Her unwinking gaze examined every detail of Christa's appearance. She could find no fault with it, but she disliked Christa's warm gay manner. It at once made her suspicious.

'Trying to get round me,' Julia Chalford decided, 'but it won't work. I'm much too cute.'

Christa answered all the questions with a direct honesty that was certainly disarming – even to Julia Chalford. And she had to admit that the girl was a *lady*; but really, as she had anticipated, Christa was not in the *least* suitable to be the wife of a man whose entire interest lay – and must always lie – in farming.

Then suddenly, on one of her impulses, Christa broke out:

'Mrs. Chalford, are you very disappointed because Tony wants to marry *me*?'

For an instant Julia felt uncomfortable – a rare condition for her. She tried to laugh.

'What a strange question, my dear girl.'

'Well, I somehow feel you *are*,' said Christa growing valiant. Because she was so much in love with Tony she felt an overwhelming desire to get closer to this woman. She believed that honesty might help to achieve it. 'Oh, I know I'm very much a Londoner,' she went on, 'but I'm sure I shall soon learn all about farming, and become madly interested in it. Tony is so marvellous – I want you to feel happy about our engagement. I do realize that he must mean an awful lot to you.'

Even Julia Chalford had to soften to such a generous appeal. In a more friendly way she said:

'He does, of course, mean much to me. All my boys do. We've always been a very united family.'

'I understand,' said Christa, 'and it must be a shock to realize that your son is about to take a wife and desert you.'

Julia froze again.

'I don't think Tony will ever *desert* me,' she said.

'No, of course not exactly,' stammered Christa, finding it a bit difficult not to say the wrong thing. 'He adores you.'

Mrs. Chalford raised a brow. '*Adore*' was a word she never used. It was part of the vocabulary of those whom she termed 'affected'. But she said:

'Well, as I have just remarked – we are a very united family. Tony is my eldest son and I rely a great deal on his management here. Richard, who is away on holiday at the moment, is an excellent farmer, and Pip will make one in time. But Tony has the business head, and I am retiring more and more from the business side and leaving things more to his judgment.'

'Tony and Pip look at bit alike – is Richard the same? Are they all fairish like you?' asked Christa.

Mrs. Chalford nodded towards the piano.

'No, Richard is not like the others. He has this artistic side which is such a pity, because he would have been an even better farmer without all that music and poetry nonsense. He plays the piano – or thinks he does.'

'He sounds awfully nice,' said Christa and got up and moved towards the array of photographs. She picked up the one that Mrs. Chalford had indicated.

So this was Richard. Certainly not like either of his brothers.

It was an enlarged snapshot of him taken when riding. He was bare-headed. Man and horse looked as though carved in one. It was a handsome face, and Richard had a friendly attractive smile. But she knew instinctively that Richard was the one of her three sons who counted least with Mrs. Chalford.

She heard the older woman say:

'Now I'm sure you would like to go up and see your room. I've got to say a word to Mitza – she is our Austrian cook.'

Christa followed Tony's mother from the room. Once more, walking behind that tall commanding figure, she received the impression that Julia Chalford would always expect to be the leader, and took it for granted that her leadership would never be questioned.

CHAPTER FIVE

'WELL, darling, what do you think of my home?' Tony was sitting with Christa in the small room where all the late Mr. Chalford's books were kept and where Tony did much of his writing and accounts at the big walnut roll-topped desk. Tony had just poured her out a glass of sherry. They raised their glasses to each other.

'It's all a bit overwhelming. I'm rather dazed,' she said with a light laugh.

'Oh, you don't have to be,' said Tony lazily. 'You'll soon get used to it – and to us.'

'Do you think your mother would be shocked if I smoked? I saw her expression when you handed me your case last night and I did not take one. I hope that you noted *that* sacrifice. For you, darling,' she added looking at him through her lashes.

'Of course you can smoke, darling,' he said warmly.

He found her, as usual, very provocative and made for man's delight. He had not really been alone with her much since they arrived yesterday. He seized the opportunity, this Sunday evening, to take the glass out of her hand and kiss her with an abandon which he rarely showed. She relaxed and kissed him back hungrily. Then, because he thought he heard footsteps, he released her. With a rapidly beating heart, she sat back in her chair and took her cigarette case out of her bag.

41

'I wish to God you were going to marry me before the first of June,' muttered Tony.

'We do seem to be rather in love, don't we?' murmured Christa.

Tony leaned down to light her cigarette and take one for himself.

'You ought to hear what everybody says about you,' he said.

She smiled. She knew he was pleased because she had made a success with the friends who had dropped in last night for sherry. Pip was already her slave. Mitza – so she was told – had never appeared more friendly towards anyone who entered her kitchen. No doubt it was because Christa had learned to speak German at her Convent School and so could converse with the Austrian woman in her own language.

'But what about your mother? I can't help wondering if *she* really likes me,' said Christa.

'Of course she does,' said Tony.

He lied and he knew it. He had, in fact, known from the start that his mother would not like Christa, even though she could find nothing definite against her. But in Tony's new state of passionate desire he was, for the first time in his life, determined to defeat his mother. He was not going to let her stop his marriage. When he had had a few words with Mrs. Chalford alone last night he had drawn from her the admission that she thought Christa 'wrong' for him. He then made it plain that he intended to go on with the engagement.

'Please welcome her for my sake,' he had ended.

It seemed that Mrs. Chalford had given in, because she had been much less forbidding for the rest of the evening. She had even gone so far as to get out family albums and show Christa the photographs she had wanted to see of Tony when he was small.

This morning, too, Mrs. Chalford had been quite exemplary in her behaviour towards Christa. They had all gone to church at Amersham and when they had returned Mrs. Chalford conducted Christa on a tour of the farm. She had introduced the girl to everybody as 'Mr. Anthony's fiancée'. She had begun to speak of the forthcoming marriage as a *fait accompli*. Nevertheless, Christa had gone to bed *wondering*. Wondering whether she was not up against a hostility that was both premeditated and eradicable. Wondering whether she could ever grow fond of such a mother-in-law. *'Fond,'* no! That was already apparent, but she could respect her. After twenty-four hours at Queen's Lacey, she found much to admire in the older woman; in her efficient control of this big farm.

She could also sense the 'iron hand' on those three sons, and wonder how ruthlessly it could take a grip of her own life once she became Tony's wife.

She liked Pip. He was like a schoolboy still – immature despite the fact that he had done his National Service. He was his mother's mouthpiece and shadow, and he leapt to Tony's commands. Tony gave orders. Tony discussed finance and prices with his mother over the dinner table. But Tony occasionally stood corrected by *her* and acknowledged her mastery. With Christa, *he* was the master – strong and possessive. It was that side of him that she had first liked. She had told Mummy she enjoyed being '*bossed*'; imagined it would be quite pleasant to have a strong-minded husband who would look after her. But, Tony with *his* mother was another person.

Tony was talking to Christa now about his mother.

'She's not a person who shows her feelings much, darling. You mustn't take any notice of her if she appears casual. She's like that, even with *us*.'

Christa's wide sweet mouth curved into a rueful smile.

'She certainly isn't as easy to get on with as my mother.'

'They're different types,' said Tony, and because he was so much in love, he did not add that he found her own mother too 'young and modern' for his liking. He had a preconceived notion that all mothers should be elderly and dignified.

It was as well that the two mothers would not often meet; for certainly *they* would never see eye to eye. And thank goodness Christa was tidier than Mrs. Morley who never seemed to know where anything was in her mews cottage.

Now he had something on his mind and he must come out with it before taking Christa home. She was leaving Queen's Lacey tonight. She did not want her mother to have to make the early start to Covent Garden.

Last night Julia had made it plain that she would be most upset and disappointed if Tony and Christa did not accept her offer of the unused wing for the their future home.

. Tony was a little afraid of the way in which Christa would respond to the idea, so he approached it carefully. First he asked her what she thought of the Queen Anne wing. He was pleased when she replied that she preferred it to the rest of the house.

43

'I love the Jacobean period, but I really prefer Queen Anne or Georgian architecture,' she said. 'I think that wing is simply heaven; like a little house on its own. I adore those square-paned windows and the proportions of the rooms are so good.'

'Do you think it could be made attractive?' asked Tony eagerly.

'Yes – why?' she asked innocently.

After he had told her what his mother had suggested, Christa sat very still. Her first instinct was to say 'no'. But when she saw the look in Tony's eyes she hesitated to damp his ardour. He went on to enumerate the many advantages to be gained by falling in with this plan. The housing problem was acute, and, as his mother said, there was nothing suitable for them in the district. He must be on the spot and what better than living actually on the farm?

Christa looked gravely at him.

'Surely you could always drive over to Queen's Lacey from any place of reasonable radius,' she began.

'I quite agree, darling, and I want us to have our own home eventually of *course*. This is really a question of *faute de mieux*. We can have our own sitting-room and two bedrooms and a bathroom. Mother and I have talked things over and agreed that we should spend some money on it, and you can do it up exactly as you want.'

'Ye-es,' said Christa in a halting voice.

'You could make it most attractive – I know you like interior decorating,' went on Tony, trying to press his point and to please her at the same time. 'Mother says she wouldn't interfere in the way we lived. We would be absolutely on our own, only our domicile would cost us nothing.'

'But Tony darling, we wouldn't be on our own.'

'Yes, we would – we'd have our own sitting-room, darling. It would only mean eating with the family and that would be a help to you. None of my married friends seem able to get domestics easily nowadays. You wouldn't have to do anything here, what with Mitza as cook and all the outside domestic help we can get at Queen's Lacey.'

Christa bit her lip. She could see the advantages of Mrs. Chalford's plan, and from Tony's point of view, of course, it would be admirable. He was still coaxing her. She could have electric central heating put in, he said, because he knew how she felt the cold. And she could turn the wing into her very own home. *But it wouldn't be her home,* she argued to herself. It would still be Julia Chalford's – with Mrs. Chalford at the head of it.

'Oh, no, I really don't think it is a good idea, Tony—' she began, but he interrupted, taking one of her hands; fondling it.

'Oh, darling, don't turn the idea down too quickly. It really has such wonderful advantages for us.'

'But I still wouldn't be the mistress of my own home,' said Christa in a low voice.

'But you *would* – you could manage our little wing exactly as you wanted it. It would only be a question of meals—'

Now it was Christa's turn to break in.

'But it would be so awkward. What about the catering? I mightn't want to eat the same food as your mother.'

'Oh, come, darling, you needn't eat what you don't want,' said Tony with a laugh. 'And you said at dinner last night, Mitza cooks superbly.'

'There are other things. Entertaining our own friends and so on. *That* would be awkward.'

'Why? You would be absolutely on your own in your own sitting-room. We could ask what friends we wanted,' persisted Tony. 'And you must admit it's glorious here at Queen's Lacey. We would never find anything else as perfect.'

Christa's heart sank. Tony seemed already to have decided in his own mind to take over the wing. He must have decided it even before he mentioned it to her.

She was much in love and anxious to please him, but she had always considered herself a resolute sort of girl who could hold her own. Now she seemed to be swept along on a strong tide that threatened to carry her into dangerous reaches. It was an uncomfortable sensation. It scared her. She went on arguing against the plan for a moment longer – as though trying to keep her head above water.

At last Tony said:

'Let's go and look over the wing – come on, darling. You've only seen it once.'

Tony could be very persuasive when he wanted; and all that easy charm of his was being manufactured to dazzle her. Despite herself, Christa went with him and began slowly to change her mind. She even ended by admitting that it would be very foolish to turn down Mrs. Chalford's handsome offer. Walking arm in arm with Tony through the rooms and up the staircase which had the beautiful original banisters carved out of rosewood, Christa felt her heart go out to it. It was pure Queen Anne. The big sitting-room had fine windows at each end and quite a lovely Adam fireplace. If she liked, Tony said, they would have a polished floor put down. It was a grey day today, but yesterday Christa had seen the wing with the sun warming every corner. The drawing-room windows faced east and west, and upstairs due south. It was very much on its own yet had to be approached through the main building. Therein lay the snag, thought Christa. They wouldn't have their own front door. She wouldn't even have her own little kitchen. But when she made this observation, Tony began to coax and bribe.

'I'll get a tiny kitchen made for you so if you ever felt you couldn't face the family, we could stay over here and make our own omelettes.'

She gave him that enchanting look through her sweeping lashes and said:

'You *are* spoiled! You love to get your own way.'

He looked back at her laughing tolerantly – blind to the implications of the future; to everything but his present desire for her.

'I only want you to be happy, and naturally at the same time I want to please my mother. You do understand, don't you? She's given us boys everything. The whole place is run for us. I think it would be a tremendous joy to her if she could persuade us to live at Queen's Lacey.'

'And you really think I won't get on her nerves – or she on mine?'

'I don't think my mother ever gets on people's nerves,' said Tony a trifle haughtily.

Christa thought: 'I suppose one of the nicest things about Tony is his loyalty to his mother. Perhaps it means that he'll love me and be loyal to me in the same way. They say that a man always treats his wife as he does his mother.'

She, too, was blinded by desire and the wish to please everybody.

'Darling, let's live here, if only for a few months or a year at most,' pleaded Tony, 'then perhaps something will come on the market which we can buy, and we'll have our own place.'

'Are you certain that your brothers won't mind?'

Tony laughed and replied easily:

'What young Pip wants couldn't matter less – but in any case he thinks you're the cat's whiskers.'

'And Richard?'

'Oh, one hardly ever sees Rich. When he *is* in the house, he's either strumming that darned piano, or reading. But then you like books and music. You two will get on. I don't think you are likely to see much of either of my brothers.'

Then Christa drew a deep breath and said:

'All right – if you truly believe it'll work, I'll agree. We will try it.'

'And if it doesn't work we can always move,' said Tony. And now he caught her in his arms and kissed her with fervour, delighted that he had made her change her mind; knowing that his mother would be equally pleased. He repeated:

'We can always move.'

Long afterwards, when the rot had set in, Christa was to remind him of those words.

CHAPTER SIX

THE next few weeks in Christa's life rushed by with quite frightening rapidity. Soon there would be no more for her of the hard routine of early rising, summer or winter, in order to go to the Market to buy flowers. No more opening up the little florist's shop in the King's Road and helping Mummy to arrange the sweet-smelling flowers and plants. No more rushing back to the cottage to get meals; or quiet evenings spent with Mummy reading or sewing, or listening to the music which they both loved, on radio or gramophone. Christa felt that she had become a different person. She already led a different life. She wore Tony's ring on her finger: a fine solitaire diamond which had cost him a lot of money. But he had insisted on buying it for her. He overwhelmed her with generosity. He was literally storming the quiet haven of the Morley's cottage; driving up from Coleshill late every afternoon in order to spend the evenings with her. Or taking her down to Queen's Lacey at weekends.

He gave her no time to think – to change her mind. The man who was by nature cool and aloof and a little contemptuous of emotion, was not himself during these all-important days. His mother knew it and deplored the fact; feeling that this girl, Christa, had come into his life and altered him – not for the best. She did not like Christa any the better for it; she did not really relish the idea of Christa's living at Queen's Lacey.

As for Sarah Morley she knew nothing but a shattering fear for her daughter.

In her opinion this was infatuation at its worst. She did not believe that either Christa or Tony knew their own mind nor, in the passion of their urge towards each other, were they capable of wisdom or logic. The fact that Tony was flinging his money around, dazzling Christa just a little bit, made no impression on the older and more experienced woman. She believed herself to be a judge of character. Tony was the peacock spreading his tail; displaying all his best qualities in order to attract the female. It was the kind of emotional dishonesty which Mrs. Morley had always abhorred. She knew that it happened hourly, daily to thousands of young people. It was 'the marriage trap' with a vengeance, but she could not bear her beloved Christa to become a victim.

When Christa had first told her she had agreed to live at Queen's Lacey, Mrs. Morley had, however, spoken bluntly.

'It will never work, darling; it rarely if ever does. Young people ought to start life in their own home.'

'But it's only for a bit,' Christa argued (Mrs. Morley was ready to swear it was against her own inner convictions), 'and the wing is so lovely – you'll adore it. And we shall be quite apart from the rest of the family except for meals.' Then she had added: 'Don't worry, Mummy, *please*, I know what I'm doing. I've talked it over with Tony and Mrs. Chalford, and she and I are actually getting along much better than we did that first time. Last week-end at Queen's Lacey was really very pleasant.'

Yes, thought Sarah Morley, she's pleased because she's got her own way. She's the spider who has lured you into her web and once she's got you there, she'll change her attitude and eat you right up!

But she could not say *that* to Christa about the woman who was going to be her mother-in-law. It would be positively criminal to try and set her against Mrs. Chalford and cause mischief from the start. But what was that saying about '*there are none so blind as those who will not see*'?

When Sarah Morley actually met Tony's mother all her doubts about the wisdom of this marriage became a grim certainty. It could not survive such a woman – more especially now that Christa had agreed to live under Mrs. Chalford's roof.

They met at the engagement lunch. Mrs. Chalford with punctilious formality held the party at Claridge's. She wore her usual impeccable tweeds and an expensive if unbecoming hat. She had also ordered an expensive meal, and champagne. Everybody talked and laughed a lot, but Sarah Morley's spirits had sunk low. For from the first moment in which she had looked into Julia Chalford's cold shrewd eyes, she had disliked her. She had sensed the hostility behind the tight-lipped smiles. She had not even been comforted when Julia Chalford addressed Christa as 'dear' or appeared to be tolerant and gracious. Sarah had come away from Claridge's, bursting to say:

'That's a thoroughly unpleasant and destructive woman. Oh, Christa, my dearest one – be careful of her – or she'll destroy you and your marriage!'

But Christa had seemed pleased and happy. She said:

'I think it all went off very well. Mrs. Chalford was awfully nice to me, and admired my dress. She told Tony I had great taste in clothes. You know, I think her bark is worse than her bite and I shall quite like her once I get to know her better. She's wonderful to those sons of hers, isn't she, Mummy, and they adore her.'

So Sarah Morley maintained silence, and suffered in her solitude from bitter fears for Christa's future happiness.

Christa, if she had had any doubts in the beginning, had none at the moment. Her love for Tony had changed the whole of her existence. She tasted the delights of being loved and admired and sought after. She felt that she had achieved quite a little triumph in making friends with Julia Chalford.

But she was secretly very worried about her own mother. Mummy looked ill and tired and seemed unable to keep up to the usual work in the shop. Tony agreed that he did not think Mrs. Morley was looking at all well and on his advice – Tony loved to be consulted and to give counsel – she sent for her cousin Judy Masters and installed her straightaway both in the mews cottage and at The Greenhouse.

But whenever she had any time at all in which to think Christa fretted about leaving her mother – more especially when she was so unlike her gay sparkling self. She tried to induce the older woman to see their doctor and have another X-ray done – because the last had not been very satisfactory. But Sarah Morley had a horror of illness – more especially of operations – even of medicine. She boasted that she had only one bottle in her medicine cupboard and that was a simple cough mixture. She refused stubbornly to give in to her aches or pains and now she was not going to let illness – or the fear of it – spoil Christa's wedding.

One evening Tony arrived unexpectedly when Christa and her mother were entertaining a couple from the mews cottage next door. The girl, Dana, was a model. Her husband played the violin in a television orchestra. They were always hard up. On that particular evening they came in for coffee and a cigarette, unconventionally attired. Bill in *matelot* canvas trousers and a check sports shirt. Dana in the same sort of shirt with a pair of scarlet jeans.

They were a feckless couple but kind and friendly and on one occasion, a year ago, when Christa was laid up with flu, Dana had come in and looked after her while Mrs. Morley was at work. They were not a pretentious pair but Christa got on particularly well with Bill who had composed several charming songs that she could sing. She had an untrained voice but it was light and sweet.

From the moment that Tony arrived on the scene the atmosphere changed. He assumed what Mrs. Morley called his 'haughty attitude'; conversation lagged, and finally the young couple rose and left. Then Christa said to him:

'Don't you think they're a sweet pair? Isn't Dana *beautiful*?'

Tony replied:

'I suppose so. But not my type. I haven't much use for women in jeans, and I though the young man quite appalling.'

'Oh, darling, he's a *very* fine musician,' Christa had protested warmly.

Mrs. Morley had kept a rigid silence. Her personal opinion was that Tony could be an absolute prig when he wanted, and a snob too. Then Christa restored the good humour by pretending to be mortally offended and handing Tony her ring.

'Take back your diamond, sir. I thought *I* was your ideal. *I* also wear jeans. You obviously can't want to marry me.'

Of course he had relaxed, laughed and told her that she was adorable and that if she liked jeans, she could wear them.

Mrs. Morley had left them alone and gone to her kitchen to make fresh coffee. She was conscious of that persistent frightening pain in her side. And of the still more frightening belief that Tony was a fraud. She was ashamed of herself because she had wished fervently that Christa *had* been handing back that diamond, and was never going to see Tony or any of the Chalfords again.

Meanwhile Richard had not come back from France.

Christa had still to make the acquaintance of this particular future brother-in-law. When he was last at Queen's Lacey Mrs. Chalford had spoken with cold disapproval of her second son. He had promised to return in a fortnight and had now written from a place called Pessac-sur-Dordognes, on the Loire, to say that he was extending his holiday. He and his friend Jimmy had had an accident on the outskirts of the town. Nothing serious and the young men had escaped injury but the car needed repairs and would have to be in a garage for at least another ten days. He and Jimmy were having what he called 'a glorious trip' through the wine country. He said that he thought it would not matter much if he prolonged his annual holiday. He loathed trains and infinitely preferred the idea of motoring back with Jim. Let old Tony and Pip and Gomme 'cope' for the few days longer.

Mrs. Chalford read this letter aloud at the dinner table. Pip looked up and grinned.

'I don't blame him,' he said.

Mrs. Chalford raised her brows.

'I understand him preferring to drive back, but he might remember that there is work to be done on the farm.'

'He might also remember,' put in Tony, 'that I am about to be married and that he has got to be back in time for the wedding. You did warn him that we've fixed it for 1st June, didn't you, Mother?'

'I never forget what you ask me to do, Tony,' she said in her cool precise voice.

Christa, who was now beginning to feel a little more at home in the long panelled dining-room, the walls of which were hung with portraits of former Chalfords, put in her say:

'If I were Richard I'd bribe the garage to go slow on the repairs. It's simply heavenly in France at this time of year. I was over there last May for a week with friends of mine.'

There was silence. Pip eyed Christa with furtive admiration, then glanced out of the corners of his eyes at his mother. She looked at her future daughter-in-law, crumbled her bread on her plate and said nothing. Tony coughed, and said:

'Yes – it's pretty nice over there in May but if he *doesn't* get back for our wedding there'll be trouble. I want him for my best man.'

After the meal when they were alone, Christa teased Tony about this.

'Sometimes you scare me – you're such a martinet when you want to be. Don't hurry the poor boy back from his holiday even if he misses the wedding. Find another "best man" darling.'

Tony was astonished and allowed himself to show it.

'My darling girl – there is such a thing as *duty*. You can't go off and leave a job just because you're one of the bosses. If Richard was *employed* by somebody, he couldn't write to his employer and say he was waiting for his car to be repaired.'

'You're terribly conscientious, aren't you, darling?'

The lovely golden eyes twinkled, at him, but the twinkle was lost on Tony who replied:

'I try to be.'

'Oh, dear,' said Christa with a little grimace, 'I can see I shall have to mind my p's and q's when I am Mrs. Anthony.'

Tony's mood changed. The charm broke through the surface.

'You shall to exactly as you like when you are Mrs. Anthony, my darling, but Richard does important work on the farm you know. He is the expert, really.'

Christa reached on tiptoe and kissed his chin.

'Does it mean my poor Tony ·will have to do some extra work?'

She was teasing him again. He did not really like it but she was blind to the fact. They dropped the question of Richard playing truant in France. Tony began to discuss their forthcoming trip to Paris.

One of the greatest thrills was getting that lovely wing decorated and furnished. Julie Chalford was being quite co-operative, except that she kept wanting to give things to Tony. It was good of her but awkward for Christa. She didn't always like them, but Tony seemed delighted, and what could Christa do but accept? There was, for instance the embarrasing affair of the curtains. Mrs. Chalford had found two pairs of curtains that used to hang in her drawing-room. They were expensive and well lined. She suggested that they might 'come in' for the sitting-room in the wing which her son and his wife were to occupy. But the brocade was of a particular shade of mustard which Christa had always hated, and she could not see the colour fitting in with her schemes. But Tony argued.

'They're such good stuff and all that, and curtaining is so expensive these days. Wouldn't it be sensible to use them?'

'Yes – but oh the *colour*!' protested Christa.

'Well, do tell Mother you'll have them, darling. Don't let's offend her.'

Christa said no more. The danger of 'offending mother' began to loom rather largely on the horizon. But whenever it confronted her, she deliberately banished the sinister inference, and told herself that she must not be too selfish, nor could she expect Tony or his mother to share hers and Mummy's tastes. After all she could *dye* the curtains, and hope Mrs. Chalford wouldn't be offended by *that*.

On went the time. . . .

Christa's little pile of pretty clothes grew larger and was finally transferred to a new and expensive suitcase which had been sent to her as a wedding present from her Aunt Claire, Lady Baintree, who was Mrs. Morley's eldest sister. She lived in Bath and was crippled with arthritis, therefore unable to pay visits to London. But she sent a generous cheque with the suitcase, and Tony always seemed interested in this aristocratic member of his fiancée's family and suggested that they should drive down to Bath to see her one day after the honeymoon.

The engagement and the date of the wedding had been announced in both *The Times* and *Telegraph*. Congratulations and presents began to pour in. Not so many or so expensive from the Morley side because they had few relatives and not such a wide circle of friends as the Chalfords. A frightening number reached Tony. Christa seemed to spend most of her time writing 'thank you' letters, unpacking parcels with Tony when he came up in the evenings, or packing them up again ready to be taken down to Queen's Lacey.

The wedding which Tony had first told his mother was to be quiet had developed into a big affair. Mrs. Chalford – or Tony – kept finding fresh friends or distant relatives whom they must not 'offend'. (That dread word, thought Christa.) Over one hundred and fifty invitations had gone out and most were accepted.

Christa had made it plain to her fiancé that her mother could not really afford such a big wedding nor had Mrs. Morley the strength for it at present. But in this, Mrs. Chalford openly interfered. Tony was one of the best-known gentlemen farmers in Buckinghamshire. He just could *not* have a small insignificant wedding, she declared. She, Julia, would like to pay for the reception at Claridge's (the hotel she always favoured on these occasions). Both Mrs. Morley and Christa fought against the idea but Tony in the long run made it difficult for them to refuse.

'If my mother wants to help – do please allow it,' he said. 'She

53

can afford it – she'll be awfully upset if we say no. After all it *is* a big day in our lives. Mother's terribly good at organizing and you' – he had smiled at Christa's mother – 'need not do any more than you feel able to do.'

Sarah Morley protested.

'It's wrong. I want to feel I am marrying off my own daughter. But what can a poor little florist do?' she added. 'And if you've got one hundred and fifty relatives and friends it is a bit awkward. We just haven't got the money for a huge reception and I admit it. It has been difficult for Christa and myself to live since the war – let alone save.'

Christa could see the points of view of both the mothers. In the end it was Sarah Morley who made the whole thing easy for her daughter by giving in.

'I only want what you two children want,' she told the young couple.

'Oh, does any bride really know just what she wants immediately before her wedding day!' sighed Christa.

On went the time – remorselessly for Sarah Morley. Gaily and crazily for Christa . . . until the 1st June – her wedding day dawned.

CHAPTER SEVEN

HOLY TRINITY CHURCH in Sloane Square was packed.

Pip and a young cousin at Oxford acting as ushers, had taken their instructions from Mrs. Chalford and divided the guests without paying too much attention as to which side they should be placed. For as she acidly remarked, there were many more Chalford guests than Morley.

Richard seated himself beside Tony in a front pew. The organ, rich and muffled, played for the waiting congregation. Richard kept wondering wildly if he had done everything that he had been detailed to do. But Tony seemed to be taking things in his stride with calm self-assurance.

Richard patted his waistcoat pocket. Yes, the ring was safely there. And he had the Airways tickets for the young couple's flight to Paris, tomorrow morning. Tonight they were staying in London – at Claridge's.

When Tony had broken the news to Richard that he and his wife were having the unused wing at Queen's Lacey done up for their future home and that for the moment after the honeymoon they would live with the family, Richard had felt rather annoyed.

'I think it's a damn fool plan,' he announced bluntly. 'You ought to have a place of your own.'

'We know that, thanks,' was Tony's stiff reply. 'But it suits us to live at Queen's Lacey for the moment.'

Richard had grumbled:

'With a girl living in the house one's got to be careful how one looks and dresses. I can hardly strip to the bone on Sunday afternoons and sunbathe in the orchard, and all the rest of it, can I? It's going to be awkward.'

He had received no sympathy so continued to grumble to himself. Of course he could see exactly what had happened. Mama wanted to keep her 'Tony-boy' at home. Richard was slightly cynical about his mother's attitude towards Tony, although never jealous. He envied no man. He was a law unto himself, and he did not expect to be shown preference by others. If he guessed that he was not as high in favour with his mother as Tony or Pip, it caused him little or no distress. On the whole Mrs. Chalford treated them all much alike. Richard had no cause for complaint.

But he did feel uneasy about Tony's wife living at the farm.

Now Richard turned his head; he picked out one or two familiar faces and particularly that of Ursula Corby. She had come to the wedding with a woman friend from Amersham. He felt a bit sorry for Ursula. Nice of her to show up under the circumstances, he considered. She must have hoped for some time that Tony would marry her. Richard wondered why Tony hadn't done so. She was very smart; with bright pink flowers in a chic hat on the smooth dark head. Just behind her were the Thorntons. The sight of young Susan caused Richard less pleasure. He wished she hadn't come.

In the pew immediately behind him was his mother. She had been forced to abandon her tweeds for the occasion and put on a navy-blue dress and coat. She wore with it a narrow sable tie which she had had since her girlhood. It spent most of its existence lying between tissue paper with moth balls for company. Richard stared critically at this woman who was his mother and to whom he bore no resemblance whatsoever. He had often wondered how she had ever given birth to him. His respect and affection were concrete things but he could not say that she made an attractive figure. Today her choice of a hat was almost as bad as Susan's. A black straw hat that did nothing to help soften her angular features. She was unsmiling. Richard, who knew her so well, was sure she was feeling neither comfortable nor happy.

Over the other side of the aisle sat a frail-looking attractive woman with ash-coloured hair – Christa's mother. The tall girl beside her was her niece Judy. Richard thought that Christa's mother looked enchanting. She was a porcelain figure in pale rose-pink. Amazing to think that she was so efficient and ran quite successfully that florist's shop in Chelsea. Tony said she was a sick woman. Richard felt sorry.

His gaze returned to Susan Thornton who sat between her father and her aunt. She made it so embarrassingly obvious these days that she felt for him a kind of suppressed passion which was half genuine and half a schoolgirl's 'crush'. She was twenty-four but looked seventeen, and behaved as though she was still adolescent. She had never really grown up. Richard had long since decided that she had an immature mind as well as that thin childish body. With her short-cut, darkish hair, she looked her best in riding breeches or the slacks and jerseys which she wore around the farm. She looked her worst today, he thought, poor Susan. Smart clothes didn't suit her. And she had atrocious taste. She had chosen a dress of a bilious green colour which made her look sallow.

There was a stir in the congregation. Everyone stood up.

Now he heard Tony mutter:

'This is it. . . .'

Richard and the bridegroom moved to the chancel step. Richard passed a hand over his hair and turned his gaze in the direction of the figures coming slowly up the aisle. First the choirboys, then the Vicar, and now the white-robed figure of the bride with head slightly bent, her arm through that of a short jolly-looking man with thick grey hair. He, Richard presumed, was Brigadier Filing, an old family friend who had been at school with Christa's father. He was retired from the Army nowadays and lived at his club in Pall Mall. In the absence of any near relative, he had consented to give Christa away.

The choirboys filed into the stalls. The Vicar turned and faced the congregation. Now Richard saw his future sister-in-law for the first time. He saw her quite clearly and experienced an extraordinary jolt of the heart – of his whole spirit. She was of course like that snapshot he had seen, only much more beautiful. So beautiful that he felt dazzled. With an eye for detail, he noted the simplicity of her dress – he did not know what the material was – but it was a stiff white brocade, fitting closely over the breast, and drawn tightly into the smallest waist Richard had ever imagined. The collar was high and the sleeves long and tight, which gave her a nun-like appearance. The veil (Tony had taken care to tell Richard that it was Limerick lace, loaned by Lady Baintree) framed one of the most haunting faces Richard had ever seen. He watched her move to her place beside Tony (she seemed to float rather than walk) and hand her bouquet of white roses and stephanotis to the pretty girl in pale blue who was her only bridesmaid.

The Vicar opened the service:

'*Dearly Beloved we are gathered here together. . . .*'

Richard no longer saw Christa's face, only her straight slender back. He felt odd – shaken in some peculiar way.

'Dear life!' he thought, 'I didn't think she'd look quite like that. . . .'

And for a single crazy moment he wished that she did *not* look like that; feeling in this one dazzling flash of time that she had fired all his inner hunger for true beauty and then left the hunger unslaked – and himself in torment.

'Dear life!' he muttered again and tried to concentrate on the service.

Julia Chalford was also staring at the bride and bridegroom. She knew nothing but a bitter jealousy – a kind of cold fury because this girl was about to become Tony's wife and there was nothing she could do to prevent it.

Sarah Morley saw only the slender figure of her daughter. A fog of tears blinded her vision. She was losing her darling; losing her to the wrong man – of that she was certain. She was conscious, too, of that pain in her side – a pain so fierce today that it threatened to defeat her courage and endurance. If it went on, she would have to sit down. She knew that she was almost at the end of her tether. She had been ill all night. Nobody knew. She was going to let Christa have this day – *her day* – and not spoil it, whatever happened later on.

Lady Corby also stared at the backs of the bride and bridegroom – more especially at the tall handsome bridegroom. She, too, was conscious of jealousy, less fierce than Mrs. Chalford's. But she felt deeply disappointed. She had been in love with

Tony ever since her husband died. She had been certain he would return her affections. It had been a hideous blow to her when she had first learned that he was going to marry some little girl from a florist's shop in the King's Road. But she had to admit now when she saw Christa that Tony had not picked a 'dud'.

Susan Thornton, standing very stiffly to attention, stared forlornly at the best man, and felt an agony of frustration and despair. Her hands – how she loathed the tight compression of her gloves – picked at the white booklet of hymns which bore the gilt-printed initials A.C. and C.M. She wanted to burst into tears. The last time she had seen Richard alone she had asked him to take her to the cinema in High Wycombe, but he had politely but definitely refused. Yet they used to be such good friends. He had always been so nice to her, in a casual fraternal sort of way. He was so *handsome*, she thought – that brown hard face of his filled her with intense desire. It was *murder* being in love with a man who did not love you. If only she wasn't so thin and scraggy and didn't look so awful when she was dressed up. If only *she* could have been more like that fair-haired ethereal bride who had lured Tony into marriage. Then *she* might have got Richard.

'Oh, *Richard*,' she uttered his name soundlessly, and was glad that it was time now to kneel down and pray so that she could bury her face in her hands.

The bride, herself, had noted vaguely the sun-tanned face of the one Chalford brother whom she had not yet met. She thought how good-looking he was. But now all her attention was turned upon her bridegroom. As was right and proper, she thought with a small secret smile, she felt more intensely in love with Tony today than ever before. The doubts of yesterday had gone. She was confident that she was not making a mistake. Once or twice during the ceremony he had turned to look at her and she saw in his eyes what she thought to be a love deep and sincere enough to satisfy her soul's needs. This really was a tremendous thrill. She was going to love every moment of her wedding. It was exciting, solemn and gay, too – all things rolled into one.

Mrs. Chalford had given her a string of real pearls – from her own jewel case – as a wedding present. Christa was wearing them. Tony's present was a beautiful stole of blue Norwegian foxes; her choice. She had always wanted a really glamorous fur and although Tony had said she wouldn't wear such a thing at Queen's Lacey much, he had admitted it would be wonderful for parties, or nights out in Town.

Mummy had been splendid and dug into her small nest-egg of savings to buy what she could for the trousseau. This diamond star that Christa wore at her throat, was Mummy's own brooch which she had worn at her wedding to Christa's father.

'My day for wearing diamonds is over; you must have it, poppet,' Sarah had said.

The only shadow on Christa's happiness today was the fact that Mummy looked so ill, despite her carefully tinted cheeks. But Mrs. Morley had assured her that it was just because she was over-tired, and she would rest during the next few days and let Judy cope with the shop.

Now the ring was on Christa's finger. Christa found herself signing her maiden name, *Christa Sarah Morley*, for the last time. The Vicar said:

'Let me be the first to congratulate you, Mrs. Chalford.'

She thanked him and shook hands. Tony bent to kiss her – perfunctorily – because he did not care to exhibit his emotion in the vestry. Christa hugged and kissed her own mother.

'Mummy *darling*!'

'All the happiness in the world, my dearest,' Sarah whispered back.

Then Julia Chalford ... behaving very nicely ... touching the bride's flushed cheek with her lips ... added her congratulations, and the words: 'How nice you look, dear.'

Christa in the emotion of the moment kissed the woman back with a warmth from which Julia shrank. Under her breath, Christa said:

'I *promise* I'll make Tony very very happy. Don't worry.'

'I won't,' said Mrs. Chalford coolly.

A few moments later, Christa was in the hired Daimler driving to Claridge's with her husband.

She smiled at him through her lashes, clinging tightly to his hand. The stephanotis on her bouquet trembled slightly. Her breath came quickly.

'So here we are!' she said.

'You look beautiful,' said Tony. 'I must say I like having such a beautiful wife.'

She sat back so that she could not be seen as they drove through the traffic down Sloane Street. All the deepest of her feelings came to the surface. She asked:

'You do love me, *don't* you – really *really* love me.'

'Of course I do,' he said, and lifted the slim hand with the new wedding ring to his lips.

It was the right reply and the right gesture. She was in a daze of excitement. Yet somehow she felt as though a small chill wind shivered through her warmth. It was as though she needed more from him. What more – poor Tony, she asked herself wryly. Mummy had told her last night, when they were having their final heart-to-heart, not to expect too much ... so many men, she had said, seem afraid of their own feelings – particularly Englishmen who were repressed from the time they went to their Preparatory Schools; taught to cover up their emotions.

'You've always been rather too impulsive and warm-hearted. All people are not like you, darling, and the honeymoon's a difficult time anyhow. Husband and wife have got to adjust themselves to the new partnership. They can't always meet on common ground right away.'

Well, thought Christa, it was sound advice and I must follow it.

Now on to the arduous duties of the reception; Christa and Tony, side by side, shaking hands as the long line of guests filed by. So beautiful did the bride look that even Ursula Corby meant it when she pressed Christa's hands and congratulated her.

Ursula remarked to a woman friend as they moved off:

'I must say I like the look of Mrs. Anthony.'

The friend who had lived in the district longer than Ursula and known the Chalfords for years, put her tongue in her cheek.

'I don't think it will be a success all the same. Mrs. Chalford will make a formidable mother-in-law.'

'Oh, I get on very well with her,' said Ursula.

'*You* do, dear, but I wonder about Mrs. Tony. We shall see.'

Richard did not have any conversation with his newly made sister-in-law until the last guest had been welcomed and the reception was in full swing. Champagne flowed. Smoked salmon and pâté sandwiches were handed around. Mrs. Chalford had organized a handsome wedding breakfast, with the best wine. But the bride's mother had chosen the cake. It was an exceedingly fine affair; three tiers of frosted ice; the top encrusted with sugar roses and silver bells.

Bride and bridegroom began to circulate amongst the guests.

60

Christa talked to so many people whom she did not know and who were Tony's friends, that afterwards she could not remember who they were. Pip had just come up to her looking flushed and as untidy as usual, given her a smacking kiss and said: 'Hullo, sis!'

Then a low-pitched voice – unfamiliar to Christa – said behind her:

'What an intolerable youth you are, Pip, do go away.'

Those around who heard, laughed. Christa turned her head. She looked into a pair of brilliant hazel eyes.

'I'm Richard,' said the voice, 'we haven't met yet, although I've heard a lot about you.'

'Oh, of course, Richard! And I've heard about you,' said Christa, and held out a hand

He took the hand. It was very slender yet firm. He looked down at the slim fingers with the pointed rose-varnished nails. He said:

'Tony ought to have your hands sculptured. They're the kind you see on Greek statues – just not true!'

She was astonished and delighted. She flushed a warm pink. How unlike the rest of the Chalfords – this sun-browned young man with the amusing mouth and eyes that expressed such open admiration. He did not appear to be troubled by Tony's or Pip's inhibitions. Like Pip, he bent to kiss her, the merest brushing of his lips against her forehead.

'I shall *not* say "Hullo sis",' he murmured. 'But I *will* say I think it's very decent of my brother Tony to give me a goddess for a sister-in-law.'

'I've never been called a "goddess" before', she giggled.

Richard grinned.

'I have a passion for Greek history. You are the nearest thing I've ever seen to my conception of those divine-looking creatures who used to wander around the ancient temples, on the "burning isles".'

Christa blinked. He noted the length of the wonderful lashes.

'It doesn't make sense,' she said, 'I've been told you're the real farmer of the family. You oughtn't to be talking about Greek islands.'

'Well, I'm certainly not going to spoil your wedding by discussing mangel-wurzels or pigs,' he retorted.

They both laughed. Richard added:

'Anyhow I take back all I've ever said about Tony having no taste.'

61

'Of course he has taste!' exclaimed Christa with a show of indignation.

'I believe it now,' said Richard with that rather brazen look into her eyes which she found singularly disconcerting. *'By the way, how you gonna like it down on the farm?'*

'That sounds like the old song.'

'It is and it goes on: *"After you've seen Paree!"* '

'Well, I'll tell you after I've come back from "Paree",' said Christa, her eyes full of laughter.

'You know Paris, don't you?'

'Yes, I adore it.'

'All the same you and Tony ought to do what I've just done and tour the wine country.'

'I'm sure I should like that but we want to go on to Rome.'

'Ah, Rome!' said Richard softly. 'I went to Rome the year I first came down from Oxford. It's perfectly splendid. You haven't lived until you've stood on the steps of St. Peter's, and seen the sky on a summer's evening with that lucid golden light shining behind the hills. And the fountains . . . *oh*, those fountains!'

'Three coins and all,' she said.

'Three coins and all,' he echoed solemnly.

'You know Rome well?'

'Well enough. One needs to stay there a year. Two weeks' holiday is too short. One sees everything and nothing.'

'I shall go crazy there,' she exclaimed.

Richard thought: *'You* will, *Tony* won't. He'll be bored stiff and he's not capable of "going crazy" over anything. Perhaps over *you*, who knows?'

And Richard looked at Christa's full underlip which had a slight charming cleft in it. There was passion in this girl behind the façade of delicate purity, he decided. As for that rare combination of fair hair with golden eyes – dear life! how had Tony induced such a divine creature to love him?

To have *her* at Queen's Lacey . . . to be able to see, to speak with her daily . . . to look upon that dazzling golden beauty. It was for Richard a moment shot with dangerous electric currents. For she had been made his brother's wife only an hour ago.

Christa murmured:

'Aren't I lucky – to have Tony for a husband and you and Pip for brothers?'

Richard looked at her strangely, then, turning, picked a glass of champagne up from a tray carried by a passing waiter and took a long draught.

'Yes, very lucky,' he said and moved away from her.

Tony came up.

'Darling, come along – they want us to go and stand by the cake. The Brigadier is going to make a speech.'

Christa forgot Richard. She tucked an arm through her husband's. They moved towards the table, smiling and chatting to the crowd as they threaded their way. Mrs. Chalford, who was standing near the entrance talking politely to Christa's mother, saw Richard striding towards her, with a deep scowl on his forehead.

'Where are you off to?' she asked.

'I want some fresh air – it's too hot in here.'

'Really, dear, you ought to stay and talk to people.'

Richard shrugged his shoulders and turned to the little woman in rose-pink who stood beside Mrs. Chalford. He recognized a faded likeness of Christa. He shook hands with Mrs. Morley.

'I do congratulate you,' he said. 'You have a lovely daughter. My brother is very lucky.'

After he had gone, Sarah said:

'What a charming looking boy – not a bit like the other two. They are so fair.'

'Yes,' said Mrs. Chalford, 'Rich has always been shall we say the odd man out – a bit of a mixture – an excellent farmer but too restless – his is rather an artistic temperament, I fear.'

'Ah!' thought Christa's mother. 'But I am sure he is warm-hearted and lovable and much more *human* than Tony.'

There was a hush among the guests. Brigadier Filing was beginning to say pretty things about the bride; how long he'd known her; what a lucky chap the bridegroom was. Christa looked at her husband with the happy dewy look of a young bride very much in love. Then toasts were made, more champagne was drunk and finally bride and bridegroom cut the cake.

'Where's Rich got to?' Tony said towards the end of the reception.

Nobody had seen him. Then Pip came up to his elder brother and handed him an envelope.

'These are your air tickets. Everything's fixed for your car and so forth,' he announced, 'but when I saw Rich just now he asked me to apologize to you and Christa. He was took ill or something and has gone off home.'

'*Took* ill!' repeated Tony, frowning. 'What on earth do you mean, Pip?'

'Oh, I don't know. He said he had developed a cracking head or something. Anyhow, he's vanished.'

'There's a nice thing! Our best man, too,' said Tony crossly.

'Never mind, darling,' said Christa. 'I'm sorry poor Richard's got a bad head but we don't really need him now.'

'He must always do the wrong thing,' said Tony darkly.

'Never mind,' repeated Christa in a soothing voice. 'Actually I thought your Richard was rather attractive.'

But she immediately capped the statement by adding in a silken whisper: 'Though not as attractive as my husband. No man could be!'

Easily flattered, Tony's frown vanished. He pressed her hand and said:

'Go and change now, sweet, and let's get away from this crowd.'

PART TWO

CHAPTER ONE

A YEAR and some months later Christa walked into the kitchen. Mitza stood at the long scrubbed table, hands and wrists deep in flour while she kneaded the dough in a big yellow basin. The air was full of the scent of baking scones.

It was warm and homely in this, Christa's favourite of all the rooms at Queen's Lacey. For it was the only one that she felt belonged less to the Chalford family than to the Austrian cook, and where she, Christa, could relax and be herself. Mitza's small short-sighted eyes peered at the young lady. She nodded and clicked her tongue against her teeth.

'You haf come for a cup of tea, *hein*? You haf another headache, isn't it?'

'Yes,' said Christa and put a hand to her forehead wearily. 'It is! Dear Mitza, you always seem to know what I want and why I want it. Mitza, you *are* a poppet!' and she put an arm round the stout plump little woman and kissed her cheek.

Mitza wiped her hands and switched on the electric kettle.

'A nice cup of tea and *zwei* aspirins, *hein*?'

'Thanks, Mitza darling. I've got the *zwei* aspirins.'

Christa's listless voice indicated the state of her mind and body. She had never before felt so down – so devitalized. She sat in Mitza's basket chair looking out of the windows at the courtyard and beyond to the paddock. Heino, one of the Estonians, was driving a huge sow – with a litter of squealing piglets following – across the yard. It was raining. The weather alone was enough to depress anybody, Christa mused on this last day of August. In fact they had only had one full week of sunshine so far this summer. It had been deplorably wet.

She knew now that without central heating, this huge old house was bitterly cold. How she dreaded the second winter. Not so much because of the physical discomfort, as the *mental*. To the town-bred, sociable girl, the thought of living at Queen's Lacey yet another winter, cut off from everybody except the Chalfords and their restricted circle of friends, was a menace.

She only half listened to Mitza who had begun to chat in

German. She heard her own voice answering: '*Yah*' or '*Nein*', but while she crushed the aspirins into powder and washed them down with the strong good tea that Mitza had made for her, her thoughts wandered in an interminable circle. It was as though she, her essential ego, could not escape from that circle. It described an arc, round and round to the whisper of the words '*Queen's Lacey ... Tony ... Tony ... Queen's Lacey ... Julia ... Richard ... Pip*' and back to Tony.

These revolving thoughts embraced all that had happened since she became Tony's wife. Jumbled up; confused, unhappy.

She knew that she was a bundle of nerves – unusual for Christa – and lately she had been having these headaches too often. Always flying to the aspirin bottle and to Mitza's cups of tea.

Christa looked at the kitchen clock. Three o'clock, Tony and his mother were in Aylesbury at some sort of Board meeting. They wouldn't be back till five. Pip was supervising the men who had just finished cutting the corn. They were about to put some of the chickens on to the stubble. She had heard him announce this at breakfast.

And Richard? At the thought of her eldest brother-in-law she swallowed an extra large mouthful of tea and felt it scald her throat. She choked suddenly.

'*Ach! Liebschen*,' said Mitza who was privileged now to call Mrs. Anthony by such an endearing name, 'something has gone down the wrong vay, isn't it?'

'Yes,' said Christa. 'Everything is going the wrong way!' and she gave a cynical little laugh.

She thought of Richard again but shut her eyes tightly as though she did not want to visualize that hard brown face, with the intelligent humorous eyes – nor that magnificent lithe body of his which was to be seen at odd times, moving around the farm. Always busy ... with the animals ... with the men ... with the produce ... and sometimes he himself worked on one of the tractors. Richard the farmer, remorseless like the rest of them, in what was considered the necessary treatment of the animals. Yet never personally unkind. It was he who got out of his bed at night, and went to the assistance of a cow in difficult labour. He whose hands could be as gentle as they were hard. He who once came in from the woods with a little furred creature that had been caught in a trap and fiercely denounced the poacher who had set the trap.

Whenever the old family story of Julia's tears and lamen=

tations when the labrador had been run over, cropped up now, Christa had a cynical comment ready.

'It must have been the first and last tear she ever shed. And it must have been because it was *her* dog.'

Julia was so essentially possessive. She loved only *her things* and *her* flesh and blood; such love in Christa's mind was more than three-quarters egotistical. Like Mrs. Chalford's strong attachment to Tony or young Pip; because they resembled *her*; because they approved of *her*. But Richard she did not care for so much because he was different; that was another thing Christa had learned.

Richard was different . . . yes!

She thanked Mitza for the tea, got up, put on mackintosh and boots and went out. Wryly she thought of the many pretty clothes in her trousseau; how few of them she had worn.

Tony hardly seemed to have time for her these days. He had been far too busy with affairs on the farm . . . he was organizing important plans for some new farm buildings. He spent a lot of time with architects and builders or at conferences in London or Aylesbury. Sometimes when he went up to town she went with him to spend the day with her mother. She even liked to help in the shop, and found it gay – like old times.

Cousin Judy appeared to be getting on very well and was being a great help. And her mother's health had improved since Christa got back from the honeymoon. Christa was less worried about her these days. But she shrank from any of the old 'heart-to-heart' talks. Mummy knew her too well. Christa was terrified that she would see visible signs of the inner change that was taking place. The sad transformation from the radiant bride who had gone to her wedding so passionately in love, so full of hope, into a confused, unhappy woman.

Hands in the pocket of the transparent waterproof which she had put over her cotton frock and cardigan, Christa walked despondently across the cobbled yard and down towards the farm buildings. Tony would be shooting partridges tomorrow – the first of September – over Ursula Corby's estate. He always did the right things at the right moment, and he was a good shot. Everybody said so. He had asked Christa to go with him but she had refused. She knew that she would only make a fool of herself if one of the partridges landed with the thud of a broken little body close to her feet. How she could ever have dreamed that she would enjoy country life, she thought bitterly, she knew not.

Mummy had known it of course. But nothing would have induced Christa to go to her and say '*You were right*'; if only because it would make her mother so unhappy.

It hadn't taken Christa long to find out that she had made a mistake when she married Tony.

The honeymoon, itself, had been far from an unqualified success.

Christa had gone eagerly to her marriage; with all the generosity of her warm vibrant nature she had offered herself to Tony's love. She had anticipated complete response from him. He *had* responded, but with a violent and short-lived passion. At first she had thought that she must accept a certain streak of shyness in him – a reticence that he found hard to break through. He desired her, but once assuaged, he reverted at once to being the cool and arrogant young man who considered it bad taste to reveal his feelings.

Christa tried to attune herself to this failing in him and to synchronize her emotions to his. But gradually she found it was not merely shyness that was responsible for Tony's rather awkward mechanical love-making but a lack of fire or imagination. He considered that demonstrations of affection should be relegated to the bedroom and in between times there should exist only a 'sensible comradeship'. He was ungenerous in love – and not overgenerous now that he was married – with money. He spent a certain amount on his wife in Paris but always found some good reason why she had better not buy what she wanted; or pleading currency restrictions.

At first she was tolerant. When they went on to Rome she was still blindly in love. Tony could still turn on that enormous charm that made her heart turn over, and especially when he took her in his arms.

She had had so much to give – *but it was so much more than he wanted*. That was the tragedy which began to unfold itself during the week in Italy. Gradually she began to be more aloof and simulated a coolness to match his own. She was too proud to let him think that her need for love and tenderness was any greater than his. But she was confused and at times hurt by the disparity. Later it was to have a disastrous effect on her whole emotional nature, to make her ashamed of her own ardour.

It would have been all right, perhaps, if they could have met on some other common ground. In Paris, Tony enjoyed the theatres or cafés; the night life. But in Rome he was bored. Horrified, Christa tried to please him – to divert her attention from the glorious architectural wonders and the fabulous art treasures which so vitally attracted her. She soon found that he would sulk if he was forced into sight-seeing. He much preferred cinemas or night clubs. So, for Christa, it meant a hurried rush round the famous places that roused all her ecstasy. She did not want to 'drag' her husband around with her.

The end of that honeymoon found her with her deepest instincts thwarted and her original hope that she could make Tony like the things *she* liked, at an end. He made efforts to please her but he failed. And he was always so much more cheerful and affectionate when she did the things that *he* wanted.

It was a short sharp period of disillusionment for Christa. But she faced the realization as they travelled home, that she had chosen the wrong man. *Yes – as soon as that!* And when she thought about it now, over a year later, it seemed even more plain to her.

Tony had asked her, rather casually the other night, if she were happy. She had parried with the question:

'Are *you*, Tony?'

'Absolutely,' was his reply. And he meant it.

He was wrapped up in that fantastic imperturbable sheath of egotism in which he lived immune from the slings and arrows of the misfortune of those around him. That was the extraordinary part of Tony; he was not necessarily unkind or callous and she had no doubt that if he pointed out that she was not satisfied or happy, he would be horrified. He was just *insensitive*.

CHAPTER TWO

ON the night that Christa and Tony had returned to Queen's Lacey she had been in good spirits because Tony was so much happier and more himself. It seemed almost that the two weeks away on the Continent had upset his equilibrium; that he belonged, heart and soul, to his Buckinghamshire home. It was all strange to Christa. The Tony who had pursued her in London – the debonair sophisticated young man who took her to shows, to the best restaurants, to the Academy (she had asked for that) and even to Ascot – had in fact been a fraud. He did not really exist.

The genuine Tony now revealed to her, was a slightly neurotic man in the lap of his mother and family. He worried constantly about things that were not important to Christa; affairs connected with his money, the farm, the vagaries of the Stock Market and the family Trust. These things had of course always filled his life before and now that he was married – diverted his attention from *her*, his wife. He had got what he wanted, she thought ironically. He was content now with the odd kiss, the flicker of passion, the occasional caress or spoken flattery.

The return from abroad had been on a warm June evening. As they came up the drive and caught sight of the roofs of Queen's Lacey, reddened by the sunset, Tony stopped the car and exclaimed:

'I say – it's good to be home, darling.'

Christa sat silent. She, too, admired the mild soft beauty of the old farmhouse. The lupins had turned blue while they were abroad and the first roses were opening. The fields were green with young corn. The sight aroused a sigh of content from Tony.

'We ought to have a superb harvest!' he said.

She bit her lip. She did not want to damp his enthusiasm but she had to say:

'Didn't you think Paris and Rome looked splendid at sunset, too?'

And she knew that she wanted him to take her hand and say 'Yes' with a fervour to match her own. But he laughed.

'*Of course*, but this is my *home*. It's different.'

Then as she did not speak again, he added:

'*Your* home too, now darling.'

She sighed and smiled. He was very nice really. One just had to agree with him and not embarrass him by a show of sentiment, or ask him to become a poet – overnight.

They were met in the hall by his mother. She lifted a cheek for Tony to kiss in her usual cool fashion, but her pale eyes held a glow as they rested on him.

'Good to see you back, dear. How well you look,' she said.

Feeling suddenly lost and lonely and strange in this new home, aching for affection – Christa held out both hands to her mother-in-law.

'Oh – it *is* lovely to be here!' she exclaimed.

'Yes, the farm is looking its best,' said Julia but took only one of the outstretched hands limply for a moment, ignored the other, then led the way into the sitting-room.

'You'd both like a bath before dinner, I expect, but come and let us have a chat. Tony – there's so much to tell you. Gomme has sciatica rather badly. Richard has had to engage a man to take over – I don't much care for him – you must see what you think. . . .'

Mother and son plunged immediately into a discussion of farm affairs. Christa stood aloof – slowly taking off her hat and gloves. Tony glanced at her over his shoulder.

'Excuse us, darling, won't you – we have so much to discuss. Do you want a sherry, or will you go up and start to unpack?'

'Don't bother about me,' she said in a low voice.

Turning she walked disconsolately through the hall. The wing which was to be her future home was not ready. The plumbers had only just finished putting in the radiators. Next week it was to be painted. But it would be a good fortnight before she could expect to move into the place. She felt that this was not a real home-coming.

Christa tried to laugh at herself.

'What did you expect, Christa – to be lifted and carried over the threshold and kissed in that way that makes a woman's heart almost stand still? To be made to feel that you are loved – just as passionately – as you love? No, no, my girl. That isn't the Chalford way!'

She walked up to her room – one of the big double guest rooms that had been temporarily allotted to her and Tony. She unpacked without enthusiasm. Midway in the act she went downstairs to find a telephone in the study and ring up her own mother.

Then and then only, hearing the loving familiar voice and learning that Mummy was better and all well in the little mews house, Christa recovered her spirits.

'Did you have a marvellous time in Rome?' Mrs. Morley asked.

'Marvellous,' Christa answered gaily.

But her heart sank even as she said the word for it stood out as being an untruth – a 'saving of face' – and nothing more.

Later, the family met for dinner. Pip was out with friends. Richard appeared at the table five minutes late, apologized to his mother who nodded sourly, greeted his brother and then turned his attention to Christa.

She looked small and slight sitting against the high-backed dark oak chair with its tapestried back and seat. The whole dining-room was Jacobean in atmosphere – furnished with that

71

dark polished wood. They sat at a long monks' table which was magnificently highly polished and laid with embroidered mats. The dark crimson-papered walls were hung with oil paintings. The old-fashioned sideboard glittered with Waterford glass and Georgian silver. It was sombre in here but rich and quite decorative. Richard had always liked it. He knew suddenly that he liked to see Christa sitting here, too. Her extreme Scandinavian fairness and delicate beauty were charming against such a background. She was slightly sun browned. He found that a fascinating contrast to the silver of her hair. He said:

'Hello, Christa – welcome to Queen's Lacey.'

'Thank you,' she said and gave him such a grateful look that he felt quite startled.

He asked, as her mother had done:

'Was Rome marvellous?'

'Oh, yes it *was*!' she exclaimed and now her cheeks flushed. She began to tell him about Rome and listened to his comments. They discussed it all eagerly, joining in a union of pleasurable remembrances of the loveliest of cities. They shared their knowledge and their impressions, and for a few moments Christa was happy. Her eyes shone.

Tony interrupted:

'Personally I thought Rome very over-rated. Give me my own country . . . London, too, if one must be in a town . . . but Queen's Lacey is better than all of it.'

'Quite so,' said Mrs. Chalford.

'My dear old Tony, you are so infernally insular,' said Richard. 'I like Queen's Lacey as much as you do, but I do admit that there *are* other beauties in the world. As for London – bless it – it's grand. But it just can't hold a candle to Rome. The two are not comparable. Rome has a grandeur, an historic significance, an antiquity you find in no other city in Europe.'

'It's a matter of opinion,' cut in Julia Chalford's dry voice. 'I went to Rome with your father once and disliked every moment of it.'

'I think Tony did, too,' said Christa in a low voice.

Julia glanced at her, then at Tony . . . a quick piercing look which suggested that she could already discern the smallest crack in the even surface of the young couple's feelings towards each other. She was not altogether sure that the honeymoon had been a success. But Tony – enjoying his favourite dinner of grilled steak and tomatoes washed down by excellent red wine – now turned to his wife and raised his glass.

'Your health, darling, on this, our first night home at Queen's Lacey,' he said grandly.

She raised her wine-glass in response and nodded. Her smile was a little wintry, but she said:

'Thank you, darling.'

Afterwards she caught a quizzical, baffling look from Richard. His grin was impish. He looked brown and handsome and extraordinarily attractive, she thought; although the cut of the grey suit which he had put on for the evening meal was by no means as good as the one Tony wore. He had tied his tie carelessly. His hair was a little rough. But looking down at his hands, she found them scrupulously clean – despite his manual labour. He had rather fine long fingers. Tony's, on the other hand, were broad with spatulate tips. The brothers were a contradiction, mused Christa.

'Ah well!' said Richard in a voice that matched his teasing smile. 'You and I had better leave old Tony to his accounts, and board meetings, Christa, and we'll push off to Rome, and do a sort of brother and sister tour in uninterrupted bliss.'

Christa giggled.

'*Really*, Richard!' said his mother.

The time would come when Christa was to feel that she would scream if Mrs. Chalford said 'really' again. Most of Richard's words seemed to draw that ejaculation from her. And, of course, he knew it. He was a devil, she thought; he liked to rile his mother. She could even believe that he liked to get a rise out of Tony.

She decided to join in the fun.

'That's settled,' she said. 'The Colosseum and the Catacombs for us. When shall we start?'

'Tomorrow, if you like. There's far too much work on the farm at the moment for my liking. I'm all for a couple of weeks in the sun and I'm always ready to kneel down and kiss the stones of Rome.'

'You've only just had your holiday,' said Mrs. Chalford icily and rang for the sweet.

Across the big table, Christa's golden eyes mocked Richard who flung her a warm and friendly response.

Tony took no notice as though the light bantering conversation was beneath his contempt.

And it flashed through Christa's brain then and there: 'I wonder if he is really flesh and blood, this husband of mine ... I wonder if he is not just a creature with odd appetites that have to be appeased and who then wishes to be left alone. He has *nothing* real and sincere except his passion to make Queen's Lacey pay. I wonder what he'd do if I *did* pack up and go to Rome with his brother tomorrow?'

Then ashamed of such nonsense, she forced herself to eat a lot of pastry which she didn't want, and maintained silence for the rest of the meal. Julia Chalford talked endlessly about the farm and their friends.

Afterwards, coffee was served in the drawing-room. The french windows were open to the beauty of the summer's night. Warmth, mild air, stars, and the night-scented stock and syringa smelling powerfully. The sound of a thrush singing its last joyous song, broke the stillness with piercing clarity.

Christa walked to the window. She looked out, frowning. She felt all the doubts and confusion of her honeymoon weighing heavily upon her. Oh, this could not be allowed to go on! It was as though she was plunged into a nightmare. One could not be in love yesterday, and out of it, today. *It just could not happen.*

She turned quickly to her husband.

'Take me for a walk, Tony. It looks so glorious tonight.'

He came up and put an arm around her – a thing which he did not often do in front of others. She was quick to respond and rubbed her cheek against his shoulder.

'Darling Tony, I'm glad to be home with you,' she whispered impulsively.

'Tony,' called Julia Chalford's brittle voice, 'when you've finished your coffee, do you think you could go through those papers with me? I must have everything ready for tomorrow. I'm sure Christa will excuse you.'

Christa swung round. She wanted to say to that other woman:

'This is my first night at home with my newly made husband. Can't the papers wait? Can't you let him take me out and bring back the enchantment that I seem to have lost, lost even on my *honeymoon*?'

But no words came. Tony gave her a little hug and let her go.

'Yes, of course, I'll come, Mother. I'm sure Christa will understand . . .' and he added: 'We've got a court case coming up, darling, about one of our labourers, Ted Gibble, who seems to have committed bigamy. They want to jug him and I'd like to get his wife – who isn't the wife – out of our cottage.'

'I see,' said Christa.

All her desire to walk in the garden with Tony ebbed away, leaving her as flat and disturbed as she had felt one night in Rome when she had wanted him to walk with her on the hills and he had insisted instead on her accompanying him to a night club with some Americans he had met in the bar. The floor show was going to be much more amusing for him than seeing the lights of Rome. She had not argued with him any more than she argued now. She just kept perfectly still, watching her dreams drift away from her one by one with a dreadful persistence.

Now Richard drained his coffee cup and said, scrunching the sugar:

'Isn't it rather hard on that poor creature with three kids – even say we *can* get her out – which I doubt – where can she go?'

'That's her affair,' said Mrs. Chalford.

'And I don't suppose she knew that her husband was committing bigamy,' said Richard.

'We can't help that,' said Tony.

'I felt rather sorry for Gibble – he was a stout fellow,' said Richard with a laugh. 'Gomme, who knew the set-up, told me that wife No. 1 was a fair killer who nagged him almost to death, and that he left her years ago but she wouldn't set him free.'

'Don't let's go into details, please Richard,' said Mrs. Chalford. 'I think the whole thing is revolting.'

'I agree,' said Tony in his haughty voice.

Now Christa felt her throat restrict. She came forward. Looking at Tony she said:

'In some cases bigamy is, of course, terrible and must be punished. But what can a poor man do if he's made a mistake and finds he has a ghastly sort of wife, and life is made hell for him? Must he go without love and care for the rest of his life?'

Tony laughed.

'My darling Christa, you're so sweet.'

She flushed angrily, conscious of her mother-in-law's supercilious glance.

'It isn't a question of being "sweet". It's a matter of tolerance, of understanding human nature.'

'What do you expect me to do, darling?' asked Tony. 'Sympathize with the fellow, support his wife for the rest of her

75

days and let her use our cottage which we need for another labourer?'

'No – I – oh – I can't go into all the details. It's just that I understand people's weaknesses. I feel sorry for people like that. For all you know, those two – the man and the second wife – may really love each other.'

'*Love!*' Julia Chalford repeated the word scornfully. 'They're just animals.'

'Perhaps we're all animals,' exclaimed Christa fiercely.

'Really, Christa!' the famous exclamation was directed against the younger woman now. Julia looked at Christa with the utmost disapproval, shrugged her shoulders and walked out of the room.

Tony pulled an ear. His face had coloured. He avoided Christa's angry golden eyes.

'It really isn't your affair, darling,' he said with a cough. 'You've upset Mother.'

Before she could speak again Tony had followed his mother out of the room. Then Richard came slowly up to Christa and handed her a packet of cigarettes.

'Calm down,' he said smiling, 'when you get to know us all better you won't let little arguments of this sort upset you. I'm always saying the wrong thing, myself.'

She took the cigarettes gratefully. Her fingers were trembling.

'But why should this wretched man and his wife be necessarily *animals*? They may really care about each other.'

'Oh, quite,' said Richard drily.

She went on:

'The man has broken the law and he must be punished, but I was glad when you said you thought it hard on the poor woman and their three illegitimate children.'

'I do.'

'And I think it's awful for the man if he was so unhappy with No. 1.'

Richard shrugged.

'I'm no great judge of marital disputes and disasters, but I think it is time the law altered that cruelty of keeping two people tied together for ever more just because one side refuses to take action.'

Christa drew a breath of her cigarette. She began to relax. She said:

'Richard, I didn't mean to offend your mother – how awful of me – on my first night at Queen's Lacey.'

'Oh, don't let it worry you. Mama's very hidebound, you know, bless her. Her susceptibilities were offended by the thought of a farm labourer and his wife – or wives—' he laughed – 'locked in a feverish embrace.'

Christa laughed. Here was something human, and a humour she could understand and share. Richard added:

'I'm sure you will get to understand my mother. She's a damned good sort, and wonderful to us. But she's a bit of an anachronism in this modern age; positively Victorian in her prudery at times. She's shocked by any mention of sex. We boys never really know how we got here . . .' and he laughed again uproariously.

But Christa did not join in the laughter this time. For, remembering her honeymoon with Tony, that curious prudish streak in him which had made her feel positively wanton – she was deeply troubled. She thought:

'Tony and his mother are alike. *They are terribly alike* . . . oh, heavens – *what have I done?*'

It was Richard who took her for a walk. He was gay and friendly. They talked with animation on a dozen subjects – but nothing to do with the farm. Then they came indoors again and Richard opened the piano.

'Play for me,' he said, 'you do play, don't you?'

'No, I only sing a little. *You* play for me.'

He ran his fingers through his thick hair and grimaced.

'I quite like it. But nobody else in the house does, and several times I've tried to persuade Mama to take all these photographs and flowers off the piano. It's a good instrument and it's better when it's opened.'

She stared at him.

'Do you all three do exactly what your mother wants you to do? *That* is unmodern if you like.'

He laughed.

'Oh, now and again we rebel but on the whole she gives us most of the things we want, so we return the compliment.'

'That isn't true,' thought Christa. 'She's a complete martinet and you all answer her when she whistles because she holds the money – it's a kind of dishonest control that she exercises. And in a way you're all *afraid* of her. She has a sort of mesmeric power over you. She's always had it and now you can't break away.'

Richard sat down at the piano. He ran his fingers over the keys. Suddenly Christa stopped tormenting herself with her thoughts. For here was a true musician; Richard could not read music – he played by ear – but his improvising had a sympathetic attractive quality that Christa adored. She was at once charmed and soothed. She leaned her arms on the piano and with chin on her hands, listened enraptured, humming the tunes she recognized.

Suddenly he stopped.

'Sing for me,' he said.

'Not tonight,' she said, 'tomorrow, perhaps.'

He got up from the piano, gave a yawn and smothered it with an apology.

'Afraid I'm tired. I've been out in the fields all day. Aren't *you* tired after your journey?'

'Yes,' she said.

He looked down at her and thought suddenly she looked small and sad, and not at all like the golden goddess with the radiance that had sat upon her at her wedding. He said:

'I hope you'll be happy here with us at Queen's Lacey.'

'Thank you, Richard,' she said.

They stood looking at each other. Neither realized that it had grown quite dark until suddenly the lights were switched on. Tony came in.

'Why on earth this darkness?'

'I've been playing,' said Richard abruptly.

'It's been lovely. I'm mad about his sort of music,' said Christa.

'You can have it,' Tony said. 'Mother and I call it strumming.'

'But he plays *beautifully*,' said an indignant Christa.

Richard laughed.

'You flatter me. Good night, both,' he said. 'I'm off to my bed.'

After he had gone Christa grew quiet. Tony said:

'Mother's gone to bed, too. She asked me to say good night to you.'

'Thank you,' said Christa in a small voice.

He looked at the charming figure in the sea-green silky dress which was low off the shoulder and was part of her trousseau. She had worn it several evenings in Paris. One of his swift impulses of passion seized him. He was in good spirits. The business talk with his mother had been satisfactory. Apart from the coming court case over Gibble things were going very well and the profits this year were certainly going to be higher than last.

78

He walked up to his young and lovely wife and took her in his arms.

'Love me?' he murmured.

She stood still, her heart beating a trifle fast. Something prevented her from answering at once. He put a finger under her chin and turned her face to his.

'Hey – you! Do you love me?'

'Yes, of course.' She gave him the expected answer now.

He kissed her with fervour; one hand smoothed her warm bare shoulder.

'Let's go upstairs,' he whispered.

Then she clung to him tightly, as though in sudden fear, or sorrow – or both.

'Oh, I do love you, Tony. *I do*. But I think maybe I've disappointed you – you're so far away from me sometimes – so different . . .' she began to stammer words disjointedly, still pressing close to him as though in an agony of endeavour to draw nearer to this man whom she had married only a fortnight ago.

He laughed at her in the benevolent kind of way that he had when Christa said anything that he did not really comprehend.

'Funny little thing,' he murmured.

She tore herself away from his arms.

'Oh, *God*!' she said between her teeth.

'What's the matter?' he asked in a slightly injured voice.

'Nothing, nothing,' she said, and ran upstairs in front of him. By the time he had reached the bedroom she had already gone through to the bathroom and shut the door.

She was cool and smiling, and almost an air of indifference sat upon her when, in her dressing gown, she joined him again.

'Darling,' he said and took her in his arms, and began to caress her.

She lay still, eyes tight shut. With all her heart and soul she wanted to love him – to be spiritually as well as physically close to this husband of hers. She whispered almost as though it was an appeal:

'Tony!'

He whispered back:

'It's rather odd to think I'm here with you in this room and that I have a wife. Just down the passage is that old room I used to occupy when I was a bachelor.'

79

Her lips moved against his. Her whole heart questioned him. She had meant to maintain a state of indifference and cool self-control, but it soon deserted her. Her fingers wandered over the clean-cut, good-looking face, just discernible now in the darkness. She said, quite frantically:

'Tony, Tony, tell me that you're glad, *really* truly glad, that I'm your wife. Oh, Tony, I don't think that your mother likes me.'

'Nonsense' he said lazily. 'Mother just doesn't show things in the way you do.'

'Sometimes you don't either.'

'That doesn't say I don't love you, and I'm extremely glad you're here with me at Queen's Lacey. I assure you I am.'

'Oh, my darling!' she said and pressed his face between both her hands, 'my *darling*.'

'I say!' he said as though a sudden thought struck his memory, 'tomorrow's going to be rather a big day for us all.'

'Why – what?' she was dreamy, yet excited, trembling a little.

'I'm going to see a chap whom they all say is first rate about saving surtax. And if it is the case, the Chalfords will have a lot more to spend. That includes you too, of course.'

'Does it?' she said.

And she began to laugh helplessly, drawing her lips away from his.

That was the first night of the return to Queen's Lacey.

CHAPTER THREE

Now another June had passed. It was another summer. Tony and Christa were quite an old married couple, settled in their own wing. There had been a period of happiness while Christa planned and arranged her home. Tony, on the whole, left things to her. He was not particularly interested in the home which he called 'the woman's sphere'. In one way Christa was thankful; in another she was sorry that he did not enjoy hunting with her for treasures and admiring the bargains when she found them. But he paid the bills – up to a point. And that point ended when Mrs. Chalford stepped in.

Walking through the rain this wet dismal day, Christa could

not restrain the thrill of irritation that ran through her at the memory of her mother-in-law.

It wasn't working – this living under the family roof. She was quite positive, too, that Tony would make no effort to move. Of course she had been silly ever to risk that happening, but it was so perfect for him, nicely housed between mother and wife, able to enjoy the family meals as usual; bribed by Julia who blandly announced that she would not dream of asking them to pay for their board.

When, one night, Christa had said to her husband: 'But we would feel so much more independent if we did pay . . .' he had answered that he saw no object. Why pay for anything one could get for nothing? That was Tony's policy, but not hers. It was all 'in the family' he kept telling her. But Christa would meet the cool and often sarcastic eye of her mother-in-law and realize that Julia was pleased because she had gained another victory, and was binding her eldest and most beloved son with just one more shackle.

Then there were those awful presents from Julia constantly pressed upon Christa. Tony did not want her to refuse them, and it made things hideously embarrassing for Christa.

Mrs. Chalford had partially persuaded Christa to live at Queen's Lacey by assuring her that her wing would be her own little world. But in came the curtains, the rugs, the bits of furniture, the pictures and ornaments – one by one destroying Christa's colour schemes or personal taste. Always accompanied by the words:

'Why waste good money? You can have this for nothing, my dear. . . .'

The final straw had been that wardrobe – a huge Victorian mahogany piece, a long mirror in the centre, and two semicircular cupboard doors on either side. Christa, returning from a visit to London, found this installed in her bedroom. She stared at it in horror. It looked like a colossal idol balefully glaring at her, aware that it had no place in her light gay bedroom with the carefully chosen rose and silver wallpaper. She had planned to have cupboards built in across one wall.

She turned to rush indignantly down the stairs and demand an explanation when she met Mrs. Chalford coming upstairs with her eldest son.

'Oh, hullo, Christa. I was just bringing Tony to see the new wardrobe,' said Mrs. Chalford. 'Are you pleased with it?'

Christa tried to keep calm, but she had not had a very happy afternoon in the old mews home, because she had thought her beloved mother was looking very ill again, scarcely able to control the pain which she so bravely tried to hide.

Christa snapped at the elder woman:

'Nobody warned me that the wardrobe was going to be "wished" on me. It absolutely ruins my lovely bedroom.'

Mrs. Chalford's freckled face tightened but she gave her frozen smile.

'Never mind, dear, it will save you a lot of money. Nothing is more expensive today than built-in wardrobes. You may remember that this one was in the room you and Tony occupied on your first night home from Italy. I got three of the men to move it up to your wing for a nice surprise.'

Christa tried to protest. Tony cut in, with a restraining hand on his wife's arm.

'Very decent of you, Mother. Let's go and have a look at it.'

By the time they had all finished looking at it, with Tony uttering words of admiration and thanks, and Mrs. Chalford continuing to point out that it was foolish of them to spend money when she, Mrs. Chalford, could provide what was needed, Christa trembled with anger. For once she ignored the warning in Tony's eyes: she spoke her mind.

'I'm sorry, Mother. You mustn't be offended but I don't really like it, and this *is* my home, and I *was* told I could arrange my rooms as I wanted.'

'So you can, dear, but it would be madness to make Tony spend so much money when you've got this good wardrobe for nothing. It was his grandmother's and after all—'

'Well, I'm not his grandmother,' broke in Christa, her face flushed and her golden eyes blazing, 'and I don't think things like this should be done while I'm away and unable to say what I want or don't want in my own bedroom. I *don't* like it being implied, either, that I *make* Tony spend money. If he hadn't *got* you and Queen's Lacey he would *have* to furnish his own home like other men.'

Mother and son stared at her. Mrs. Chalford had gone a dusky red. Tony looked gloomy, pulled at his ear and pursed his lips. He was obviously angry with her, Christa thought. He said:

'Well, I thought it was a most handsome present, Mother, and I'm sure Christa will change her mind. I quite agree with you about not spending money unnecessarily. These chaps do charge a hell of a lot for built-in wardrobes.'

'*I* don't wish to interfere with Christa's arrangement of the house. I must apologize. I made a mistake in thinking the wardrobe would be a nice surprise,' said Mrs. Chalford, turned and walked downstairs.

After she had gone there was an unpleasant argument between husband and wife.

'You thoroughly upset Mother and I think you were damned ungrateful and tactless,' said Tony.

Christa retorted: 'Naturally you're on her side; nobody in this house is anything else. Everybody is terrified of her – except perhaps Richard. You've grown up to believe that everything she does is right!'

Tony gave her a cold and scornful look that made him look exactly like his mother.

'What an unattractive thing to say. I think your day in town must have upset you. No doubt you and your own mother were planning what to do about the cupboards.'

'What if we were? Mummy has marvellous taste.'

'That's only your opinion.'

'Very well – why should I like what your mother gives me any more than you like what *my* mother gives *me*?' demanded Christa wildly.

'I haven't noticed your mother giving us anything,' drawled Tony.

Christa gasped.

'That's a perfectly rotten thing to say when you know that we haven't a bean and the Chalfords are so hideously rich. I dislike most of the things your mother gives us; and she only does it to annoy *me* – not because she really enjoys giving me a present. She resents me, too. She's jealous because you married me. And if she could make *you* regret marrying me, she would. She—'

'I think you'd better stop, Christa,' broke in Tony in a low menacing voice. He took a cigarette from his case and tapped it and rolled it between his lips, looking at his wife through half-closed lids.

Then she burst into tears and ran out of the room and out of the house, knowing that she had made a hopeless mistake, and that she had nobody but herself to blame for it. She must have been mad ever to believe that a man as temperamentally different from herself as Tony could be the right husband for her. Even more mad to agree to come and live at Queen's Lacey.

Of course it had ended in Tony going out into the grounds to look for her, finding her crying her eyes out in some remote corner, and stepping down from his high horse. He kissed and tried to console her. He did not want her to be unhappy and he hated quarrelling, he said. He apologized for the ungentlemanly allusion to her mother's impecuniousness (that piece of pomposity made her smile) and said that if she disliked the wardrobe so much he would try to reconcile things with his mother, and send the offending piece back to the old house.

Then of course Christa said that she would try to like it. In her generous fashion she met Tony handsomely by going so far as to seek out her mother-in-law, and beg to be forgiven.

'I didn't mean to be ungrateful – I suppose I'm just not feeling frightfully well,' she said.

'That is quite all right, my dear,' said Mrs. Chalford in a voice that would have put a thin film of ice over anything. But she had given the girl a sharp look and added: 'You aren't by any chance—'

'No, I'm not,' Christa interrupted hastily, and went crimson. 'Nothing like that.'

When she repeated this conversation to her husband that night, she suddenly asked him, with curiosity, if he thought that his mother would like them to have a child.

'Oh, I think so,' answered Tony vaguely, 'but I don't want to be bothered with children at the moment.'

'Would anybody think of asking *me*?' Christa said with a raised eyebrow.

'Don't be silly, of course darling. But you told me only the other night you didn't want children at the moment.'

'Yes – all right,' she said.

No – she did not want a baby. She would hate to think that it might be like Julia Chalford. Weeks of intimacy with this family had not increased her admiration for Tony's mother. Her whole outlook was avaricious, prejudiced and self-centred. And Christa disapproved of the way she favoured Tony while she enslaved and subjected to her will, poor young Pip who was such a silly fool, but so nice. And how she nagged at Richard! But then of course *Richard* was not like the rest of the Chalfords.

He was much more like Christa herself.

Christa faced that fact continually, but as though it was disloyal and rather frightening, dismissed it. They had fun together whether it was over their shared knowledge of books, or their music. Sometimes in the evenings now he would play her songs and she sang for him. Tony, whom she knew did not care for music except as a background, always thanked her politely for singing. 'Awfully nice,' he would say. But once the music began Mrs. Chalford invariably found that she had something to do in her own room, picked up her tapestry and departed as though in silent disapproval of the duet by her son and daughter-in-law.

Sometimes, Christa showed Tony that she was aggravated by these pinpricks. He had no comfort for her. He thought her ultra-sensitive. Even Richard laughed at her, but gently and with pity, she thought.

'You take things too much to heart, my child,' he said to her one evening.

'Child, indeed! You're the same age as I am,' she answered, tossing her bright head.

'But you're awfully young for your age,' he declared. 'When I first met you I thought you were a sophisticated young lady of London. But you're really just a kid – you get so het up about silly little things.'

'I suppose I'm made that way,' said Christa.

'Well you shouldn't let Mama see that you notice what she says. It only makes her worse.'

'Why is she like that, Richard?' Christa had asked him, with a genuine desire to make things better between herself and Tony's mother. '*Why* does she hate me?'

'Who says she does?'

'You know it.'

'Then if it is so, it's jealousy, my dear. You've married her Tony-boy.'

'But doesn't she want her own son to be happily married?'

Richard gave her a sidelong glance out of those handsome provocative eyes of his, and grinned.

'She used to like being the one who made Tony happy.'

'Then she's terribly selfish.'

'You'll never understand her.'

'Do you?'

'Yes, in a way. Hers is the possessive mother-love of a woman who has, herself, been frustrated in marriage, and, and whose sons constituted her whole world. She resents any intruder into that world.'

'Intruder – yes that's what I'm made to feel!' said Christa bitterly.

But Richard refused to take her seriously. He compelled her to laugh at everything, as he did.

'Sometimes I don't know how you *do* go on laughing. I just can't. Things madden me,' she said.

'Poor Christa,' he said, and suddenly there had been a deep sympathy flowing from him – acting like a caress upon her jarred nerves.

She was sure that he saw and understood more than he cared to admit. He, too, was as restless as the devil, despite his love of the farm, but he worked so hard that he drove himself into a state of exhaustion. He went to bed early, slept soundly and rose early. He did not stop to think too much – of that she was sure.

She tried to emulate his example, but failed.

She tried to turn Tony into a companion, even though he was such an indifferent lover. She failed in that too.

It could not be said that the fifteen months of her marriage had brought her either fulfilment or the affection and companionship she had always hoped for in marriage. She went up to London as often as she could to see her mother, but whilst Mrs. Morley could congratulate Christa because she looked so brown (Christa was glad of the deceptive tan), she knew that the girl was neither well nor happy. They had been too close to each other for too long for Sarah Morley to be deceived. And for Christa the visits gradually became occasions for worry and distress rather than pleasure. Her mother grew slowly worse and it was developing into long-drawn-out torture. She had become much too thin, and admitted at times how often she suffered: but still she refused to go into a nursing home or see new doctors. From Judy, however, Christa heard more of the truth. Judy was deeply concerned. Judy saw her aunt these days when Mrs. Morley was not made up or putting on a gay brave façade for her daughter's visits. Christa implored her to take further advice – but in vain; so the girl could only stand aside helplessly and wait for whatever might happen to this brave and beloved woman.

Tony, whenever he accompanied his wife on a visit to the mews cottage, was polite and pleasant to his mother-in-law. He often turned on the famous charm for her – and for Cousin Judy too. Judy was quite won over by him and became one of his great admirers.

But between Sarah and Tony's mother there could be no real friendship. They had met only once since the wedding reception; just before Christmas last year, when Mrs. Chalford held her annual cocktail party at Queen's Lacey. Christa went up in

Tony's car and drove her mother and Judy down to attend this function which was held on a Saturday. It was a big party. The whole of the district attended it. Queen's Lacey looked its best festooned with holly and mistletoe and made even more beautiful by Richard's arrangements of chrysanthemums which were old Chean the gardener's special pride.

Christa looked lovely and gay and helped to receive the guests standing at her mother-in-law's side. Julia put on her most pleasant air of welcome for the occasion. Anybody except Sarah Morley might have been deceived into thinking that young Mrs. Anthony had 'fallen on her feet' by making this marriage and that all was well. But the mother had returned to London full of apprehension, and positive that Christa was anything but content. Then, again, she had seen the look of sheer naïve pleasure in Christa's eyes when Sarah praised Richard and said what an enchanting young man he was, and how different from the others.

'Yes, I like my brother Richard,' Christa had said lightly.

But Sarah – all too sensitive – had detected more than ordinary feeling behind those casual words and it had troubled her. It would never do for Christa to fall in love with her own brother-in-law. Sarah went so far as to mention to Christa that it might be better for her to start looking for her own house and get away from Queen's Lacey. But Christa said that it was impossible for the moment – Tony wouldn't hear of it.

Christa's headache eased as she neared the biggest of the barns where they kept the clover seed. She liked it and often went down there; the dim fragrance soothed her and it was warm and dry, even on a wet cool day like this. She found the place deserted, except for a chicken that had got in by mistake and was pecking away at some scattered grain. It scuttled away flapping its wings, as Christa opened the door.

She unwound her scarf, took off her mackintosh, and lay down on a bundle of sweet-smelling hay. There was a stillness in here, as in a church, she thought. A glorious peace. Here nobody would disturb her. But she was never alone at Queen's Lacey. Even in her own bedroom she had no privacy. Tony would enter at any time he wanted. Not so much to draw near to her, as to talk endlessly about his latest success in matters connected with the farm. He was more than ordinarily busy at the moment, and delighted because a new builder had given him a lower estimate on the proposed building than he had anticipated. It amazed Christa that Tony and his mother could both seem so inordinately pleased by the saving of a few pounds; despite their wealth.

The two aspirins and Mitza's tea were having an effect. Christa was growing drowsy. Last night she had slept badly. After a moment or two now, resting on the warm sweet straw she fell asleep.

Some time later Richard opened the door of the barn.

He had been talking in here this morning to Hawthine, the new man who temporarily replaced the incapacitated Gomme. Before going out to the cornfields, Richard had taken off his pullover and flung it over one of the cross beams supporting the loft. Now, finished with work for the day, he remembered to fetch the pullover.

As his eyes grew accustomed to the dimness he suddenly saw the reclining figure of the girl, her scarf and transparent nylon coat on the hay beside her. A little startled, he drew nearer and stared down at Christa. For a moment he had a ridiculous and terrifying fear that she was dead – that he had stumbled upon her dead body. She lay so still, on her back, both arms flung up above her head. Then he saw, with relief, the rise and fall of her breast and knew that she breathed. Her face had a pearl-like luminosity in the shadows. Her hair was untidily tumbled across her forehead. He thought her very beautiful and desirable like this. He could see the marvellous length of her lashes against her soft cheek. He drew in his breath, feeling a strange constriction of his whole heart. True beauty always moved Richard. From the first moment that he had met Tony's wife, his senses had been dazzled. Now that he knew her better he was not so much dazzled as perceptively, deeply aware of her attractions. He was sorry for her too. He knew that she should not have married his brother and that she was not happy at Queen's Lacey.

What distressed Richard was the expression on the face of his sleeping sister-in-law ... the sad lips slightly parted ... the contracted brow ... she looked as though she was suffering. Perhaps, he mused, in her dreams she was finding fresh cause for despair. He turned away strangely moved and troubled. He did not wish to disturb her, nor had he the right to break in on those desolate dreams.

But a gust of wind suddenly caught the old door. It creaked and swung to with a crash. Christa sat up.

'Oh!' she gasped and pushed her hair out of her eyes.

Richard gave his swift youthful grin.

'The Sleeping Beauty awakes,' he said, and gave a mock bow. 'What, pray, are your highness's commands?'

She got up, smoothing her crumpled dress. When she had first come to Queen's Lacey she had worn smart narrow slacks and gay shirts, but his mother had expressed such strong disapproval of women in trousers that to please her Christa no longer wore them. So this afternoon it was a flowered cotton; pink and grey, and with it a grey cardigan. There were pearls around her throat, and in her ears. Now he noticed that one of her earrings was missing. He pointed out the fact. She bent down to look for the earring but could not find it. He began to hunt with her, suggesting that it might have rolled away under one of the sacks. Their shoulders touched. They drew away from each other sharply. Richard found the pearl. As she clipped it on to her ear, she felt her heart pounding. She knew that it ought not to pound in such a way because Richard was with her and they were alone and so close in the warm scented barn. He said:

'I can't say I fought my way through thorn bushes or slew dangerous dragons in the effort to reach you, and wake you up, as in all good fairy stories, my dear.'

She laughed.

'I'm sure you didn't.'

'And you missed the kiss,' he added boldly, 'you woke up on your own account.'

Her eyes danced at him now from under the long lashes.

'How often have you tried to wake up sleeping princesses?'

'Not very often. I haven't time.'

'You do talk a lot of nonsense, Richard.'

'It's the Chalford prerogative.'

'Maybe Pip wouldn't mind – but Tony would be furious if you said he talked nonsense.'

'And, in fact, he talks more nonsense than the rest of us, does old Tony. But he puts it over in such a way that he makes one believe he's full of knowledge.'

'Once,' said Christa, 'I thought *I* was full of knowledge. Now I realize that I don't know anything.'

'You're in one of your sad moods.'

'Do I have sad moods?'

'You know you have.'

'Your mother would say it is my artistic nature. It hurts being an artist in any way, doesn't it?'

'I don't let my nature hurt me any more,' said Richard grimly. 'I said goodbye to the artist in me when I left the Army.'

'Why when you left the Army?'

'Well – while I was doing my National Service I decided that I disliked soldiering and that I was a musician, and I meant to become a great composer. Then I came home and down to earth again and realized that I wasn't nearly as brilliant as I imagined. That all I could really do well was farm, and I was glad to be at Queen's Lacey again and carry on with the good work so I don't worry about my artistic nature any more. I'm too darned busy.'

'That is where I find you such a contradiction, Richard. You're the best farmer of the three and yet you're the only one of the family who ever opens a book or plays a tune.'

He shrugged his shoulders.

'That's the way it is! Appearances can be deceptive, you know. I'm always pretty rough and ready too – but old Tony who looks like the best-dressed and most romantic hero in any woman's novel, is—' Richard stopped.

'Is what?' she asked as Richard stopped.

He was silent.

'You began to say something about Tony – you didn't finish,' she said.

'Oh, nothing,' said Richard abruptly. 'Let's get going – I want my bath.'

'Very well,' she said meekly and picked up her waterproof and scarf.

Outside the barn a high breeze tore at her hair and made her shiver. It had stopped raining. Richard looked at the fields. Yesterday the men had cut down twenty acres of barley. The tangle of ears lay there crushed down by the rain.

'A fine sight,' he nodded.

'Yes,' said Christa forlornly and had never felt less like admiring a field of barley.

As they walked together across the courtyard to the house, Richard asked her, casually, what she and Tony were doing tonight.

She answered that they were going to Ursula Corby's at Forty Green where she had promised at last to learn to play Canasta. She had been holding out against it all these months.

'Tony likes it, so I *must* try,' she said valiantly.

Richard made no reply. He wondered whether brother Tony ever tried to please this wife of his. So far he had thought it a very one-sided marriage. And Christa must by now be alive to the fact that Tony's famous charm could be as easily turned off as on.

'I shall be out tonight, too,' he said in the same abrupt voice.

'How unusual for you, Richard.'

'I've been asked to dinner at the Thornton's,' he said. 'I've refused so often that I must go or Mother says I really will offend the old boy. He's our next-door neighbour and so on – *voilà!*'

It was Christa's turn to keep silence. The kitchen door opened. Tessa, Richard's spaniel, rushed out. With her ears flapping she joyously leaped upon him. She had been kept indoors today because they had been putting the chickens in the stubble.

Christa watched thoughtfully while Richard caressed the animal.

She thought about him going to the Thorntons. Susan would of course be there. Susan, who everybody knew was in love with Richard. Christa had met her once or twice and thought her a rather difficult girl, but so obviously did she adore Richard that it was painful. A latent spirit of feminine mischief made Christa suddenly give a sidelong glance at Richard and say:

'Better go and put on your best suit and tie and dazzle poor Susan.'

He turned on her quite angrily, glaring down into the clear gold of her eyes. Sometimes he found them as appealing and mournful as his spaniel's and it hurt him. Because of the hurt he snarled:

'I don't want to dazzle any girl, let alone Susan. See you in the morning.'

He moved off and almost collided with his mother in the hall. Mrs. Chalford said:

'Have the men gone off?'

'Yes,' he answered.

Julia clicked her teeth.

'Their laziness today infuriates me. I can remember the time when they used to be still working in the fields until eight at night. Oh, well – this is 1956. I think the country is absolutely going to the bad.'

Now Richard who had been looking taut and angry burst out laughing.

'Dear Mama! So says you, and so said your Mama, and her mama before her. And so, I presume, shall I say, and my children after *me.*'

Mrs. Chalford shrugged her shoulders. She turned her attention to Christa who was thinking:

'What a funny one Richard is. . . . He plays a lone hand but he does consider the possibility that one day he will have children. I wonder what sort of girl he will marry?'

Mrs. Chalford addressed Christa:

'Tony has been looking for you everywhere. Where have you been my dear?'

'Oh, I didn't expect you back so soon. I fell asleep – in the barn.'

'What an extraordinary thing to do!' said Mrs. Chalford haughtily.

Everything I do or say is extraordinary to her, thought Christa, and walked through the kitchen, a little comforted by the unmistakable love that had shone in the short-sighted eyes of Mitza, as they followed her progress.

Later, up in her bedroom dressing for the party, Christa tried to snap out of her mood of depression. She yearned suddenly to draw closer to the man to whom she had been married such a short time. She ought to be still madly in love with him, and he with her. How was it possible that a violent all-absorbing passion could vanish so swiftly? It was as though all the stars had shattered to fragments and the lights had gone out and she was living in a confused world of dark apprehension – a cycle of disappointments that came round and round, unendingly.

Once she was bathed and dressed, she presented herself to Tony for inspection.

'Nice?' she asked coaxingly.

She wanted to flirt with her husband. She wanted the old Tony who used to arrive at the mews cottage and tell her that she was the loveliest thing on earth and that he could not live a day more without her. Now to her delight, he appeared suddenly to become that Tony. He was looking well-groomed and clean, handsome in that dark grey lounge suit with a blue tie. He was attractive enough to stir any woman's heart. And he gave her his most charming smile.

'You look very smart,' he said.

She had put on a short dinner dress of black stiffened tulle. It had a belt of sequins, and was off the shoulder. She wore with it turquoise earrings and a turquoise choker around the long slender throat. The effect was so stunning that it aroused even Tony from memories of business projects. He was in high spirits because he had presided over a very successful board meeting today. And his mother had complimented him on the way he had tackled a difficult situation. He pulled the enchanting figure of his wife against him.

'Can I kiss you? or what about the lipstick?' he whispered.

'Love me, darling, *love* me again as you used to,' she whispered frantically.

'I've never stopped loving you,' he said in a surprised voice.

'You *have*!' she argued fiercely. 'You've become terribly matter-of-fact – too busy for me – I know you don't think I fit in down here and—'

'Rubbish, darling,' he broke in. 'Absolute nonsense. It's only that you're such an intense little thing. Women are different I suppose, but I'm a man and have got my business and—'

Now it was she who broke in, raising her flushed face, looking up at him with the brilliant eyes that begged for an understanding that he could not give.

'What's *business* got to do with our love? Can't you sometimes stop thinking about making money on the farm or doing something that your mother wants? You're with her so much more than you are with me. It isn't that I want to be stupidly jealous, only to feel that you're really *mine*. Not *hers*.'

'Really, darling—'

'Oh, don't use that word *really*,' she said between her teeth.

He frowned – incapable of seeing through the fog of his own self-righteousnes – of reaching down from the unassailable peak on which he had placed himself, in order to touch the depths of her despair. So he gave her a little shake and murmured:

'You're looking gorgeous. I'll show you how much I love you later tonight.'

She went cold. She drew herself out of his arms. The heart which had been beating so madly slowed down, down, *down*.

She walked to her dressing-table and ran a comb through her hair; the strange gold of her eyes looking almost black with her passionate disappointment. Tony's words had been in the nature of a rejection. The humiliation of it blasted all her desire to share the ecstasy of the sudden perfect moment. He had merely given the hint, the promise of ecstasy – relegating the kiss to a more convenient future. He added:

'Oh damn – look at this, now we shall be late!'

She swung round to him, rose-red lips pressed mutinously together.

'Why?'

'You've put lipstick on my collar.'

'I apologize. How very tactless of me. What a nuisance for you.'

He took the apology seriously – his own sense of humour completely wanting.

'Oh, that's all right.'

'It isn't,' she said, her voice trembling. 'It isn't *at all* all right. I was a fool to think you could ever forget everything and go crazy just because you love me. I'm nothing but a damned fool, and I know it.'

Now he stared at her over his shoulder as he untied his tie.

'Really, darling—' he began in an injured voice.

She put her hands to her ears and ran out of the room.

She ran down the stairs and through the passage into the main house. In the hall she met Richard. He too, had bathed and changed. He was in the act of lighting a cigarette when he saw her. He left the match suspended and the cigarette unlit. A little exclamation came from him.

'My, *my*! All this glamour for my Lady Ursula?'

She could hardly speak, she was so angry. So hopelessly aware that instead of drawing nearer to Tony she had only widened the gulf. Richard noted how flushed she was. He thought he had never seen anyone look more enchanting.

'You're like something by Degas.'

She gave a breathless laugh but her eyes remained angry.

'*Lac des cygnes*. Black swan instead of a white one.'

'Very effective. The blue choker against your tanned throat is marvellous. Somebody really ought to paint you.'

His eyes were travelling over her delicate shoulders and the little ankles. She wore high-heeled blue satin sandal shoes. He added:

'Not at all like the sleeping beauty in the barn. Do you know you looked then rather like a sad little girl, asleep.'

Christa broke into a laugh that was definitely sarcastic. He had begun to sense that she was at high tension.

'Maybe I am a sad little girl,' she said. 'And maybe I don't like living at Queen's Lacey, and I want to run away soon, then everybody will be very much more peaceful. I don't think I ought ever to have come.'

The muscles of Richard's face tautened. He lit his cigarette and put it between his lips.

After a pause he said:

'Look, sister mine – take my advice and don't get yourself so het up whether it's over my brother Tony, or my mother, or living with us at Queen's Lacey. We may all live under the same roof but each one can still have his own separate existence. Don't worry so much about what *others* say or do. Nothing can destroy your own secret existence. It's inviolate.'

'It isn't!' she argued, feeling an almost childish desire to quarrel with him; with everybody.

'If I had more time I would try and make you see that you are wrong and I am right. Meanwhile mix yourself a gin and French and cool down. It will all be the same in a hundred years you know. We shall lie buried in the churchard at Amersham and instead of the Chalfords another family will be living at Queen's Lacey, disturbing themselves and others.'

Her hot anger suddenly left her, but she was near to tears. She turned away. When she spoke it was like the 'sad little girl in the barn' he thought; no longer the seductive sophisticated young woman in her 'swan-lake' dress.

'Oh, Richard, a hundred years is a long time!' she said in a desolate voice. 'But I'm rather glad I shan't be alive then. It would be *awful* to contemplate living for another hundred years.'

A pang tore at his heart. He knew now that she was very unhappy. Like a brother he wished to comfort her. *And not like a brother*. This was the most frightening thought of all. He suddenly disliked Tony. He must be crazy – sadistic – making this charming girl so miserable? For no other reason, of course, than that he was so confoundedly wrapped up in himself. But the instinctive honour that was rooted in Richard – the integrity that must be preserved, knowing that he could so easily love Christa not as a sister *but as a woman*, dismissed these thoughts. He walked towards the front door.

'Good night. Try and have a good time at Ursula's. I'm off,' he said gruffly.

She looked after his retreating form.

Richard had a swift striding walk. Carrying his mackintosh over one arm, head bare to the wind, he marched down the drive without looking to the right or left. He was walking to the next-door farm.

He was going to spend the evening with Susan. She would sit silent and tormented while he and her father discussed their farms. Oh, poor Susan, poor Susan! thought Christa distractedly. What a fiendishly cruel thing love could be – love rejected, love that had died, *love that was forbidden.*

Her face went suddenly white and her eyes were afraid as she walked into the dining-room and, as Richard had bidden her, poured herself out a drink.

'*Calm down,*' he said, '*it will be all the same in a hundred years.*'

How right he was . . . how very right.

She was cool and collected again when Tony joined her. Neither of them made any allusion to the embarrassing episode of the kiss upstairs.

At Forty Green, Christa was gay and amusing during dinner. She made every effort to please Tony.

Ursula Corby had meant, when Christa first married Tony, to dislike her but couldn't. She found her charming and friendly – that rare thing, a woman without malice. Ursula stopped being spiteful about Tony's marriage. When she spoke to him alone for a moment, during coffee, she said:

'You're a lucky guy, Tony, we all think Christa's adorable. Never seen her look prettier than tonight.'

That satisfied Tony's ego. He drawled:

'Thanks a lot.'

He was smugly satisfied with Christa.

But later on in the evening when Christa grew tired of the card game and turned her attention to one of the other guests who liked music and wanted her to sing – Tony was less amused. Before that he had been unusually charming – even thrown his wife some of the old ardent glances. But when she stepped out of the card game and refused to play any more, he sulked. And in the car coming home he started a row with her.

CHAPTER FOUR

THE Thorntons lived in an old-fashioned farmhouse which was large, cold and draughty and had none of the magnificence of Queen's Lacey. It bore the uninspiring name of Hillside Farm. Joseph Thornton, who had been a widower since the middle of the war, was as old fashioned as his house; short, burly, red-faced and bearded. He had married late in life and already reached fifty when his one and only child was born. He had spent no money on the house. Indoors it had been allowed largely to sink into decay, although the farm was well run. By no means as prosperous as the Chalfords, Joe Thornton nevertheless managed to pay his way, with a particular interest in pigs which he supplied on contract to a bacon factory. Susan had been brought up by Mr. Thornton's sister; a meek ineffectual little woman who had been a half-trained hospital nurse in her youth but who had returned in order to take over the running of her brother's home and to mother the little girl.

Miss Thornton, known as Auntie Wyn, was not very good at anything; a poorish cook and bad manager, she was always running out of everything she had forgotten to order. The only thing that Aunt Wyn knew how to do well was knit. Plain and badly dressed herself, she bought modern patterns and in strange contrast produced the most beautiful up-to-date pullovers, cardigans, and even dresses. She knitted everything for her brother and her niece.

She had never been a replacement for Susan's mother because she did not really understand children. Mr. Thornton loved his motherless daughter deeply but was too immersed in the farm and the struggle to make the place pay to worry his head overmuch about a small girl.

In consequence Susan had grown up a trifle 'wild', and once she left her mediocre boarding school in High Wycombe she did as she wanted. Her great passion was horses, and she adored hunting. Being a member of the local hunt was her great joy and privilege. She led a dull life apart from her riding and some farm work. The great nights of her life were those when she could put on an evening dress and go to the Hunt Balls. But she was not content at heart. She knew that she had neither beauty nor allure for the young men in the district. In consequence, she adopted that rather defiant boyish pose of hers and often stood with her legs astride, hands in her pockets, with a look on her face which said:

'*I don't care!*'

But she did care, passionately, about everything and particularly about Richard Chalford. He had been her hero when they were children. She could remember when she used to be sent in to Queen's Lacey to tea with the boys. She must have been about ten at the time. Pip's most memorable birthday party. There were other children from the neighbourhood; little girls dressed in pretty party frocks. Some of the younger ones were accompanied and fussed over by their adoring mothers. Susan had gone alone in one of Aunt Wyn's knitted dresses which was well worn and had become elongated in the wash. It made her look very thin and was stretched to an ugly length below her knobbly knees. The only attempt to smarten her up had been the pink bow in her short dark hair.

After tea, Tony – then a very handsome boy of fourteen, just back from Shrewsbury for the holidays – was made her partner in a three-legged race. She had hoped to run the race with her beloved Richard who was always friendly and kind to her. She hated and feared Tony. She hated him particularly that day because he looked with such contempt at her. During the race she slipped and fell and pulled him down with her. He rose, his grey flannels stained with mud and grass, and glared at her fiercely.

'Clever ass!' he muttered. 'Why did I have to have *you* as a partner? You've got a jolly awful dress, too.'

She had burst into tears and run away, seeking refuge in that very same barn in which Richard had found his sister-in-law fourteen years later.

It was Richard who found Susan there and had tried to comfort the weeping humiliated little girl by giving her his pen-knife and a grubby bag of liquorice all-sorts. Then she had flung an arm around him and kissed his flushed brown cheek with a smacking kiss that drew an exclamation of horror from him.

'Cripes! Don't do that!' he had said, laughing.

But she had gone home happy, feeling that she had one friend in the world. She told Daddy and Aunt Wyn that she had adored the Chalfords' party.

But she had rolled the knitted dress up into a ball and flung green paint on it in order to ruin it so that when Aunt Wyn found it, she had had to throw it away. Susan had never forgotten Tony's unkind taunt. Nor had she forgotten Richard's awkward attempts to restore her *amour-propre*. She still had the penknife locked away with her treasures.

Last Christmas, when Richard had kissed her under the mistletoe, the adult Susan had fallen desperately in love with him.

She had little hope of that love being returned. Richard seemed so aloof these days. Now he even avoided her. She had received one or two proposals of marriage during the last three years and turned them down, with Richard still her *beau ideal*.

She had felt tremendously excited when her father had told her this week that he had asked young Richard Chalford to the evening meal tonight and he had accepted. She made Aunt Wyn hire the services of a good cook. She, herself, arranged the dinner table and the flowers. She did so want to impress Richard. She put on three different dresses and tore them all off, hating the sight of her angular over-thin figure. None of the dresses seemed to suit her. It was such a cold night that she really needed warmth but she finally chose the thinnest dress – a floral organza which she thought the most becoming. It had orange flowers on it. She shivered in it, rather than spoil the effect by putting on one of Aunt Wyn's home-knitted cardigans.

Since Tony had married Christa Morley, Susan had so often thought about the beautiful ethereal-looking Christa. She envied, with some bitterness, that Scandinavian fairness of skin, that beauty of gilt hair and lustrous eyes. Envied, too, the chic clothes, the poise, and distinction that marked Christa down from other women. Susan could not begin to emulate it. A little lipstick – that was all the make-up she ever put on. She had tried recently to use nail varnish but wiped it off in disgust. She had short nails and the broad finger tips and big knuckes of a man; wonderful hands for a horse, but when she was indoors, in a pretty dress, those fingers looked ugly and unfeminine, and she knew it.

Richard greeted her as he always did when they met – casually but kindly.

'Hullo, Susan – how's yourself?'

'Okay,' she answered and hoped he would not know how the blood pounded in her temples.

'I saw Buddy in the paddock – he looks well.'

Buddy was her roan hunter – her pride and her joy.

Her eyes kindled and for a moment her thin plain young face looked almost attractive.

'Bud's in fine form but he wants more exercising. Wouldn't you like to ride him for me one day, Rich?'

'I haven't got much time,' he said.

'Busy on the farm?'

'Just now, as you know, is our busiest time.'

'Daddy says your barley is magnificent.'

'So-so,' he nodded modestly.

'I don't think ours is nearly as good. Daddy is very disappointed because we had another heifer born last night. We ought really to buy some more cows but he says we can't afford it. Farming is all right for you Chalfords but it is a bit of a tussle for us this year, and the pigs are not as lucrative as they were.'

'I'm sorry for that, I think *we're* very lucky,' said Richard and took a cigarette from the box she offered.

They were alone in the big ugly sitting-room where one or two fine old rugs were ill at ease with curtains and covers which had been bought during the war and faded to a dull rust. They still had 'black-out' linings which increased the effect of gloom. It always worried Richard to see how shabby things looked at Hillside Farm. To know that their kind and peaceful neighbours whose farm was in friendly opposition to their own, were so much less successful. It worried him, too, because he meant so much to Susan Thornton. He was not vain enough to feel flattered by her unwelcome love. He could never bear the suffering of others. Susan's heartbreak made him feel guilty, although he could not in any way be held responsible for her pain. But what he saw in her eyes tonight was the reason why he avoided her and came as little as he could to visit the Thorntons.

'Are you shooting in Ursula Corby's party?' she asked him towards the end of the meal.

'No, I'm not shooting tomorrow. Tony and Pip are going. I don't think it will be much of a year for partridges myself.'

'Rastus and I put up a wonderful covey in the spinney down by Sagger's Copse,' said Susan and threw a piece of toast to Rastus, her black labrador, whom she had had since he was a puppy. That was ten years ago. Now Rastus was white about the muzzle and his eyes had a bluish film. Aunt Wyn complained that he smelled. He ought not to be allowed in the house, she said, or on Susan's bed. But there he slept. And smell or no smell Susan worshipped him with that single-heartedness and over-intensity which she showed in her affection towards all those people or things when she loved.

She steered the conversation round to Tony.

'How are things with Tony and his wife? Somebody told me – I don't know who – it was at Ursula's cocktail party I think – that Christa's got awfully thin and looks rather miserable.'

Richard frowned. The mention of Christa made him curiously uneasy. Remembering her as she had looked with those long lashes curving against her cheeks asleep in the barn, and the memory of her tonight in her 'swan-lake' dress, with her flushed cheeks and passionate mouth. He pushed back his cheese-plate, asked if he could smoke, and hurriedly lit a cigarette.

'How do you think they are getting on, Rich?' persisted Susan.

'I really don't know – I haven't asked them,' he said with scant courtesy and gave a laugh.

Susan went scarlet.

'Sorry. I suppose I oughtn't to have asked but I was curious. I think she's so lovely – don't you?'

A plain woman praising a beautiful one signified for Richard both pathos and generosity. He cast a more compassionate look on Susan and spoke to her in the old kind way.

'I didn't mean to snap your head off, but really, Susan, I'm much too busy to wonder why Christa's thin or if she is miserable.'

That wasn't true but he said it. Susan knew it wasn't true. She had made a study of Richard for so long that she fancied she knew every shadow of his face. She got up and looked at Aunt Wyn.

'Let's have coffee in the sitting-room.'

'I'm afraid I haven't a cigar for you, Rich my boy,' said Mr. Thornton, 'but we'll have a pipe and a chat together while Susan and Aunty titivate.'

Aunt Wyn went into the kitchen to help the hired cook. Susan whistled to Rastus and walked out into the garden, which looked bedraggled. It had had very little attention this year. How strange and troubled Richard had seemed when she had mentioned Christa and asked about the marriage. Why had he 'snapped her head off' if it wasn't that the question touched him on the raw? Everybody in the district was talking about Christa and wondering about that marriage. Nobody could get on with old Mrs. Chalford. Everybody thought it mad of Tony to allow his wife to live at Queen's Lacey. Christa was Richard's sister-in-law; he couldn't think of her in any way *but* as a brother. *Or was that nonsense?* They were no blood relation – none at all. And many a man had married his brother's widow!

Susan tortured herself with these reflections. She wished she hadn't let Daddy ask Richard to dinner. He avoided looking at her. Possibly he thought her dress didn't suit her. The orange was too bright a colour. She had caught sight of her face in the hall mirror as she walked down and decided that it made her look horribly sallow.

Nothing's going right, she thought despairingly. Even Rastus was getting a little more blind every day but she wouldn't have him put away. *She wouldn't.* He was the only person in the world who returned her love in full measure. He could not bear to be apart from her. Buddy loved her, too, she had only to whistle and he would prick his ears and trot towards her. Only when she was riding him during the hunting season, was she really happy. Everybody said how well she rode and jumped.

She walked Rastus down with her to the paddock and gave Buddy two lumps of sugar which she had taken off the coffee tray. He whinnied softly as she put her arms around his neck and pressed her face against the hot satin of it. She listened to his strong teeth crushing the sugar. She felt particularly forlorn and lost this evening, and her hunger for Richard seemed to tear her heart from her body.

The rest of the evening was a nightmare because she could not control the attack of nerves which had seized her when Richard first arrived. She realized that all hope of restoring the cheerful friendly association of their childhood was gone beyond recall. She was quite glad when at ten o'clock Richard said that he must go home as he had an early rise in front of him. She walked with him to the end of the farm road that led to the wooden gate. On a bench there, under the chestnut tree stood three great churns of milk waiting to be picked up by the lorries. It was raining again.

'Better not come any farther, Susan, you'll get wet,' said Richard lightly.

'I don't care,' she said.

'Well, thanks awfully for the dinner,' he said awkwardly and held out a hand.

In the dim dampness of the night he saw her face. She looked wretched and particularly plain tonight, he thought. The orange dress was an abomination – still he had always been quite fond of poor Susan. He was so sorry for her. She couldn't have much of a life with that father or silly old aunt. The same mistaken impulse that had led him to kiss her under the mistletoe at Christmas led him now to kiss Susan good night. He wouldn't have done it if he had given a thought to the matter, but she looked so unhappy. He bent and touched her cheek with his lips.

'Good night, my dear,' he said.

It was the match to the bundle of hay – the trigger point. She lost her head completely and flung herself against him. He had to steady her. As his arms went round the thin figure he felt the urgency of her mouth dragging kisses from his lips.

'Oh, Richard, *Richard*!' she breathed his name agonizedly.

He was speechless. His cheeks burnt in the darkness. She did not rouse his passion – only that immense pity which was the danger. 'Beware Of Pity.' Wasn't that the title of a novel? He felt her breath against his lips and the tightening of her hard young hands about his neck.

'Richard!' she said again, and it was a cry of despair rather than an utterance of his name.

'Look, dear—' he began.

But she gave him no time to finish the sentence. She dragged herself away from him.

'No, you needn't tell me – you don't love me and I know it. You don't have to tell me.'

'We're good friends, Susan,' he said, and wished to God that he had never made that gesture towards her. He hated to hurt her but could not help it now. He added:

'Let's stay friends – it can't be anything more and it's better for you to know it.'

'Better!' she repeated in a hoarse voice. 'Maybe. Oh, why, why aren't I like Christa? You admire her, don't you? If she hadn't married Tony you might have been in love with her. I don't attract you. Oh, I wish I were dead.'

Turning she rushed away from him. He could hear her sobbing as she ran, the old labrador quickening his pace loping down the road after her.

A gust of wind spattered the rain drops against Richard's face. His heart beat quickly and uncomfortably. He felt rather sick.

'What a mess life is,' he thought and began to walk with his long swinging stride down the main road towards the gates of Queen's Lacey. It had been a mistake accepting old Thornton's invitation. Susan was becoming impossible. He hated the thought that he had helped to humiliate her. But he could do nothing about it.

What pounded in his mind were those things Susan had said about Christa. 'If she hadn't married Tony you might have been in love with her.'

What a staggering remark! Of course Susan was jealous of Christa. She had had no right to say a thing like that. It was in atrocious taste.

It was more. It was the second trigger to be touched that night ... confirming in Richard's mind the certainty that Susan's despairing words held more than a grain of truth.

If Christa hadn't married Tony you might have been in love with her.

'I damn nearly am,' he muttered the words to himself as he walked through the wind and the rain.

He walked at such a pace that he was out of breath when he got home. He was also in a furious rage, as unaccountable as it was violent. He heard voices in the sitting-room. The door opened. The figures of his mother and younger brother emerged. Mrs. Chalford was in the act of taking off her horn-rimmed glasses and putting them in their case. She held a book and her tapestry under one arm. She looked at Richard's taut face.

'Hullo, Thundercloud,' she said with a somewhat humourless effort to be jocular, 'you don't look as though you've enjoyed your dinner party. Pip and I had a nice peaceful evening, didn't we, dear? The others aren't back yet.'

Richard made no answer but started to mount the stairs. Mrs. Chalford called him back:

'Really, Richard, I was speaking to you, dear.'

'Sorry,' he said, 'I didn't hear.'

'Didn't you enjoy your dinner?'

'Very much, thanks.'

'How's poor Susan?' put in Pip yawning.

Richard snapped at him.

'To hell with this "poor Susan" business. Good night.'

'Really Richard,' came from Mrs. Chalford again, 'I can't say your manners are very charming.'

'Sorry,' he repeated tensely and ran up the stairs two at a time.

Mrs. Chalford heard his bedroom door slam. She sighed.

'I can't think, why Richard is so bad-tempered at times. He never used to be.'

'Good night, Mother,' said Pip, who had no wish to be drawn into a discussion about Richard. Julia raised her cheek for her youngest son's kiss. She always felt well-disposed towards Pip. He had such a nice chubby face and was so completely hers. As she went towards her own bedroom she thought wistfully of Tony. *He* used to be completely hers, too. Clever, handsome Tony. What a change there had been in him since that wife of his came to Queen's Lacey. Such an *undercurrent* going on. It was obvious that the girl did not care for her any more than she liked Christa. Their antipathy was mutual. However, thought Julia walking into her bedroom, there was not much need to worry about Christa removing *Tony* from his mother or home. He still seemed to be the same dear devoted son. But of course she, Julia, had to share him with that silly pretty thing he'd

104

married. What sort of a wife was she to Tony? There were moments when Julia had her doubts about the way things were going between the pair.

One thing was certain – she must never let Tony leave Queen's Lacey. While she had him here, she could watch over him. She must also always control the purse strings, then she would never really lose any of the boys.

It must have been an hour later, as Julia was winding up her bedside clock and preparing to put out her light, that she heard the scrunch of car wheels on the drive. Tony and Christa coming back.

Julia got out of bed and put on her dressing-gown; a masculine, tartan affair. Her faded auburn hair was plaited and confined with a rubber band. The strong bulb from her reading lamp threw up the sharp contours of her face and made the freckles stand out. She looked as though she could never have been the handsome vivacious redhead who had been wooed and won by Tony's father nearly thirty years ago.

She walked on to the landing, meaning to have a word with Tony and say good night. They generally came in through the main building. Tony would probably have a glass of beer or cider – then they would go through to their own wing. As Mrs. Chalford leaned over the banisters she heard her son's familiar voice on a brisk loud note of irritation:

'Don't be so ridiculous, Christa.'

Julia drew back, her brows raised. A look of satisfaction came into her eyes.

Oh! So he's finding her ridiculous – that's new. He wouldn't have used that word to her twelve months ago.

Julia stayed up on the landing, drawing back so that she could not be seen but hoping to hear a little more of what appeared to be a 'tiff' between husband and wife.

Sure enough she heard it. Christa's reply was flat and dispirited.

'Honestly, Tony, everything has always got to be exactly as you want it or you sulk. It wasn't my fault.'

'I'm sure it was,' thought Julia Chalford nodding her head grimly to herself. 'Tony doesn't sulk or if he does nowadays *she's* made him. . . .'

The couple had stopped in the hall, Tony's voice could be heard clearly by the eavesdropper.

'Stay here a minute, Christa, I'm going to have a drink. I want to talk to you.'

From Christa:

'I don't want to stay and be nagged at.'

'Look, Christa, I'm not going to be accused of nagging. You knew when we went to Ursula's that I wanted to play Canasta.'

'Well, we did play. I tried to learn but you know I hate cards and Ursula admitted that I have no card sense. She was very nice about it – much nicer than you.'

'Ursula has excellent manners and is a good hostess. Naturally she wouldn't say what she felt.'

'But Tony,' Christa's voice was rising, 'I played Canasta for a solid hour. Now didn't I? And then that Mr. Belfort or whatever his name is, who used to be an opera singer, heard that I was fond of music and suggested that we should try Ursula's piano. Everybody else seemed to enjoy the music except you.'

'Belfort's an old bore and it's time he stopped singing.'

'I can't agree and I don't think you know much about music, anyhow, Tony. Mr. Belfort still is a very fine tenor.'

'That's your opinion.'

'Oh, what did you want me to do, then?' came from Christa on a weary miserable note. 'Refuse to play and say that I *must* go on with the Canasta because my husband wanted me to? I find Canasta a dreary game.'

'Much less dreary than listening to your duet with old Belfort.'

'Thanks. I won't bore you with my music again. I'm going to bed. Good night, Tony.'

A door shut.

Upstairs, flattening herself against the wall, Julia Chalford stood with that grim smile on her face. She nodded to herself once or twice, then tiptoed softly back into her own bedroom.

Downstairs, Tony finished his drink, turned out the lights and walked through to his own wing. By now his bad temper had cooled. He realized that he had been unwarrantably difficult and after all everybody at the Corby's had complimented Christa on her delightful singing. It was just that music had absolutely no meaning for Tony. He felt cheated because he wanted to play Canasta.

Once he was undressed, he went through to the bedroom, meaning to tell Christa that he was ready to forgive her. But she had turned on her side and seemed to be asleep. He shrugged his shoulders and went to sleep as soon as his head touched the pillow. Then, and then only, Christa's eyes opened and the big tears began to well slowly down her cheeks.

She wondered if it might not be a good thing if she got away from this house and the whole family, and went up to town to stay with Mummy for a day or two. Tony might not be pleased and there would be trouble about getting away (and of course Mrs. Chalford would say unpleasant things about it). But, all the same, Christa decided it might be for the best. Her nerves were on edge. Mummy was so soothing. Longingly Christa thought of her old home. Her sympathetic, peaceful mother. It would be such fun, living with her again. Even though Christa might have to do the cooking – and here there was Mitza – it would be *heaven*. Just she and Mummy alone again. Sharing a talk and a cigarette, perfectly relaxed. In Queen's Lacey she always seemed to be living at tension – as though waiting for something to snap.

'I'll tell Tony tomorrow that I'm going and that he must do without me for a few days,' Christa thought.

But it was not to be. The blackest day of Christa's life was to dawn for her on the morrow.

It was such a clear golden day, that 1st of September. Tony had woken up early and was in a much better mood because he looked forward to his partridge shooting. Ursula always organized a first-class syndicate and she had told him last night that her keeper thought they should get a fair bag.

Christa was drinking her early morning cup of tea and preparing to announce her intention of spending a few nights in town, when the telephone bell rang. Mrs. Chalford, when she had been persuading the young couple to live at Queen's Lacey, had had an extension line put in for them.

Tony, just about to go into the bathroom, said:

'Answer the phone will you, Chris?'

She disliked that shortening of her name, but said nothing. She presumed that Tony meant to be friendly. Well, she wanted him to be in a good mood when she gave him her ultimatum.

It was Judy on the line.

Christa began:

'Oh, *hullo*, Judy! As a matter of fact I was going to ring Mummy and suggest coming up this morning.'

She paused and glanced at the bathroom door. Tony had just vanished. Then Judy spoke again. The colour drained from Christa's cheeks. She sat upright; her fingers clutched the cobweb chiffon of the nightgown she was wearing.

'Oh, *no!*' she breathed.

A moment later Tony heard her calling his name. Shaving

brush in hand, he came in and looked at her. He saw that she was white and that her eyes were stricken. He put down the shaving brush and hurried to the bedside. In his own way he was still in love with this pretty, attractive wife who was so different from the Chalfords.

'What's the matter, darling? Have you had bad news?'

In unutterable grief she flung herself into his arms and pressed her cheek against his shoulder. For a moment or two he could not get the facts from her.

She had lost the one irreplaceable being who mattered to her above all others. Her mother had died in her sleep last night. Judy had just found her.

CHAPTER FIVE

DURING the weeks that followed Mrs. Morley's funeral Christa drew a little closer to her husband again. Almost as close as when she had first fallen in love with him, although it could never be quite the same between them after the sharp disillusionment of the last year. However, the death of the mother whom she had adored forged some kind of link; not that Tony had known her or cared for Mrs. Morley long enough to share such bitter sorrow. But he loved his own mother and could respect Christa's grief.

In the beginning, Mrs. Chalford, too, was shocked out of her ordinary attitude of icy disapproval and tried to be kind to Christa. In an awkward fashion, to be sympathetic, too. But she was never at ease where emotions were concerned and only too pleased when Christa went up to London and stayed there. Tony also stayed at the cottage for a night or two and would have remained longer, but Christa assured him that he could be of no further help and begged him to go home. She knew that he wanted to go and that he was hanging around London only out of deference to her. Tony was at his best when he had to organize and take control. He had arranged the funeral and done his best to make things easy for Christa and her cousin.

Christa was grateful and told him so.

'Thank you, darling Tony, for being so kind,' she said just before he drove back to Coleshill.

'That's all right, darling. Come back to Queen's Lacey as soon as you can,' he said.

After he had gone, Judy said to Christa:

'I think your husband is absolutely *delightful*. Poor Aunt Sarah used to seem worried about your marriage, but I can't think why.'

Christa had no answer for this. She could not discuss her marriage with Judy, or even think about it just now. She had to go upstairs to the bedroom that her mother once occupied and start the morbid task of getting Mrs. Morley's things packed away, she wondered how she was going to go on without Mummy in the world.

Everybody had to lose their mother – Tony had said that himself, even while he shrank from the prospect of the inevitable end of his own mother.

But Christa felt that Mummy had had far too short a life and that this was too sudden an end. She had been so sweet, so lovely, and always so kind. Her one consolation lay in the knowledge that Mrs. Morley was beyond further suffering.

Christa kept wishing that she had made a visit to her mother earlier. It was terrible to think that their association was now forever ended. Soon the little home would go, too. Judy did not feel that she could carry on the shop, alone. So the business must be sold.

So, Christa thought as she stared round her mother's familiar bedroom, shivering and melancholy, I shall be quite alone in the world except for Tony and *his family*.

The tears began to flow. She fumbled in her bag for a handkerchief. With it she drew out a note. Through the tears she stared at it. It was from her brother-in-law, Richard.

Last week-end Christa had gone down to the farm to please Tony, and had taken Judy with her. Judy seemed to get on very well with Mrs. Chalford who thought her a sensible sort of girl, and the whole family had been very kind to Christa. Mitza in particular – the only one actually to shed tears with her *'liebschen'*. It had, in fact, been the most peaceful week-end Christa had ever spent at Queen's Lacey, except for Richard, who was so deeply embarrassed by the disaster that had befallen her that he gave her a wide berth. He did not speak to her, except for a few muttered words of sympathy. She began to wonder if she had offended him in some way. Then, with her mind and heart full of memories of her mother, she gave Richard no further thought.

Until two days ago, when she had received this unexpected letter. It was written in Richard's rather big untidy writing. The ink was smudged, as though he had written in a hurry.

Dear Christa,

I fear that you may have thought me a boor unmindful of your terrible loss, and the sorrow you must be feeling. But I have thought about it and I am writing this to tell you how I personally feel about death. It may not be of the slightest interest but I do feel that we mortals waste too many tears weeping for those who have finished with the impossible problem of life. They find suddenly such a glorious solution that it should be a cause for congratulations rather than for mourning.

Do not be sad about your mother. She has solved the problem a little younger than need be, perhaps, but the solution is, in fact, Death's recompense.

I am in touch with a Danish farmer who would like his son to take my place and learn what we can teach him for a few months while I take his place in Denmark. If my mother approves I shall probably arrange this. So I may be away this winter. But I want you to know that I feel deeply distressed for you.

Do not go on grieving – will you? Or feel alone. You are one of us now, and Queen's Lacey will shelter you.

Richard.

She had thought this letter as extraordinary as it was unexpected. An old-fashioned sort of letter – obviously written with much thought and with difficulty. She had read it many times. It was the outstanding letter of the many she had received from distant relatives and old friends.

But this one letter from Richard brought Christa inexplicable comfort. The phrasing, the philosophy seemed so much part of his make-up, of the fascinating Richard who belonged to the farm, to the earth, and yet was capable of walking on the starry heights. Who possessed spirituality and compassion.

Only he, of all the Chalfords, could have written that letter. She knew every word by heart now. She had wept less since she had dwelt on the meaning that lay within them. Why, indeed, weep for her poor little mother who had been so often harassed by lack of finance, sacrificed so much for her child, and lost the love of her own life so early? She had found 'the glorious sol-

110

ution'. *Death's recompense*, as Richard called it. That was a nice idea.

But the other part of his letter disconcerted Christa. Why was Richard arranging to leave Queen's Lacey? Why this sudden idea of exchanging places with a Danish farmer? Surely his mother would not like it; Christa had so often heard her say that Richard on the farm was irreplaceable. Besides, she would not want to loosen her grip upon any of the boys, even if the Danish substitute worked as well as Richard.

From this thought Christa's mind moved to another. The prospect of life at Queen's Lacey without Richard in the house. Not the queer awkward Richard of last week-end, but the old Richard ready to laugh and jest with her. The Richard who played while she sang with that light, charming touch of his, the Richard of swiftly changing moods, with a love of stimulating conversation.

She would miss him terribly. She did not want him to go away.

Grief for her mother was punctuated by uneasiness, and a little niggling dismay, every time she anticipated the long winter at Queen's Lacey without Richard.

Such dismay was followed immediately by a sensation of guilt – of disloyalty to Tony. Tony was her husband. His companionship should be enough for her.

It was well into the third week in September before Christa finally returned to live at Queen's Lacey.

With the assistance of Tony and the family solicitors, she had sold The Greenhouse at a profit; also the lease of the mews cottage. Reluctantly she also disposed of most of the furniture and effects, with Tony's approval. But as she remarked to Judy sadly, poor Mummy had never had much of value in this life and she left little. She had already given her best piece of jewellery to Christa for a wedding present.

The day came when Judy returned to Devonshire and Christa bade a permanent farewell to the little cottage. The couple from next door were there to see her off; Bill and Dana, heart-broken over the sudden death of their charming neighbour, were deeply depressed to see Christa go.

'Keep in touch with us, Christa,' they said.

'You must come down and stay with me at Queen's Lacey,' said Christa.

But she knew that she would never be able to ask them because Tony did not like Bill, and Mrs. Chalford would most certainly disapprove of the pair of them. They were the 'Chelsea types' that she abhorred.

Tony was too busy to fetch Christa that day because he had an important date in High Wycombe. He sent Pip up with the car. Christa was quite pleased to see her 'littlest brother' as she called Pip. He was a cheerful uncomplicated sort of boy. But she could not control her depression as the car moved away from the mews. She looked back at the cottage with the shut windows and the locked door and at Bill and Dana, waving her farewell.

Good-bye to Mummy and to the little home that had always seemed such a refuge and a joy. Good-bye to her girlhood – to her whole past life. Now she would be thrown completely on the Chalfords – Queen's Lacey would be her one and only home.

She felt that it might all be much better if she and Tony could have had a home of their own.

Nice though Julia had been since Christa's mother died, Christa was sure that the 'niceness' would not last long. They were too hopelessly antipathetic in their relationship towards each other.

Pip took a glance at his sister-in-law. He had not got an understanding temperament, and was even more shy of emotion than Tony, but he wanted to try and do his best. Christa looked so forlorn today, so unlike herself. She had lost weight, and much of the sunburn she had gained at Queen's Lacey this summer. There were big shadows under her eyes. She looked older. He glanced a trifle nervously, too, at her dress. On this September afternoon she wore a pale blue suit, Pip had an uncomfortable memory of what his mother had said at dinner last night.

'I really do think, Tony,' she had said, 'that Christa ought to wear mourning. After all – it was her *own mother* – and going about as she did last week-end in those gay clothes shocked me.'

Tony had answered:

'I don't think it matters much. Christa's not as conventional as you are, Mother, and Mrs. Morley was the same, you know. Christa says that Mrs. Morley always said there was to be no mourning worn for her, just as she asked that there should be no flowers.'

'Well, I thought that was very unattractive, and that is why I *sent* flowers!' said Mrs. Chalford in a prim voice.

'Incidentally, Mother,' Tony said, 'yours was the only wreath that came and it was extremely awkward knowing what to do with it.'

'It should have been placed on the grave,' said Mrs. Chalford coldly.

Pip had sat silent, as usual, during these sort of discussions, but Richard chimed in.

'If people say they don't want flowers or mourning, surely their wishes should be respected.'

Mrs. Chalford looked at Richard over her glasses.

'Really, Richard I don't know that your opinion was asked for.'

Pip formed no opinion on the matter one way or the other, but he had grown up so closely under the shadow of Mrs. Chalford's wing, that he felt sure that her ideas were right and proper.

Of course he adored Christa, but he thought perhaps she ought to wear black just now.

As they drove down the Western Avenue, Christa asked casually:

'Is Richard going to Denmark?'

'There's been some talk about it,' said Pip, 'but Mother and Tony are against it. I haven't heard anything definite.'

Now, despite herself, Christa's heart gave a throb of relief. She turned the conversation from Richard to the farm.

'How are your beloved chickens, Pip?'

'Had a bit of trouble,' said Pip gloomily, 'hundreds of them with gapes. Hell of a business treating them.'

'What are gapes?'

Pip explained the disease. She listened, her mind only half on what he was saying, but she turned her attention to him fully again when he mentioned the name Susan.

'I had a very nice little letter from Susan on behalf of her father and herself,' she said. 'You know, I feel very sorry for that poor girl.'

'So do I,' said Pip and added with a laugh, 'she's crackers about Richard.

'Of course, I think Richard is crackers too,' Pip volunteered.

Christa had to smile. Pip, in spite of the pipe he sucked, always spoke and behaved as though he was still a schoolboy. She said wryly:

'I should have thought Richard had the best brain of the three.'

'Oh no, Tony has.'

'You mean academically.'

Pip grimaced.

'Well, we all three got a degree by the skin of our teeth but Tony's is a first-class business brain.'

'Business brain,' echoed Christa. 'Yes. But Richard has something more original – something very deep.'

She broke off, realizing that she might have shocked Pip who had preconceived notions (in imitation of his mother) ... for instance, a woman must say that her husband is more clever than any other man even if he isn't. Pip continued:

'Rich is a funny fellow. He used to write poetry as well as play the piano when we were kids. Yet he's the best farmer of us all.'

'A complete contradiction,' said Christa, and added, 'You admire him very much, don't you, Pip?'

'I get on jolly well with Rich,' said Pip.

'And you're scared of Tony.'

'Oh, I say!' protested Pip blushing. 'You do say odd things.'

'Dear Pip,' said Christa with a laugh, 'you're so well brought up.'

'Sometimes I don't understand you,' Pip added.

'Sometimes I don't understand myself,' she agreed with him and this time laughed without humour.

It had stopped raining by the time they reached Queen's Lacey. Christa looked at the herbaceous border as they drove up to the house. It was a mass of light and dark purple Michaelmas daisies, interspersed with golden rod and dahlias, but they were flattened and drooping. The front lawn appeared to be half under water. As they drove through the courtyard and round at the back of the house Christa could see nothing but mud. Never had Queen's Lacey looked more depressing. Pip climbed out of the car and volunteered the information that they had had three days' solid downpour.

Mitza came out of the kitchen and gave Christa a royal welcome, peering at her with short-sighted eyes that gleamed rapturously.

'So! She is back home my *liebchen*, I haf missed to give you tea and cakes and haf for you tonight an *apfel strudel* made.'

'Dear Mitza!' said Christa and as she embraced the little plump Austrian, felt the tears pin-prick her eyeballs. But those emotional tears dried speedily as she heard the precise voice of Tony's mother:

'Hullo, my dear, so you are back again. Tony is in his own room, I think, changing. He got very wet going round the farm just now. Everybody must wear gum boots and leave their indoor shoes ready to put on at the front door. The mud is so bad.'

Just like a schoolmistress, Christa thought, but tried to be pleasant as she walked with Mrs. Chalford into the hall. Pip was taking her luggage out of the car. She seemed to have brought a lot with her today; everything there was to bring, she thought sadly, for she would never return to the house that had been Mummy's.

'Just a little hint, my dear,' she heard her mother-in-law speaking. 'I think it's rather bad for Mitza that you make such a fuss over her, and really, there's no need to *kiss* her.'

Christa gave a short laugh.

'Do I have to be given a lecture as soon as I get back?'

Julia flushed. She was not in a good mood. She had just had a rare dispute with her eldest son on the subject of money. In her opinion he was spending too much on his wife and the 'wing', but when she said so, he took Christa's part. He wanted her to have the best of everything, and did not think she overspent, he said. Unusual for Tony who used to be as thrifty as herself, Mrs. Chalford reflected. But of course it was his wife's influence. Mrs. Chalford had thoroughly enjoyed the three weeks down here without her daughter-in-law, and was not at all pleased to see her back.

Christa added:

'Mitza is always very sweet to me, and I'm not a snob, you know. I don't see why I shouldn't give her a kiss when *she* gives *me* such a lovely welcome.'

Mrs. Chalford eyed the girl resentfully. Certainly she looked pale and unwell but she knew how to stand up for herself all right. Mrs. Chalford felt that there was little hope of ever being able to control Christa as well as the boys.

'Oh, please behave exactly as you wish, Christa,' she said icily. 'I didn't intend what I said to be a *lecture* – merely a hint.'

'Thank you,' said Christa almost as coldly as the older woman.

Her nerves were raw. She lit a cigarette and felt her fingers trembling. She had no heart for battles with Julia Chalford or anybody else.

Mrs. Chalford suddenly remembered Christa's recent loss and modified her astringent welcome.

'Well, my dear, now you've settled up everything at home you will be able to concentrate on your life here.'

'Concentrate?' Christa echoed the word, unsmiling.

Mrs. Chalford lowered her gaze. She felt slightly venomous towards Christa not only because of her acute jealousy but because there was something aloof and intangible behind this girl that the older woman could not grasp or conquer. She said with pretended lightness:

'Yes – on your life with Tony. It's quite a job being a farmer's wife, you know.'

'You make it sound as though I ought to be milking the cows or churning the butter,' said Christa. It was unlike her to be even mildly unpleasant to people but Tony's mother did seem deliberately to rub her up the wrong way.

Tony walked in as she said the words. Mrs. Chalford threw him a quick glance.

'I'm sorry,' she said meekly for his benefit, 'I didn't mean to make you cross, dear. I don't understand why you think I'm *getting* at you, or what I have done to make you be so hostile. I've tried to make you feel so very welcome in our home. Oh well—' and with a sniff she walked out, giving her son another glance which suggested sadness and bewilderment.

Christa, still trembling, was furious. Hypocrisy nauseated her. Mrs. Chalford had so subtly changed her tune once she saw Tony. He, with a frown on his handsome face, walked up to Christa.

'Oh, hullo,' he said coldly. 'I didn't hear the car. I was having a quick bath.'

'Hullo,' said Christa flatly.

'Why was Mother upset? On your first day back – really darling! You must be very tactless with her.'

Christa's temper, already frayed, snapped.

'So *I* am the tactless one and it is *my* fault! Why not hers? Why jump to the conclusion that I am to blame for any hostility that exists between your mother and me?'

'Darling, I overheard what you said – that sarcastic remark about milking the cows, etc. It seemed to be unnecessary if not rather rude. I don't blame Mother for being upset.'

'If I was rude – she asked for it,' said Christa. 'You didn't hear the beginning, did you? You didn't hear her being sweetly sarcastic, telling me that now my mother is dead I can settle down and make a good farmer's wife for you – as though I've been a bad one up to date.'

Tony stared gloomily at his wife's beautiful, angry face. He had been looking forward to seeing her but he had to admit that

116

it was more peaceful at Queen's Lacey without her. Why must she bring such a spirit of discord into the place? Mother was always a bit sharp, and a disciplinarian, but perfectly amicable when you got her to yourself, or didn't deliberately rile her. In fact, Mrs. Chalford had been particularly generous to him this week and written him a fat cheque – apart from his usual allowance.

'I know you will be needing a bit extra,' she had said. He started to inform Christa of this. She only heard half his story then flared out:

'Oh yes – she may have given you a cheque, which delights you and that's the way she gets you and Pip – with the money – plus making you believe it your duty to kow-tow to her. Well, her cheques don't impress me. It isn't *my* way of loving. If she really loved you she'd try to be more tactful with *me*, and not do her best to upset our marriage.'

'I think it's monstrous of you to suggest she is trying to do any such thing.'

'It's the truth. She dislikes me. She shows it in a dozen different ways. I'm *not* a good farmer's wife. I don't understand animals and growing barley and ploughing land and all the rest of it and you knew it when you married me. I never pretended that I could come here and step into line with your mother who has farmed all her life.'

'I know that – but you did say you'd try to step into line when we first decided to get married, Christa.'

She stubbed her cigarette-end on an ashtray and came closer to him – her eyes flashing.

'And haven't I tried? Are you telling me, as she tried to do just now, that I've failed to be a good wife and that I must turn over a new leaf now that I have lost my own home, and should apply myself more diligently to the life you all lead down here?'

Tony moved his hand impatiently.

'Look – this is most unpleasant and unnecessary. I didn't say our marriage has been a failure – I don't even think it.'

'But you wish I were more like your mother.'

'I didn't say so, Christa.'

'But you *do* think it!'

'For heaven's sake—'

'Very well – then if you're satisfied with me please ask your mother to stop nagging at me. She never comes outright with criticism – it's all underneath – it's all lowdown and beastly, and

117

I just can't take any more. If I'm going to go on living at Queen's Lacey it must be on the understanding that she leaves me alone – and lets me get on with being *myself*, even if she doesn't like what I am.'

And now, tired and dispirited, Christa burst into childish tears and hid her face in her hands. She looked so young and desolate, weeping like that, Tony softened. He was still in love with her in the physical sense. Even if he could not understand her, he had opened his eyes to the fact that he had chosen a wife who did not strictly fulfil the obligations demanded of a 'farmer's wife', and whose ideas were so opposed to those of his mother. He took the trembling figure in his arms.

'Christa, darling, don't – I hate you to cry. I'm very distressed about this – really I am. Do stop crying, darling, and let's behave in a more adult manner. We can't just have a hell of a row. It gets us nowhere. Besides, we will both only lose our tempers and say things we might regret. Christa – we still love each other – don't we? Damn it, we've barely been married sixteen months.'

She was unyielding in his embrace, her tears flowing in scalding rivulets down her cheeks; but after a moment she controlled herself, pulled a handkerchief from Tony's breast pocket and blew her nose.

'I'm sorry . . . I admit I'm being rather stupid,' she whispered.

He led her to the sofa and sat down, keeping his arm about her.

'You misjudge my mother, you know – she doesn't really mean to be unkind. She's just not our generation.'

Or the last, thought Christa, or the one before. She's an early Victorian – a prude – a hypocrite – and a bully. She's got three sons under control and now she wants me to knuckle under with them. She'd got Tony and Pip, anyhow, if not Richard. Richard was trying to break away.

She sat silent while Tony did his best to conciliate her. He was very nice and even admitted after a while that his mother was, at times, hard to understand and get on with, but that she, Christa, must remember that mother was no longer young and had had a tough fight bringing up her sons, and had achieved remarkable results. She was used to being mistress of the house, and so on – to all of which Christa listened, knowing that only half of it was true. The part Tony did not admit was the most salient (he did not wish to admit it, of course): the fact that his mother did not like *her*.

At length, however, he dragged from Christa the promise that she would 'try again'.

She went along to their own wing. She stood in the doorway feeling her heart lift slightly at the attractive sight of the drawing-room on which she had spent so much time and care. Despite several small pieces of furniture and one or two pictures that had been forced on her by Mrs. Chalford, the general effect was charming. Curtains of yellow silk brocade framed the long windows gracefully and toned with the pale yellowish-green of the paintwork. In contrast the covers were vivid red, and there were all Christa's books in a handsome Regency book-case, and on an oak table, the fine blue Bristol glass which her mother used to collect and had left to her. This was more home than the rest of Queen's Lacey. But what struck Christa most forcibly were the flowers. Two great bowls of yellow and red roses at one end of the room and in a far corner, a Chinese jar standing on a stool, full of glorious Michaelmas daisies, vivid purple, against boughs of copper beech.

She knew instantly whose handiwork this was. Her eyes shone.

'That must be Richard. How good of him.'

Tony looked down his long thin nose.

'He asked me if I thought you would like some flowers and as I am no good at arranging them, I said carry on, so long as he did *not* put mud on the new carpet with his filthy boots.'

Christa thought, 'I don't think I'd have minded if he had. Fixing those flowers was such a sweet thought.'

But feeling the urgent need for friendship and understanding with her husband she held out a hand to him and said:

'I am glad to be home – really I am, darling!'

'I should think it very odd if you weren't,' said Tony in a haughty voice. He took the hand that she held out, but she felt that jolt that he seemed bent on giving her whenever she made a gesture towards him. *Why* must he always spoil the moment? she wondered dismally.

She looked again at Richard's flowers.

She thanked him when they met, later on that evening. She had changed and was down before Tony. Richard was alone in the sitting-room, running his hand over the piano keys. The rest of the family had not yet put in an appearance.

'Hullo, Richard, how *nice* to hear the piano again,' said Christa moving across the floor.

He stood up. He seemed to her more deeply bronzed by the

sun than ever. He was never as well tailored as Tony, for he seemed disinterested in clothes. Every night that she could remember, Richard had changed into this old grey suit. But his shirt was very white and clean and the blue tie well chosen. He gave her a quick look.

'Welcome back,' he said.

He thought she looked extremely thin and pale and had lost her radiant good looks. But he had never been more drawn to her. It was a magnetism that shook his equilibrium.

'Thanks, Richard,' she said, 'and thanks *awfully* for those wonderful flowers. You do fix them marvellously. What a success you would have made running a shop like poor Mummy's.'

'I've always liked arranging flowers,' he said and added with a brief laugh: 'Tony calls it "pansy".'

'Which hardly suits *you*,' she smiled.

'Have a cigarette or a drink?'

'I'll wait for the others.'

'Pip brought you down, I hear?'

'Yes. And I hear that you've decided to go to Denmark or something.'

He turned from her and began to whistle in a rather nervous way.

'I've thought about it but Mama seems very much against it. There's such a lot to do at Queen's Lacey, and I suppose she's used to my taking the initiative in my particular job. She doesn't seem to like the idea of a Danish substitute.'

Christa could not control the fact that she was enormously relieved. Something made her ask:

'Why this sudden desire of yours to farm abroad? I always thought you were heart and soul here at Queen's Lacey.'

'Oh, I am really, I suppose,' he said and whistled again. But as she moved to the window and looked out, he let his gaze return to her. She had certainly lost weight. He looked thoughtfully a moment at the incredible slenderness of Christa's waist. She was wearing a fresh floral skirt with a wide white belt, and off-the-shoulder organdie blouse. The back of her neck looked to him childish and extremely pure in outline. The fair hair clustered in tendrils like a child's.

'I'm in love with her,' he thought, and it was a thought so definite and intense that it took away his colour and made him tremble. He had known it right from the very first moment that he had seen Christa on her wedding day. But it had taken a year and a half to make him admit it even to himself. It was terrible but undeniable knowledge. He was in love with a woman who was his own brother's wife.

'Oh, God!' he said, soundlessly.

'If only the weather would improve,' she was saying, 'and look how dark it's growing. We'll have to put the lights on for dinner. It really is the end of the summer.'

'Yes,' he said. And he went back to the piano stool and began to play a silly jogging tune that made her raise her brows. It got on her nerves. It wasn't at all the lilting rhythm of the music Richard generally liked to play.

'Oh, *don't*!' she said with a laugh, and leaned her arms on the piano, her long lovely eyes narrowing between their thick lashes. 'Play me the *Liebestod* from *Tristan*.'

'You found last winter pretty grim here,' he said, ignoring her request. 'Mud and rain and then snow and more mud. It's ruddy cold in the Chilterns. Why not admit it and clear out from Coleshill, *dear*?' He stressed the name sarcastically.

She stared at him, her smile fading.

'What's wrong with *you*?' she began.

'Nothing,' he interrupted rather rudely and banged down the piano lid. 'But take my advice and get Tony to make a move before autumn ends.'

She drew away from the piano.

'You mean you'd like it if Tony and I moved to a home of our own?'

'You'd like it better too, wouldn't you?'

'Naturally, but—'

'Well – you've been here at Queen's Lacey over a year. If I were you, no matter what Mama says, I'd clear out.'

Christa suddenly flushed to the roots of her hair.

'That sounds like a broad hint that you dislike me being at Queen's Lacey. It isn't flattering and it's most unlike you.'

'That's my charm,' said Richard with a loudly ugly laugh, and banged his chest with a clenched fist. 'I'm never the same – a creature of many moods . . .' he aped a silly feminine voice.

The shocked blood receded from her face. She stared at him open-mouthed. Then the drawing-room door opened and Julia Chalford, carrying her usual tapestry under her arm, came in.

Richard spoke a lot during dinner – mostly to his two brothers or his mother, on the subject of the farm. Pip announced that Susan Thornton had pneumonia and had been taken away to a nursing home in High Wycombe.

'You ought to go and see her, Rich,' said Pip. 'I bet it's a broken heart and not pneumonia.'

'Oh, for heaven's sake, don't start that tripe again!' Richard almost shouted the words, got up and walked out of the dining-room. He did not reappear for coffee nor was he seen again by the family that evening. Pip muttered:

'Can't think why he was in such a foul temper.'

Tony shrugged his shoulders. Mrs. Chalford looked up from her tapestry work to say:

'I think he's been *very* odd lately. His manners have become deplorable.'

Christa sat silent. She felt stunned. Rudeness or ill manners were things she least expected from Richard. And his sudden change of attitude towards herself was inexplicable. Something had bitten him; she knew not what, but she felt curiously thwarted. The only thing in this house that had sustained her all this long time at Queen's Lacey had been a friendship shared with Richard. Now he seemed bent on removing it (and himself) from her. She would be more than ever alone.

The evening seemed long and boring.

Christa felt utterly outside the family circle. Her thoughts turned to the mother whom she had lost. With a sharp stab of anguish she remembered that Mrs. Morley was no longer up there in that little house in London; that no matter what went wrong, Christa could never again go to the telephone and speak to her. Feeling morbid and tired, her mind leapt to the memory of the most poignant line the poet Tennyson ever wrote:

Oh death in life, the days that are no more!

Christa stood up, hands clenched, fighting the inclination to break down and cry. She kept thinking about Richard too, and what seemed to be the end of their understanding ... their friendship. It had been important to her. It was hateful to her to suppose that he did not really want her to go on living at Queen's Lacey.

Why should she be hurt? What should it matter to her whether Richard liked her or not?

Mrs. Chalford glanced up at her over her spectacles. She thought that her daughter-in-law looked tired and miserable. She said:

'Off to bed?'

'Yes, if you don't mind,' said Christa swallowing hard.

'Not at all,' said Julia politely, 'you look as though you need some sleep. Perhaps tomorrow you'd like to come in the car with me to Buckingham. There's a sale there, and I am going to see some cattle. We might stop on the way back at Padbury. I'm very fond of their bread, and we'll get a couple of loaves. They have been baking it, there, you know, for the last three hundred years.'

'Thank you,' said Christa in a strangled voice, 'I'd like to come with you.' But she almost ran out of the room, afraid of showing her tears.

She sat on the edge of her bed and took out the letter that Richard had written her and which had been so much on her mind. That beautiful, thoughtful letter.

Every line of it had expressed his deep understanding of life and of death, and his compassion for her. She could not reconcile the writer of that letter with the Richard who had snubbed her so unmercifully this evening.

She tore the letter up and flung the pieces in the wastepaper basket.

'I hate the Chalford family. I hate all of them . . .' she breathed the words to herself. And once in bed, she wept bitterly for her dead mother, for her lost illusions and the love that seemed about to be lost; for sheer loneliness. She wanted Tony to come up and hold her close, reassure her, take away the pain. But Tony became involved in a very long discussion with his mother on the cost of feeding cattle and the plans that he and Richard had made for dealing with the new herd.

When he came up to his wife, he felt remorseful about it, but it was too late. She had cried herself to sleep.

CHAPTER SIX

TIME moved on, another winter came, and towards the end of November the first heavy fall of snow spread a white carpet over South Buckinghamshire, and sparkled on the roof tops of Queen's Lacey farm.

Christa was warm enough in the wing that she shared with her husband, but meal times in the old house and the evenings too often spent in Julia's drawing-room were a misery to her. She shivered in the big cold dining-room and felt annoyed every time Julia, with a sly glance at her, invariably took off her cardigan and murmured that 'it was quite warm'.

This year, Christa had a succession of colds which lowered her vitality. She lost a bit more weight. The only room in which she felt truly welcome, and into which she would steal for comfort, was the kitchen. Mitza kept warm in there and the Austrian was shocked by the thin white face of the young Mrs. Anthony; made her drink hot chocolate with whipped cream on it and tried to induce her to eat. Her quick eye noticed that Christa had no appetite and that often her plate came in from the dining-room with half the food still on it.

There were changes at the farm. Gomme did not recover from his sciatica and became permanently incapacitated. He was pensioned off and a new man named Saunders took his place. Saunders was not a success. He got on well with Richard, but badly with Mrs. Chalford and Tony. He was a modern worker – disliked the hauteur with which he was treated by Tony and his mother.

One of the Estonian boys, Vorrow, left after Betty, his wife, had a row with Mrs. Chalford who had criticized the way she kept her cottage. Heino, the other Estonian, brought in a friend, but he was lazy; and now at table there seemed generally to be discussions about staff troubles – a general atmosphere of discontent.

As far as Christa was concerned, her own discontent went even deeper and threatened to become an incurable canker – a live thing eating away her former enjoyment of life, even her appreciation of beauty – of art.

As Christmas approached, Tony's wife faced up to the fact that she and Tony were only doing what they could to conceal the fact that their marriage had failed. Tony was less troubled by his personal life: he was for the most time engrossed in his job. Christa had to spend too much time alone and indoors. That made matters worse. She felt penned up, hemmed in by the walls of Queen's Lacey, breathing an atmosphere which became daily if not hourly less agreeable to her.

She supposed that Tony tried to maintain the old spirit of eager devotion but just could not manage it. She knew now that he was capable of passion but not love, and that even that passion was a feeble flicker, fitful and swift to die. He understood only the most blatant things. If you went to bed with a temperature you were ill. If you cried you were unhappy. If you laughed you were gay. But what went on deep down beneath the many façades that human beings can present to the world – he did not trouble about – it held no interest for him. So if Christa neither wept nor laughed much but went woodenly about this life she led at Queen's Lacey, trying always to adjust herself to circumstances, he took it for granted that she must be all right. So far as he was concerned, they 'got on', even if they were no longer passionate lovers. He hoped, of course, that she would eventually have children, but none came. His mother kept telling him that Christa *ought* to have a baby and that it would make her 'more normal'.

Julia was also having trouble with Richard. Everybody in the house thought he was odd. He seemed to have become thoroughly anti-social. Whereas in the old days he used to join in the family life and be the humorist – the boisterous, laughing one – he was now morose and moody. He appeared at meals – talked little and snapped at those who argued with him. He spent much of his spare time at the home of his friend, Jimmy Oxley, and announced that he intended to take an extra fortnight's holiday next year and go to Arosa, ski-ing with Jim, soon after the New Year.

Julia imagined that it was all because she had definitely put her foot down about his exchange with the Dane. She was growing a little tired of his peculiar attitude. He was not only out of tune with the family but his work was deteriorating. He had made several mistakes lately, and seemed not to care. He had, Mrs. Chalford said to the rest of the family, lost his former enthusiasm.

She knew in her heart that he was trying to get away from her and his home. He had always been such an excellent farmer and so hard-working and reliable she was determined not to give him his freedom.

They had a blistering row one cold afternoon in December. It was already dark when, at half past four, he came in, took off his muddied boots and walked in his socks across the hall. Mrs. Chalford waylaid him, ready with a furious accusation.

'You never told me that you forgot to put in that order for seed. Now we can't get it for another three weeks, and that's much too late for sowing. I thought it had been done a month ago – why didn't you tell me about it?'

'I thought I did,' he said. His face had thinned and he had lost a lot of his summer tan. He avoided his mother's angry gaze and began to walk up the stairs. She called him back.

'Richard – this can't go on. We'll begin to lose money if you make any more silly mistakes and I don't like not being told serious things that happen on the farm. Apart from this seed affair, I've only heard this afternoon that you've been making an allowance to Mrs. Gibble ever since she left Queen's Lacey, helping to keep those children of hers – why, may I ask?'

He glowered at her.

'You had the poor wretch turned out of her cottage. Gibble is in gaol for bigamy, and Mrs. Gibble has nothing – she needed help and we oughtn't to have turned her out.'

'My dear Richard, the court settled that case. I found Mrs. Gibble alternative accommodation and there my responsibilities ended.'

'I don't agree. I never did. Those three boys of hers were fine little chaps and they were born at Queen's Lacey. I think we owed her a bit more.'

'I scarcely think,' said his mother, 'that it behoves you to dispense charity on *my* money.'

'If you don't mind my saying so, Mother, it was on *my* money.'

Her freckled face reddened. Richard had the power of annoying her as neither of the other boys had ever done.

'I'll trouble you to remember that it is *Chalford* money.'

'Remind me, too, that it is only given me, as to Tony and Pip, in the form of a salary for services rendered, and that you could stop the cheques at any moment,' he cut in, 'and that without it I shouldn't have a penny. Yes, I quite understand.'

'Richard, I will not have you speak to me like this.'

He controlled himself with an effort.

'I'm sorry. I don't want to be unpleasant. You know perfectly well I am deeply grateful to you, Mother, for all you've ever done, but I regret ever coming back to Queen's Lacey. After doing my National Service I ought to have struck out on my own.'

She bit on her thin dry lips. She could have struck him across the face, she was so angry with him. Certainly her absolute power over this one of the three boys was diminishing – almost gone. Sheer perverseness of spirit forbade her to give in – to tell him to go.

'If this is all leading up to the fact that you want to walk out on your job here, you're wasting your time, Richard.'

'Supposing I said that I want so much to become independent that I intend to go,' he said, 'even if it means hardship.'

'I'll cut you out – I warn you – you won't get a penny from me, either now or ever, if you leave Queen's Lacey,' Julia said in a low harsh voice.

At that moment Christa came in from her own wing.

Richard threw a glance at her. He so rarely looked in her direction these days. But when he did look he was well aware of the alteration in her as well as in himself, of the listless way she went about the house; just as he knew the failure of her efforts to interest herself in the farm, or to become a companion to his mother. And above all, he knew about the failure of her marriage.

These things were clear to Richard who alone of all of them had the vision, the power to comprehend. Because of it, he walked in impenetrable darkness with Christa, yet without her, unable to reach out a hand and offer one single word of comfort.

He knew, of course, that his own surly behaviour must have offended her. But to be himself – to let her see how he felt – that must never be.

So he threw her a curt greeting.

'Evening Christa. It's been damnably cold again. I must turn on my bath. It's getting late.'

She watched him go up the stairs and heard him whistling. Her eyes were shadowed. The lids felt heavy. She was never very well these days and her last cold had left her with an irritating cough.

Mrs. Chalford kept telling her that it was because she wore such ridiculous lingerie (she had seen Mitza ironing the wisps of chiffon and lace). She had tried to nag Christa into wearing woollen undergarments, and refused absolutely to believe that the wool set up an irritation that Christa must avoid.

The two women rarely showed open hostility these days but walked warily around each other like cats. Christa felt always that Tony's mother was waiting to spring, but so apathetic had Christa become since the long dark winter set in, she had not even the heart to fight. She listened to adverse criticisms or endured the little spiteful jabs thrust at her by Julia, and remained silent. Her apathy extended, too, to her old friends – few of whom she ever saw now; although Brigadier Filing had come down on Sunday and lunched with the family. He had enjoyed Mitza's cooking and Tony's choice of wine – told

Christa she was a lucky girl to live in such a beautiful place, and had gone away again, believing the bride, whom he had given away last year, to be very happy.

Once or twice Christa drove up to London with Tony and shopped, or they went to a theatre. But she hadn't felt like making the effort lately. The drive back in the snow and the darkness did not make it worth while.

She had begun to think that she was a doomed being – one of those creatures born with a star of misfortune hanging over their heads. She could remember in her youth hearing about an unhappy friend and saying to Mummy:

'How awful to be like her. Nothing seems to go right for her. How lucky I am – I've got you and Jack. . . .'

Yes! She had had Mummy and her first love then.

She thought about Jack sometimes, in these bitter days. His death had certainly been the worst of her misfortunes. For if he had lived and she could have married him, none of this would have happened. He had understood her so well; but then he understood everybody in a way that Tony seemed incapable of doing. If dear Jack could come back now he would shake his head at her and say: *'Why ever did you do it, darling? He wasn't right for you. You weren't being very intelligent!'*

Now she knew that for herself.

Even poor old Aunt Claire was taken from her – not that she had ever seen much of the crippled aunt in Bath. But she was touched to tears when she received a lawyer's letter telling her that Lady Baintree had died and left her a legacy of £2,000. Tony had invested it for her. He prided himself upon choosing the right things on the Stock Exchange, so it brought her in a small income which might be useful one day, perhaps. It had never pleased her to feel penniless, entirely dependent on her husband.

During this last fortnight, Tony had been like a bear with a sore head because so many days' hunting had to be postponed. He looked forward to his blood-sport, she thought with sarcasm, as he never did to any form of entertainment shared with her.

Watching Richard's figure disappear upstairs, she was reminded of the fact that there had been no music in this house since October. Not once had Richard touched the piano; nor had she sung. Everything that she loved deep down within her was frozen. As frozen as the pools out there in the yard. She only wished that her heart could freeze too, and grow numb. But it didn't – it remained sensitive to hurt. She could not always get on top of the hurt. And she knew that it was not companionship from Tony that she so much missed now as some contact with Richard. *It was Richard whom she needed.* It was a staggering thought, but having once entered her mind it stayed there and would not be banished.

Christmas came. The first Christmas that Christa had spent without her mother. She missed that dear and cherished presence sorely when she woke up on the morning of 25th December.

The weather had changed. It was fine at last, though with patchy sunshine and a very cold north-east wind that tossed the leafless branches of the tall elms. The sort of wind that made Christa shrivel up. Tony said it was healthy and Mrs. Chalford seemed to thrive on it. She put on only one extra woolly under her tweed costume. She seldom wore an overcoat.

Tony had no Christmas present for her. It was her fault. He had asked her what she wanted and she had said, 'Nothing, I'd like you to choose.' But he had said he was bad at choosing presents so they had better wait until she felt like going on a shopping expedition. For the last fortnight she had been in bed with a heavy flu cold, this time with a temperature. She got up feeling less energetic than ever.

Mrs. Chalford had never been much of a present-giver. She presented each boy with a cheque; somehow Christa had grown to hate the sight of those cheques and that signature: *Julia Mary Chalford*. They seemed to her like horrid little links in the chains with which Julia bound the family to her side. Such impersonal gifts. Christa's mother used to hunt for days until she found something beautiful which she knew her daughter would like – no matter how small or inexpensive.

Mrs. Chalford was very correct in her behaviour. She presented a small cheque also to Christa. Christa thanked her and gave her mother-in-law a new bag to hold her tapestry work, for which Julia, in turn, thanked the girl. Both were excessively polite. Pip apologized because he had no presents for anybody and was forgiven by all, and delighted with the gloves lined with sheep's wool that Christa had chosen for him. For Richard, she had a fountain-pen, having heard that he had lost his favourite one. He thanked her perfunctorily, and then laid a small parcel on her plate muttering 'Merry Christmas', rushed through his eggs and bacon and departed, announcing that he would see them all in church. Christa opened her parcel, conscious of the fluttering of her pulses and the heightening of her colour. She was stupidly pleased that he had, at least, remembered her, for it seemed that as he had done this, he could not feel altogether antagonistic towards her.

She was even more pleased when she saw what he had chosen.

It was a beautifully bound edition of the life of Kathleen Ferrier whom he knew had always been one of Christa's favourite singers.

Mrs. Chalford turned a sharp eye on the book and asked what it was. Christa told her and she shrugged her shoulders. She did not even know who Kathleen Ferrier was. Neither did Tony. Christa's starved heart warmed suddenly on this bitter cold morning, for there seemed some significance in the fact that Richard had chosen this particular biography. For when Christa and Richard had talked together one summer's afternoon, it had been on the subject of the great singer who had died so tragically young. Christa could recall the whole conversation.

Richard had been in the mood to philosophize. The world had lost that glorious voice save on gramophone records, but she had left a courage and inspiration behind her which enabled her to live on, he said. For the brave there can be no permanent death. That is reserved for cowards.

Typical of Richard. It seemed to her that the gift of this book was his silent way of bidding her take courage now. He must, then, know how much she needed it.

With a full heart she looked at the brief inscription in the book.

For Christa from Richard. (And the date).

That was all. But it made her suddenly ridiculously happy.

'He must know, too, that I am rather a coward,' she thought, and took her book and walked out of the room.

Tony's voice followed her:

'If you're going out for a walk, don't be late for church, Christa.'

'I won't,' she said.

She went out, wrapped in a thick coat and with a scarf over her head. She took Richard's spaniel with her, not for the first time. She had got into the habit of exercising Tessa whenever Richard left the animal behind. Until lately she had not even known whether he realized it, but the other day he had suddenly addressed her during the evening meal:

'I saw you in the paddock with Tessa. Nice of you to give her a walk. I never take her when we're ploughing. I lost one pet that way. Never again.'

This Christmas morning, for the first time for months, she felt that she and Richard were friends again. It was extraordinary what a thrill his simple present afforded her. It made her realize how greatly her life had slowed down since her marriage to Tony; what a little it took to please her now.

Walking home past the gates of Hillside Farm she ran into Susan and her old Labrador at her heels. Susan had recovered from her pneumonia and was quite well again but she had not been seen at all at Queen's Lacey; neither had Richard paid another visit to the Thorntons. Even Pip had stopped teasing Richard about the girl as it had become such a sore subject. And there had been strong rumours in the district that Susan was having an affair with one of her father's labourers.

Tony, in great disgust, had been the first to repeat the news, which had been slyly imparted to him by his own head man. These farm people always got to know everything about each other. Tony condemned Susan as a fool, and even called her 'a little tart'. Mrs. Chalford said she would never have Susan in the house again.

'Really, these people are disgusting – just animals,' she had said, tight-lipped and with the look of nausea in her eyes which always entered them when she was forced to the subject of sex. Richard had taken this up and announced that he did not see why his mother should persist in her refusal to admit that there was an animal side to all human beings.

'Nature, my dear Mama,' he had said. 'Just plain nature.'

'Then we are taught to control our natures,' she had retorted. 'Susan had a good Christian upbringing and ought to know better.'

Christa had sat listening to this. She made no comment. She had long since learned not to air her views at Queen's Lacey. They far too seldom coincided with either her husband's or her mother-in-law's. But far too often they were in utter harmony with Richard's. But on this occasion she knew that he was inwardly suffering (unnecessarily) from a guilt complex. He could not be blamed for Susan's behaviour. But he shouldered some of it.

'I didn't want her, poor child. She wanted somebody, and this fellow came along.'

'A cowman – it's *deplorable*,' exclaimed Mrs Chalford. 'I'm very sorry for Joe Thornton and that poor old aunt. She avoided me when I met her in Beaconsfield yesterday and I'm not surprised. If it were a daughter of mine, I'd be very humiliated.'

Richard gave her a grim smile and a parting shot:

'Nevertheless, Mama, if you had a daughter and she was very plain and unattractive and you couldn't find her a husband, you wouldn't blame her for taking love where she found it. The said cowman is a tall and rather good-looking fellow. He's Austrian, as a matter of fact, and they're full of charm, you know.'

'That makes it worse. *A foreigner*.'

'Foreigners have feelings,' Richard had said with a laugh. 'Go and ask Mitza.'

He had been still laughing when he left the room.

His mother made a few acid comments both about him and the wretched Susan. Only Christa sat silent, pitying Susan from the depths of her heart.

She looked at the unhappy girl with that same pity this morning, though she concealed it under a friendly smile.

'Merry Christmas, Susan.'

'Merry Christmas – if it is. I *loathe* Christmas.'

'I used to like it,' said Christa. 'We always had a lot of fun at home, my mother and I.'

Susan, who wore corduroy slacks and a polo-necked jersey and had had her hair recently cropped as short as a boy's, looked rather like a boy today. It suited her when she didn't try to be too feminine, Christa thought. What a shame, because she seemed such a thorough woman at heart.

Now Susan's gaze turned to Richard's spaniel – painfully familiar to her.

'Tessa's looking fit. I thought in the summer she was getting fat. Perhaps it's because you're exercising her.'

'I do when Richard can't.'

Christa saw the other girl's face tauten.

'How is Richard?' The question seemed torn from her.

'Very well,' said Christa. 'I've got to get back shortly as we all go off to Amersham for the Christmas service.'

'I used to go,' said Susan. 'But I can't any more.'

'Why not—?' began Christa, then paused.

Susan burst out:

'I expect you know. I'm in disgrace. My father and aunt are going to the Christmas service but they don't want me with them. I've even resigned from the Hunt. Nobody there said anything to me, but they *look*.'

'I can't think why,' said Christa gently.

'Oh, you're human and perhaps you don't think badly about me. But you *know*, don't you?'

'I've heard stories about you, Sue, of course'

Susan tossed her head, and hit the frozen earth with a stick she was carrying.

'I'm the scarlet woman – the bad girl of the district!' she said with a bitter laugh. 'Didn't you know? I'm involved with Anton Graff, our head cowman. When Daddy found out, he gave Anton notice, but he's a wonderful worker and he got a job at Lady Corby's. So I still see him. They can't stop me, either. Are you shocked?'

'No, I'm not shocked,' said Christa. 'I only hope it's all worth while for you.'

'It isn't, really,' said Susan in a strangled voice. 'Just because he is a labourer, my father and aunt are dead against me. But I don't care. I'm not a snob. And Anton's so much in love with me. I seem to appeal to him, and I've never appealed to any man before. I've been in love – terribly in love – but it's never been returned. It was new and rather a pleasant change to be adored, so I let Anton adore me and I'm still letting him. I miss my hunting and I never see anybody now except Anton. Dad and Aunt Wyn are miserable and I'm miserable, too,' she added, and her features contracted as though she were about to cry.

Christa felt an unbearable pain for this girl – a pain which was repeated in her own heart. She put an arm around Susan, as she would about a younger sister.

'Poor Sue, I'm so sorry. How perfectly wretched for you – the whole thing.'

Susan dropped the stick and burst into tears, leaning her face against Christa's shoulder. She wept for a moment as though her sobs would choke her, then controlled herself and apologized.

'You don't need to,' said Christa. 'I understand, you know, and I only wish I could help. Perhaps you and Anton will marry, if that is what you would like.'

'Of course I needn't marry him. I can go and live with him, and I expect that is what I'll do in the end.'

'I shouldn't if I were you,' said Christa, 'unless you feel one

133

hundred per cent sure that it is going to bring you real happiness. Living with someone may sound exciting but the glamour is apt to fade when you have no rights as a wife and get looked down on as some man's mistress.'

'I didn't think the world was all that moral these days. I thought it was rather smart to be a "mistress",' said Sue with a miserable laugh.

Christa sighed.

'Don't get cynical, poor old Sue. I assure you the world still has plenty of moral people in it and I'm sure it would break your father's heart if you left home to go and live in sin with Anton.'

Then Susan burst out:

'The dreadful part is that I still adore Richard.'

Christa turned away. The pain in her heart was increasing.

'Richard!' she repeated the name in a blurred kind of voice. 'Oh, of course . . . it's Richard you love.'

'Everybody knows,' said Sue bitterly.

Christa thought: 'I love him, too, but nobody knows. *Nobody*.'

'Do you think I'm awful?' Sue asked, and her reddened eyes looked at the other girl mournfully. Still, she was envying Tony's wife her beauty and her poise, even though she noticed that Christa looked thin and ill.

'Of course not,' said Christa in her gentle voice. 'Why should I? It's just bad luck that he doesn't love you.'

'Life seems to enjoy making the wrong people love each other. If you hadn't been Richard's sister-in-law he'd have been in love with you. In fact, I think that's the trouble – he *is*!' burst out Sue, the muscles of her cheeks working as she tried not to cry again.

An icy gust of wind caught Christa. She stood rigidly there on the frozen earth, her eyes staring at the stark trees and the hoar-rimmed bushes. The bleak landscape on this Christmas morning could not have been more empty and desolate than her heart, but those tactless words uttered in childish jealousy by Susan thrust a knife into that tender heart. At once, therefore, it was filled with all the agony and shame and despair of the uttered truth. This then must be why Richard avoided her and hurt her by his outward indifference. He loved her. *They loved each other*. Unlawfully and most unhappily, they loved, and it had taken Susan to say it aloud. The unthinkable, the forbidden thing. And as it broke through the crust of despair that surrounded Christa it was too much for her to bear. The blood tore to her cheeks. Her eyes grew large and stricken. She leaned down, put a hand on Tessa's collar, and said in a smothered voice:

'How dare you say that! You have no right, It's a monstrous suggestion. I don't want to speak to you any more.'

Susan began:

'I'm sorry, Christa, I did not mean to upset you. But it is true—'

'You had no right to say it and no possible cause—' interrupted Christa and turning walked away – the spaniel bounding ahead of her, barking joyfully.

She left the lone figure of Susan and her old tired Labrador behind her. She shut her ears to Susan's voice calling out, beseeching her to come back. She quickened her footsteps. She wanted to get away and never see Sue Thornton again. There are some things that should never be said – never – she thought, and what Susan had just blurted out is one of them.

But as Christa walked back to Queen's Lacey and up the elm drive she was mocked by her own inner consciousness. It whispered, *You know it's true. You know. It explains everything. ... Your own feelings ... Richard's behaviour ... everything.*

She met her husband in the hall. She ignored him as had become a habit with her now, kicked off her boots and walked across the polished floor on her stockinged feet. Pip had also just come in. Mrs. Chalford was coming down the staircase, wearing her dark blue coat and skirt and the old sable tie. She was drawing on her gloves and had a prayer book under her arm.

'Ah!' she said as she saw Christa. 'I thought you were going to be late.'

'Hurry up, Chris,' said Tony.

Then Christa lifted up a face so white, so taut, that even Tony who rarely noticed when things were wrong, stared at her and said:

'*You* look as though you've been nipped by the cold.'

'I'm not coming to church,' said Christa.

'My *dear* – Christmas morning—' began Mrs. Chalford flicking her sandy lashes.

'You must come,' put in Tony fretfully.

'I don't feel well enough,' she said. 'I'm ill.'

135

'What's wrong?' he asked walking up to her, but she shrank away and hurried through to her own wing without looking at her mother-in-law. She spoke as she went.

'I'm sorry. I apologize, but I can't go to church. You must all go without me.'

Pip, who was reluctantly removing his pipe from his mouth and putting it in his pocket, ran a finger through his curly hair and muttered:

'Poor girl's come over queer.'

'I say – I must go and see–' began Tony.

Mrs. Chalford clicked her teeth and broke in:

'No, I'll go, Tony, take my prayer book.'

He took it doubtfully, but his mother's attitude brooked no argument. Mrs. Chalford walked through the passage into the wing and found Christa in the drawing-room. She had switched on an electric fire and was crouching down in front of it, her hands spread to the warmth. She was shivering, and she looked small and shrivelled. She seemed to shrink still more as she saw her mother-in-law advancing towards her.

'What is it, Christa?' asked Julia. 'Do you feel faint or something? Shall I fetch brandy?'

'No. I don't want anything. I shall go up and lie down in a moment.'

'But you seemed perfectly well when you went out for your walk.'

Christa stared at the older woman. There was no real kindness or sympathy on that hard angular face. Help she might offer but only because she thought it to be her duty. She hates me, Christa thought, and she would hate me still more if she knew what Susan had just said, and how I feel about it. Oh, *I wish I were dead*!

'What *is* it?' Mrs. Chalford demanded impatiently, somewhat annoyed by Christa's silence.

Then Christa said in a small bleak voice:

'Please go to church and leave me alone. I shall be quite all right.'

'Oh, well,' said Mrs. Chalford and shrugged her shoulders. 'It's very strange, and people will talk if you don't come with us on *Christmas* morning!'

Christa clenched her hands. If only they would let her alone. If only Tony's mother wouldn't nag, nag, *nag*. Never more had she wanted to be alone. She was in a state of shock. She didn't want to talk to any of the Chalford family, even to *him*. Rich-

136

ard. Least of all Richard. *Most of all*. Oh, *Richard, Richard, Richard*!

At last Mrs. Chalford, getting no further, departed. She objected to any form of defeat especially from this daughter-in-law of hers for whom she had neither affection nor understanding. In a bad mood she rejoined her sons. Richard was there now. The car was ready at the door to take them to Amersham.

'Christa is going to lie down. I think she must just have felt faint,' announced Mrs. Chalford.

Richard, smarming back his unruly hair, cast a lightning glance at his mother.

'Is Christa ill?'

'It doesn't seem to be very much, but she won't come to church,' said his mother in an aggrieved voice.

Richard made no comment. In the car going to Amersham, he stared out at the ploughed fields, at the fruits of his labours, at the sudden beauty of the snow when the fleeting sunlight caught it and turned the grey bleakness into diamond-like brilliance.

In his coat pocket he could feel the slim fountain-pen that Christa had given him for a Christmas present. He remembered, too, the warmth, the rather shy gratitude that lit up that small pale face when he handed her the Ferrier biography. That moment shared with her had been brief, yet enough to make him deeply aware that he had ignored her and hurt her for far too long. For he was of some account with her – that swift, glad, even tender glance had expressed such pathetic pleasure. It had been unmistakable.

He listened to his mother and his brothers discussing Christa's health and her long-continued cough. He did not join in.

The Christmas mid-day meal, as far as he was concerned, was a farce. It was even more painful to Christa. Mrs. Chalford put on a coy show of being merry and exhibiting 'good will'. Mitza had cooked a splendid turkey and her plum pudding was a work of art. Tony and Pip ate hungrily; Richard more slowly, trying not to look at Christa whom he knew instinctively swallowed her own meal without appetite. Mrs. Chalford kept saying to her:

'You ought to eat more – now pass her the potatoes, Pip . . . I do dislike this pecking at good food. Come along now, Christa – another slice of this delicious pudding and see if you can't be the one to get a sixpence.'

Christa set her teeth.

'Where's your cap, my dear? Come on, we're not going to let you off, are we, boys?'

Christa sat rigid while Pip, who was beside her, put an emerald green tissue-paper cap with a silver star on her head – scarcely with adept fingers. He shoved it clumsily down on her forehead disarranging her hair. She smiled bleakly and pulled a cracker with Tony. She got the biggest half and was asked to read the motto aloud.

She began – it was some childish doggerel – then started to cough. Mrs. Chalford interrupted:

'I don't believe you are taking that syrup I gave you, Christa.'

She got no further. Christa snatched the cap from her head. By nature, the most sweet-tempered of mortals, she was conscious suddenly that every nerve in her body was being hammered by this woman – hammered until she could not stand the pain of it. She got up and said:

'I'm sorry, I don't feel awfully well, please excuse me.'

'I say, what's wrong?' asked Pip with genuine concern.

'Shall I come with you, darling?' put in Tony, half rising.

Mrs. Chalford removed her own cap and patted her lips with her table napkin.

'I don't see there is any need to break up the party. It's only her cough. Christa makes such a fuss.'

Richard had sat absolutely silent throughout this part of the meal. But he had seen Christa's face just before she removed her paper crown – the trembling of her fingers, the sick despair in her eyes. He, alone, knew the reason for that despair. His mother was a detestable bully. He stood up:

'I think the party's over, anyhow, I'm going off,' he said.

Mrs. Chalford sniffed.

'I have not finished my crystallized fruits.'

'I'll have one with you, Mum,' said Pip, endeavouring as usual to be amiable. Tony took a cigar from the box that had been one of his mother's presents.

'I'll get the port,' he said.

He would not have considered it a good Christmas dinner if they had not finished up with port and nuts. He was not much troubled about Christa. She never seemed to feel very fit these days.

Richard walked into the hall. He had meant to have one of Tony's cigars but no longer wanted it. The whole *nuance* of the

Christmas dinner had upset him. It had been on his mind to go straight out on the farm, but he paused and glanced towards the wing in which he presumed Christa had retired. He was seized suddenly with an overwhelming desire. He must go to her. He must try and comfort her.

He walked to her private drawing-room which he rarely visited these days. He knocked on the door. As nobody answered he looked in. Then he saw Christa lying on the sofa with her face buried in the cushions. She was crying. Tearing sobs that shocked him, and made his own senses acutely aware that her deep hurt, her hopelessness were also his. He shut the door behind him. Walked quickly to the sofa, knelt down and put an arm around her.

'Christa, don't, *don't* cry like that. Christa – my poor sweet, *don't*.'

She turned to him. Her face was hot, contorted and streaming with tears. It was inevitable that he should take the slim shaking body into his arms and cover that poor disfigured face with kisses. Between the kisses he kept saying:

'Oh, *God*!'

She stopped crying and held her breath. Her hands clung to him with a convulsive strength. Her whole body surrendered to his embrace. When at last his lips found her mouth and they kissed with desperate passion, she shut her eyes fast whilst she held him fiercely against her. Repressions and inhibitions were gone, defences down. He knew that she loved him as much as he loved her. But neither of them dared to say it. Richard was conscious only that she was his brother's wife and that this thing could never be. He did not mind for himself so much. He had his own inner loyalties. But he must protect her. At any moment one of his family might walk in and discover them.

Just for one more moment, he allowed himself the bitter sweet luxury of holding and kissing her – not as a brother now but as a lover. Then he released her. He was more shaken than he had believed possible.

She sat up, running her fingers through his dishevelled hair, but not looking at him.

'Richard, you must go away, you *must*!'

'I will, as soon as I can,' he said tensely.

Silence. Then she looked up. Her eyes were tortured.

'Don't let's discuss it. *Don't*. We just both *know*.'

'Yes,' he said, clenching his hands.

'But I want you to know something else,' she added. 'What

139

you – what we – have just done, has helped me in a queer sort of way. Whatever I'm not allowed to do, nobody can control my *thoughts*. I shall remember this Christmas – I shall remember this moment all my life.'

'So shall I, darling,' he said.

But he could no longer trust himself to stay with her. Turning blindly, he walked out of the room.

PART THREE

CHAPTER ONE

ABOUT a year later, Christa returned from a day's shopping in London to find everybody out except Mitza who was preparing the evening meal.

Once more Christmas was here. It was Christmas Eve. Christa had not meant to go up to Town today but Tony had particularly wanted her to do so. He had to meet two friends who were just passing through Town on the way back from Hong Kong, and they had expressed the wish to make Christa's acquaintance.

Christa had one of her usual coughs which seemed to develop every winter now. She had not put on weight and she was nearly always tired. The doctor called it anaemia and was giving her vitamin injections. Nobody except Mitza worried about her. But Christa knew well her general condition was not merely physical. The cough was incidental. It was a mental state. She was just utterly miserable.

As Christa took off her gloves and glanced at the letters on the hall table, her heart constricted. She saw a thin envelope with a Danish stamp on it. The letter was addressed to Tony.

She walked into her sitting-room and switched on the lights and shivered a little. The central heating seemed to be low. It was a very cold night and they had had to drive slowly because of fog. Tony had brought her home but gone straight out again to see his head-cowman and a veterinary surgeon. One of his most valuable milking cows had been taken critically ill.

Christa lit a cigarette and sat a moment in front of the fire, spreading her hands to the blaze. She was haunted by the thought of that Danish stamp. Inevitably her gaze travelled to the sofa. Somehow the sight of those particular yellow cushions always fascinated her. Always revived for her the heart-shaking memory of that afternoon – it would be a year ago the day after tomorrow – when she had pressed her face against those cushions and wept so bitterly. And how Richard had come silently in and knelt there beside her, how his long wild kisses

141

had burned away all remembrance of any other kiss she had ever received.

It had taken her a long time to recover from the emotional shock of that brief passionate interlude. But in time she had grown composed. And it seemed that much had happened rapidly in consequence. That very next day Richard announced his intention of going to Denmark, and packed up. She hardly saw him before he left. Everything seemed to happen so swiftly and although the thought of his departure had agonized her, she understood why he was doing it, and was thankful. That reason was a secret locked in her heart and Richard's.

But he left Queen's Lacey. He left ten days after that moment of revelation with his sister-in-law. The rest of the family bade him a cold good-bye. Christa had to keep up appearances and say good-bye with the rest of them. She even lifted her face to be kissed. He barely touched that cold pale cheek but his eyes looked with sad poignancy down into hers, and for a single second he whispered his own private farewell to her:

'God bless you, my darling.'

After that she continued to live at Queen's Lacey and do her duty by husband and mother-in-law in an entirely automatic fashion. It seemed as though the scene with Richard had let loose the flood gates of passion; then they had frozen up again.

For months she walked, talked and behaved as though she had no feelings about anything in particular. Nothing moved her – even Mrs. Chalford's bullying. As for her relationship with Tony, it had developed into such an unemotional one that it made little impression on her. As she told herself drearily, passionate love was a thing that belonged to her and to Richard; forbidden and impossible though it might be. But for Tony her feelings were passionless. And he had long since ceased to be her lover, or even to pretend to be one. On one or two occasions he had grudgingly admitted his failure in this capacity and muttered: 'I must do something about it.'

Only then, Christa felt a return to any kind of normal emotion – to anger and even disgust.

'As far as I'm concerned you needn't bother to do anything about it,' she said. 'We can live together as brother and sister for the rest of our lives. It won't worry me, my dear. You get on with your farm business, and I'll hang around.'

'You really are peculiar,' he had said, shrugging his shoulders.

But that had been the end of any attempt on either side to revive the old attachment.

For Christa the only pleasure now to be extracted from Queen's Lacey lay in the job of looking after Richard's spaniel. Tessa pined for her master at first, then turned for consolation to Christa and after that followed her adoringly, and slept in her room – much to Tony's disgust.

Throughout all the long months – spring, summer, and autumn – Christa had to feed her soul's deep hunger only on the barest news of Richard. He wrote to his mother and brother about his life over there in Denmark. He seemed to be well and to be enjoying his job on the farm. Once Tony tossed one of the letters across to Christa and said: 'There's a message for you.'

When Christa read the letter from Richard, she felt as though the old wound opened up and that she suffered as she had done on the day of his departure. She read the paragraph that concerned her.

I was glad to hear from young Pip the other day that Christa seems better. Give her my love.

Coolly she handed the letter back to Tony and went up to her rooms. Then it was to put her face in her hands and give a gasping sigh.

'Oh, Richard, *Richard*! . . .'

Now, she spent an hour looking at the presents she had bought for relatives and friends. They were going to have their big party tomorrow evening instead of the usual one on Boxing Day. It should be quite a gay affair – many had accepted – and Tony had bought Christa an expensive new dress.

But Richard wouldn't be here. And she had no little parcel for Richard this year. No communication with or from him. The one thing that worried her most was the knowledge that he could not stay away for ever. He was bound to return. And she *must* prevail upon Tony to leave Queen's Lacey before Richard actually got back. Whenever she opened the subject, Tony wriggled out of it, but she was going to force his hand soon. She was going to issue the ultimatum that if he didn't give her a home of her own *she'd leave him.*

Later that evening when she and Tony and Pip were all sitting in the drawing-room in the big house drinking sherry, something happened to put an end to all the plans for Christmas Day and some days afterwards. Mitza rushed into the room, flushed and perturbed, to tell them all that she had just found Mrs. Chalford laying in a dead faint in the corridor outside her bathroom.

Christa was summoned. The men of the house gathered round perturbed and helpless. Such a thing had never been known in their lifetime. Christa did what she could, but her mother-in-law's faint was prolonged. The hastily-sent-for doctor, after examination, announced to the family that Mrs. Chalford's poor health was a little alarming although not critical. She had not had a doctor in the house since Pip was born – so her condition was unsuspected. But she had high blood pressure and what actually had happened was in the nature of a stroke. It certainly meant that she must take care of herself in future – follow a diet and be kept as far as possible from worry or excitement.

The two brothers, and Tony's wife, discussed the situation and decided that the first thing to do was to cancel the invitations to the party. Christa volunteered to do this and spent an hour on the telephone. The word 'stroke' was not to be mentioned. They did not want to frighten Mrs. Chalford. Dr. Angus said that there was every chance that she would make a complete recovery if she took care.

'We must just all pull together and do everything we can to ensure that she keeps well and happy,' said Tony in his pompous way.

'Okay,' said Pip, and puffed at his pipe with a gloomy air. He had rather looked forward to the party as an innovation in the routine of the farm. The gravity of human diseases made small impression on him. Tony, however, enjoyed, as usual, taking command in a 'situation'.

'Of course,' he said, 'I shall wire to Richard. He must come back at once.'

Christa's head shot up. She went crimson, then white.

Then she ventured to say:

'Do you think that's necessary?'

'Of course,' said Tony with an indignant look at her. 'Mother never wanted him to go away and leave the farm. It's his duty now to come back.'

Christa said no more. She had detected a look of secret triumph in her husband's eyes. How she despised him! He was not sending for Richard out of duty to his mother alone. It was a fine opportunity to force Richard home.

Pip, innocent as usual of what was going on around his

young head, exclaimed: 'I say, it will be jolly nice to see Rich again.'

When Christa went to bed that night it was with a prescience of danger. A danger she did not know how to avert. Quite clearly she could not walk out of Queen's Lacey and leave Tony at this precise moment. She was cornered. Her mother-in-law's illness made it essential for her to stay here.

Earlier Christa had spent a far from happy half-hour with Julia. She had tried to be kind and helpful but the woman, recovered from her faint, had snapped at the girl and rejected all help.

'Absolute rubbish, this business of blood pressure,' she had said. 'I can't think what made me faint. Dr. Angus is an old fool. I shall be up and about very quickly. For heaven's sake don't fuss over me, Christa. I think it's absurd postponing our party, but Tony insists. I know the dear boy's very anxious about me,' she added with a smug expression which killed all Christa's sympathy.

How awful it was, she thought, that a human being could so aggravate and upset you that everything they did began to be a cause for irritation. She could only presume that she had the same effect on Tony's mother.

Next morning the wire was sent to Denmark. That same afternoon Richard telephoned, full of a natural concern for his mother. Christa did not know what was said between the brothers but Tony told her later on with smug satisfaction that Richard was coming home immediately.

'He'll probably get a plane tomorrow morning,' he said.

Christa, who was in bed, turned her face away from Tony. Her heart was playing tricks. She had spent most of this Christmas Day doing things for Julia, conscious of a deadly tiredness mingled with constant concern for the future. She was no longer the lifeless girl who had moved around this house for over a year. She was very much the old flesh and blood Christa emotionally alive and acutely conscious of her heart's need.

It was unfortunate for Christa that on this one night Tony chose to be more amorous than usual. He sat on the edge of her bed, took her hand and played with it.

'It's been a rotten Christmas so far,' he said lugubriously. 'I'm glad you didn't decorate the table. Awful to think of poor old mother lying ill like that, not able to participate with us.'

'Cheer up – the doctor keeps telling us she'll be all right,' said Christa.

145

He bent, and suddenly to her surprise and dismay, kissed her more passionately than he had done for a year.

'Darling,' he began, 'you're looking very seductive. Is that a new nightie?'

She drew in her mouth. Her whole body – like her mind – resented him. The knowledge that Richard was coming back was, she told herself, the reason and it would destroy her. She mustn't allow it to. With a certain amount of feminine guile, she decided to use this opportunity to persuade Tony to take her away. She *must* get away. It wouldn't be *decent* for her to go on living under the same roof as Richard.

'Tony darling,' she began in a quick feverish voice, 'I want to ask you a great, great favour.'

He gave her a rather patronizing smile.

'Yes, of course.'

'Let's start the New Year by having our own home. No, don't look like that. Please, *please*, Tony, let's leave Queen's Lacey and live on our own.'

He looked shocked, then annoyed.

'Surely you're not going to start all that again. You know how I feel about it.'

She persisted.

'And you know how I feel. You've broken all your promises about us having our own home. I've been at Queen's Lacey for nearly three years now. It's most unfair to me.'

And she thought: 'And it's unfair to you, too, but you don't know it, and I can't tell you.'

The old argument continued. All amorous thoughts faded from Tony. He flatly refused to discuss the subject further. He rose and left her bedroom, bidding her a huffy good night, and slept in his dressing-room that night.

In despair, Christa switched off her light and pressed her burning cheek against the cool linen pillow.

It was not until the next morning that Tony seemed to notice that Christa looked exceedingly unwell. He spoke quite kindly to her as they walked downstairs to breakfast.

'I've got to be out on the farm with Pip most of today so I hope you feel all right. I'd like you to sit with Mother a bit.'

'What about – Richard?'

'Oh, he'll have to find his own way home. He said he didn't know what plane he'd get or when he'd fetch up here. He'll hire a taxi from the station.'

She felt a secret, wicked longing to say:

'*I'll go and meet him. No matter how long I have to wait at the airport, I'll wait.*'

Instead she turned her head and tried to speak to her husband lightly.

'I'll do what I can about Mother,' she said.

'Do cheer up,' he said, frowning.

'You know exactly what is on my mind,' was her cold reply.

'This rubbish about moving?'

'Yes,' she said. 'I want to get away from everybody and everything. I have a right to my own life.'

'I told you last night poor Mother needs me now more than ever.'

Christa felt coldly angry.

'And supposing *I* need you? I'm not asking you to leave Queen's Lacey this morning or tomorrow. I don't mind waiting a few weeks till Mother is better – so long as I know I've got my own home to look forward to in the near future. I'm asking you to let me start house-hunting *now*.'

Tony looked at her with the utmost disfavour.

He was not a man to examine cause or effect or probe deeply into human emotions. But he did know that he had made a mistake in marrying Christa. He knew it now when it was too late. She was *not* his type. His mother had said so and warned him at the time, but he had not listened. Of course he had hoped to be able to mould Christa into something more palatable both to the family and life at Queen's Lacey. He had thought of her as a sweet pliable creature. He had often been unpleasantly surprised by her spirit, her independence, the strength of character which he had come up against in his wife. He did not like doing so but he must now admit that his love for Christa had been entirely physical.

And for Tony, who was not of a particularly ardent disposition, the passionate side of marriage had been reduced to a minimum. Women were impossible – or Christa was – *far* too demanding. He had been a fool to let his infatuation run away with his good sense. He should have chosen a more practical, less ardent wife.

He put a careless arm around Christa's shoulders again.

'Don't let's quarrel. You know I'm very fond of you and I think it's sweet of you to want to be more alone with me. I dare say Pip gets on your nerves a bit. But you must admit that poor Mother's done everything to make us feel welcome here and given us a hell of a lot. It really isn't convenient for us to move just now. Dr. Angus says Mother really must have a bit more of the responsibility taken off her shoulders. Now be a good girl and try to settle down. Anyhow, let's discuss this house-hunting again at a more propitious time.'

Christa's eyes froze; her thin young body stiffened in the curve of that condescending arm. Tony dropped a light kiss on her hair and moved towards the dining-room.

She turned and walked slowly up to her room again.

CHAPTER TWO

CHRISTA went about her business that day in a kind of daze. Against all her efforts to keep control over herself, her emotional heart played truant. Every time she heard car wheels on the drive or the front door open or close she felt her pulses leap. She rushed to a window to see if Richard had come back; then was ashamed.

'I must keep my head,' she kept telling herself. 'I must try to be just like I'd be if it were only Pip coming back from abroad.'

All day Christa wrestled with herself. When it began to snow again she was half glad because it might mean that the plane might be delayed and she might not have to face Richard to-night. Yet when suddenly there was a rift in the ragged clouds and the sun shone in a pale but hopeful fashion, her blood sang because he might come after all.

As though to make amends for her guilty joy she tried to be especially nice to Mrs. Chalford who put her back up as soon as Christa entered the bedroom. She complained about everything that Christa did. When Christa observed that Mrs. Chalford must be thrilled at the idea of seeing her second son after his long absence, Julia's lips smiled sourly.

'H'm! If Richard is only bothering to come home just because he thinks I'm about to give up the ghost, he'd better stay away. I'm not dying yet. He left my house in a most untoward fashion, and poor darling Tony has had a terrible year. Richard got out of it all.'

'I don't in the least suppose he meant to,' said Christa in a feeble attempt to defend him.'

'Oh, well,' said Julia, 'I'm feeling better so, really, his coming is a waste of time unless he means to stay. That, of course, would be a different story. I'd feel more cheerful about it.'

Christa had tea with her. Afterwards it grew dark. Mrs. Chalford seemed tired and glad to be left alone to doze. So, at last, Christa was able to get away.

She always felt worn out physically and mentally after a few hours in her mother-in-law's presence. She went downstairs chafing one cold hand against the other, intending to light the drawing-room fire. Tony and Pip should be in very soon.

When she heard the car wheels, she did not look up from the fire to which she had just put a match. She had had so many scares and disappointments today, she had decided not to let her anguished longing to see Richard again become an obsession. It was only when she actually heard a familiar voice in the hall that she leapt on to her feet, feeling the colour drain from her face. *Richard had come* ... He was saying 'hullo' to Mitza. Then the drawing-room door opened. He walked in.

She trembled as she saw him move quickly towards her. He was unchanged, except perhaps a little thinner in the face. He wore old tweeds that she remembered. His roughened hair was powdered with snow. He stared at her, then broke the pregnant silence.

'Hullo – how are you, my dear?'

All her body felt taut. Her nerves were screaming with the effort not to pitch herself into his arms – not to hold him to her and say:

'Oh, my darling, *my darling*, take me away from here, out of this house quickly. I think I shall die if you don't.'

She said nothing of the kind. He had given her the lead; just as she had guessed he would, with strong masculine control. She did not even put out a hand but answered him quietly, conventionally.

'Very well, thanks. And you, Richard?'

'Fine thanks. How's poor Mother?'

'Amazingly well, considering, but of course one never knows. She'll have to be very careful.'

'My plane was delayed,' he said, 'but finally we got above the snowstorm. We didn't land at London Airport. We were diverted to Bournemouth. That's why I'm so late.'

Silence again.

No one was to guess from the man's calm exterior that equal fires of longing impelled him towards her.

149

'I have come for good. I've done my year over there, and they don't really want me any more. One of the boys has just left University and will take my place. Tony said on the phone that I must stay home because of Mama. I don't know, of course, what *you* think about it.'

She gave a laugh which had a touch of wildness in it.

'Oh, I agree. Anyhow your mother will insist on it, but I'm going to insist on having my own home, too, so I shan't be here very much longer.'

He flushed and stared at her. He found her thin and haggard and thought she looked a ghost of the Christa he used to know. But he could see that the year's separation had made no difference to her feelings for him. He saw it in her large, intense eyes. But the renunciation he personally had made a year ago still held good. He had no intention of slipping again – no matter how perilously her beauty and the tragedy of her unhappy marriage urged him to try and comfort her again. She was his sister-in-law. He was going to remember it, *this time*.

Fortunately for both of them, Tony now came boisterously into the room and saved an awkward and painful moment.

She did not see Richard alone again that day. At dinner they barely exchanged glances. After dinner, he went upstairs to sit with his mother. Tony informed Christa later that the two were reconciled. For Christa, after the anticipation, the awful excitement of Richard's return – the whole evening was a fearful anti-climax.

She slept badly, trying not to listen to Tony enumerating the jobs he was going to give Richard on the farm tomorrow. They had had trouble with the animals – especially the fowls. He needed Richard's specialized knowledge and things would be better now that Mother was happy about Richard again. She, Tony said, seemed in good form tonight, vowing that she would be up in a day or two.

Christa awoke that next morning with a feeling of desolation.

Nothing to look forward to, nothing but the impossible task of trying to make Tony take her away from Queen's Lacey. If he wouldn't – if he persisted in remaining here – then *she* would go, and it would be the end of everything.

Somehow, despite a blinding headache, Christa managed to appear at the breakfast-table. Her eyes immediately went to Richard. He might never have been away. It seemed so normal to find him sitting in his usual chair and Tessa with him in her customary position, with her head on his knees, waiting for titbits. Christa tried to make a light-hearted remark.

'Old Tess is thrilled you're back, Richard. She never had very long walks with me, I'm afraid. She's put on weight.'

He gave her the merest smile and then rose, wiping his lips on his napkin.

'I think Tess looks in pretty good trim. I'm most grateful to you for looking after her for me, Christa.'

She lowered her gaze.

'He almost hates me,' she said to herself, and felt her whole body and mind grow rigid with a kind of numbing pain.

'Hurry up, Pip,' Richard said, turning to his younger brother who was just beginning a dish of eggs and bacon. 'We've both got to give Heino a hand with that "damn bull".'

'May I ask,' said Christa in an ironic voice, 'what is the matter with the damn bull?' and she sat down at her place at the breakfast-table and had a twisted smile only from Mitza who was carrying in fresh coffee for her and beaming at her with her little love-starved eyes. Richard said:

'A prize bull that we paid a fortune for; he's tried to run amok in his stall and gashed himself very badly.'

'I'm sorry,' said Christa. Then some perverse devilish desire to make her presence felt, called Richard back as he reached the door. 'Any jobs for me this morning – everybody seems to think I'm not pulling my weight on the farm.'

Richard met her full gaze now. The expression in them gave him a shock. There was a smouldering fire deep down inside her waiting to leap into flame, and he knew it. He knew, also the hunger and madness that lay in his own heart.

He flushed scarlet, turned and walked out of the dining-room banging the door behind him.

Tony clicked his tongue against his teeth as he looked up from his paper.

'Damned inconsiderate of Richard. I'm sure Mother will have heard.'

Christa clenched her hands, feeling the points of her nails dig inter her flesh. Then she walked up to her mother-in-law's bedroom.

Julia Chalford was dozing when Christa entered her room. The girl noticed at once that the older woman's breakfast-tray had been left practically untouched. She was not so well this morning. Christa also noticed that there was a new subtle change in her; the merest twist to one side of her mouth and there was a change also in the long freckled face. She had aged these last two days. Immediately all that was tender-hearted and kindly in Christa asserted itself. She advanced to the bedside, sat down and took one of Julia's hands.

'Can I do anything for you, Mother?' she asked.

At once the hand was snatched away. The invalid's eyes opened. They were not changed. They were as hard and bitter as ever and the voice was strong enough as it said:

'Good morning, Christa. Yes, there is something I want you to do.'

'Anything, of course,' said Christa. The snatching away of that hand was merely the accustomed withdrawal of Julia Chalford into herself, her refusal to accept any contact either physical or mental, with her eldest son's wife.

Julia had sent for Christa to ask her to take over the running of the house for a few more days. She admitted to not feeling so fit this morning. But after a few days' rest she would be up and about again, she said. Neither Dr. Angus nor any of them were going to keep *her* chained to her bed.

Mrs. Chalford reached out for a sheet of paper that lay on the bed-table. She had obviously been making a list. She was extremely methodical; so studiously correct that sometimes Christa wondered if she was human – if she ever made a mistake – or forgot anything. The window was wide open top and bottom, yet Mrs. Chalford wore the thinnest of bed-jackets. Everything was very neat in here. The old mahogany furniture was highly polished. The odour in here was of polish rather than any feminine perfume.

On the mantelpiece stood a triple-framed photograph of the three boys.

All three had been taken in their University days.

They looked touchingly young, thought Christa, who had never been in this room long enough to make a close survey.

Richard with head flung back and that bright questioning look in his eyes which showed that even as a youth he had had an inquiring mind. Tony, woodenly handsome. Pip much the same as he was today.

Once again Christa turned her gaze to the woman in the bed, stared at that angular and unfriendly face and the faded red of that hair and wondered how it could be possible that any living creature could change so with the passing of the years. Yet this same woman, as Christa knew from photographs, had been a handsome girl. She must have lain in her husband's embrace and conceived these three sons and so brought them into the world. It was astonishing. She must have hated the whole affair, reflected the girl. Christa put the shopping list in her pocket. As she got up, Mrs. Chalford cast a glance at her and said:

'I shouldn't go to Amersham in those slacks if I were you. I know it is done today, but I do so dislike Tony's wife going in for such a sloppy fashion.'

Christa's heart started to beat quickly with resentment. Then her sense of humour asserted itself and she started to laugh.

'I'll go and change,' she said, 'and I'll do my best to run the house as you would like it run.'

'Thank you,' said Mrs. Chalford politely.

CHAPTER THREE

JULIA recovered.

She recovered almost completely, although the doctor warned the family that there was a possibility that she might have a second stroke unless she exerted care. So she reluctantly accepted a diet and rested more and was now not so often to be seen striding across the fields, or as some of the labourers put it, 'Poking her nose into things.'

Richard was established back in his old job on the farm. Tony took over complete control of the business side. There now commenced a new period of misery for Christa. Richard seemed to have changed completely towards her. She knew that she should be glad that he had changed – that he avoided her. He was doing the right thing. Perhaps he had, indeed, regretted the weakness that had led him to soften towards her a year ago. Perhaps the memory of the way in which she had responded to his love-making had eventually disgusted him. At any rate he seemed to want none of her now. She was alone, marooned in a sea of bitter, floundering emotions.

She tried hard to re-orientate her feelings. She endeavoured to pretend that Richard was not here. She avoided being alone with him. At meal-times, she included him in the conversation only when it was general. She hoped that she played her part well and he would imagine that she was as disinterested in him as he seemed to be towards her. She hoped, too, that he would believe that she had forgotten what had taken place between them.

Tony went his usual egotistical way. As far as he was concerned, Christa seemed better. He was relieved, too, because she seemed less 'difficult'. She did not even quarrel with his mother any more. That pleased him more than anything. But she spoilt it by her persistent appeals to him to let her look for a house of their own.

'Really, Christa, you're as stubborn as hell,' he flung at her one day early in March after she had made one of these continued assaults upon his patience. 'I should have thought it was clear to you now that *I* don't want to move.'

'Very well, Tony, then I warn you – if you *don't* give me a home of my own, I shall leave you.'

He stared at her. For a moment she had got him worried. Then his immense conceit and self-confidence returned. He burst out laughing.

'Don't be dramatic, my dear,' he said, and walked out of the room.

She stood trembling a little. Now through the window she saw Richard's figure, a woollen scarf round his neck and wearing his gum boots, coming in to lunch. The faithful Tessa followed at heel. Christa felt an agony of longing towards Richard that was so acute it seemed to take the breath out of her body.

'All right,' she said aloud, '*all right*. Then I will go. I'll leave Queen's Lacey myself. *I swear I will.*'

But she made no move – it was as though all free-will had left her and she was kept at Queen's Lacey by a mysterious, relentless force outside herself.

Then, three weeks later, just before Easter, she went down with her worst attack of flu. It left her coughing so incessantly that it disturbed even Tony who was a sound sleeper. So he moved into the dressing-room.

Mitza was filled with anxiety for her *liebchen*.

'Herr Chalford should his vife on holiday take!' she kept muttering whenever she saw Christa's white little face, and the dull look in the golden eyes which used to be so brilliant.

Mrs. Chalford, herself none too well, but refusing to admit it, grudgingly voiced the same opinion. But she never suggested that Tony, himself, should take Christa away. He was far too busy at this time of year, and Pip was taking three weeks' holiday this Easter, going on the Continent with a Cambridge friend. Tony must be here. Julia could of course see that Christa was in poor health and obviously depressed, but felt no particular sympathy. She thought Christa weak and was secretly contemptuous of her fragility. What right had a farmer's wife to be like that? She, Julia, had conquered what might have been a serious illness and was on her feet again. This girl had no *spunk*; that was what was the matter and as Mrs. Chalford could not say so openly to Tony (although she was sure he would agree) she said it to Richard.

Richard gave his mother a queer look.

'I can't agree – I'd say the opposite,' was his answer. 'She isn't a country girl, and never has been. Life at Queen's Lacey just doesn't suit her. It can be ruddy cold in Bucks as you know – and the poor girl just shrivels up. She isn't as hardy as you, Mama.'

'I am no longer hardy. But I have strength of will. Christa is a great disappointment to me. She doesn't even have children.'

Richard stared ahead of him; mother and son were alone for the evening meal. Christa had retired to her own wing. Tony was dining with Ursula Corby at Forty Green. Christa had not felt up to going with him.

Richard lit a cigarette and screwed up his eyes. The smoke got into them.

He had been so busy since Christmas that he had hardly had time to think. Christa kept more to her own quarters these days; he noticed that she often sat in her private drawing-room reading in front of the fire, instead of joining the family circle in the main house. Tony (rather grudgingly, Richard fancied) spent some of his time with her. But often he left her alone and sat with his mother. For the last six weeks, Christa had been more often than not confined to her bedroom with a temperature, and these repeated chills. Nobody but Mitza seemed to have seen much of her.

Common courtesy had forced Richard now and again to speak to Christa – but never alone; *that* he had avoided. The last time they had talked together, she had suddenly broken into a smile, amused by some light remark he had made. He had not seen her smile like that for so long that it had hurt him.

He spoke to her then in a voice meant for her ears only.

'What in God's name is wrong with you? Why do you look like you do—? Why are you always ill?'

She flushed scarlet and stared at him as though in confusion. Then she stammered:

155

'I – I'm sorry. Am I the spectre at the feast?'

'You may be a spectre, but I would like to know where to find the feast,' he laughed harshly.

'I'd like to get away,' she whispered.

'And you ought to go – right away,' was his brusque reply. 'And this has been the worst winter we've ever had.'

He went on to remind Christa that they had had that outbreak of fowl pest in January. It had carried off most of the fine pedigree stock which was young Pip's pride and joy.

'As Tony says,' ended Richard, 'We shall soon be running this place at a loss.

She had given him a long, strange look.

'Can't we have some music together again just once?' she asked.

Against his principles, he gave in.

'Very well – I'll try to come in tonight and play for you.'

Secretly he wanted more than anything in the world to make her happy. That night he opened the long-shut lid of the piano and played for her.

In February, when she was better, Mrs. Chalford, making one of her occasional 'gestures', had taken a box for the whole family for the musical play: *Kismet*. As Christa remarked at the time, it was like a school-treat with Mrs. Chalford acting as headmistress. Nevertheless, Christa and Richard enjoyed the evening.

Richard, at home, improvised a few of the catchy tunes. Christa, her spirits lifting and her whole being suffused with a joy which she had no right to feel, hummed and sang those words that she could remember.

> *'Take my hand . . .*
> *I'm a stranger in Paradise! . . .'*

Her voice sounded rich and sweet.

Richard, sitting with his mother today, could remember exactly how she had looked while she sang. Silver fair hair flung back; eyes half-closed; delicate fingers twined together.

'Stranger in Paradise,' he had echoed the words softly.

They were barred from Paradise, the pair of them! It was not to be denied that they might have found heaven together.

She had leaned over him laughing and humming, until their shoulders inadvertently touched.

> *'I saw your face and I ascended out of*
> *the commonplace into the air*
> *Somewhere in space I hang suspended*
> *until I know there's a chance that*
> *you care. . . .'*

Richard, cigarette in the corner of his mouth, half-sang and half-spoke the next few lines:

> *'Won't you answer the fervent prayer of*
> *a stranger in Paradise*
> *Don't send me in dark despair from all*
> *that I hunger for—'*

Their gaze met and the jolt of her heart was so violent that it became excruciating. Suddenly he let the piano lid fall with a crash and got up.

'Damn silly maudlin sentiment—' he muttered. 'Murdering Borodin, too. I'm going to have a drink.'

So that had been the end of the musical evening. He fetched a mug of beer and gulped it noisily, looking at her with a hard, even angry, stare, while his heart cried out aloud. He could see that he had hurt her again. She looked pale and forlorn. Finally she announced that she was going to her own room and she vanished. Like a ghost she was always vanishing out of his sight. But that same ghost refused to be banished from his mind even when he was at work on the farm. Now he felt that they were dangerous and destructive to each other.

But it was a deplorable situation that could not be allowed to go on interminably. After Easter, when Pip came back, Richard was determined to leave Queen's Lacey again. Especially now that his mother's health seemed so much improved.

Mrs. Chalford repeated her denunciation of Christa.

'Did you hear what I said, Richard? I said that Christa doesn't even have children. Surely the only excuse for marriage is a family. I don't see that she is the *slightest* use to Tony.'

Richard scowled and avoided his mother's gaze.

'My dear Mama, you shouldn't always look at marriage from the husband's standpoint – what about the wretched wife? – what does Tony do for *Christa*?'

'*Really*, Richard!' exclaimed Mrs. Chalford indignantly. 'Are you insinuating that Tony is anything but a model husband?'

'I'm not insinuating anything. I don't really want to be drawn into a discussion about Tony and his wife.'

Julia tossed her head.

'Surely we can talk together. Tony and Christa have been very much on my mind lately.'

'If I were you I'd leave them alone.'

'Do I ever interfere?'

'Since you ask me I'd say that you do, Mama, admittedly in a very subtle fashion.'

'Subtle fashion,' she repeated the words, staring at him angrily, 'what do you mean, Richard?'

'What I say – your interference is sort of under the surface. But you keep Tony away from Christa. You and he go into constant huddles about business and spend a lot of time in each other's company and any wife, under the same circumstances, would feel that her husband isn't her property. He is more yours.'

A moment's silence, then Julia gave a curt laugh.

'Of course you're talking a lot of nonsense.'

'Okay,' said Richard, and got up from his chair.

'Just a moment,' she said, 'I'd like to know what you do think about those two. *I* say they are not getting on.'

'Do you want me to agree?'

'Richard, don't be so difficult. I want your opinion – I'm asking for it – in confidence, of course. I'm worried about Tony and you should be, too. He's your brother.'

'I'm well aware of that and I worry a lot more about your dear Tony than you think.'

'Now don't call him "my dear Tony" in that jealous way. I've never made any difference between you and him and Pip. I've always been just.'

'Okay,' said Richard.

'I do so dislike that word,' said Mrs. Chalford, 'and you still haven't answered my question.'

Richard was dangerously near the end of his control.

'Look, Mama, I don't want to discuss Tony's marriage.'

'Ah, then you agree that it's not what it should be,' said Mrs. Chalford triumphantly.

'I really do believe you'd like to see it crack up, Mama.'

'That's a very ugly thing to say, Richard.' A slow red crept under Mrs. Chalford's skin.

'And let me add,' said Richard, 'that I think it's grossly unfair that you should blame Christa for the present state of affairs, providing such a state exists.'

'If it does – she is at fault. Tony is a marvellous husband.

158

He's obviously been disappointed in her but he says nothing and—'

'And does nothing,' broke in Richard. 'And any girl who had the misfortune to be Mrs. Anthony Chalford would react in the way Christa's reacted, unless she was as tough as Ursula Corby who would have tweaked his ear and told him where he got off.'

Mrs. Chalford rose to her feet. She was quite scarlet.

'Richard, I think it's very disloyal of you to infer that Tony is responsible for this ill-assorted marriage.'

'He married her. He should have stood by her – no matter how it turned out,' said Richard.

He was red, too. He glowered at his mother. He had never felt less affectionate or dutiful. He had witnessed many of the small mental cruelties which she had practised on Christa – and all her petty spite – all due to her inordinate love for Tony. He felt nauseated.

'I am a lot more loyal to Tony than you think,' he added. 'You're so prejudiced in Tony's favour that you've lost all sense of fairness. When Christa first came here she was a warm-hearted, gay sort of girl accustomed to a life that was not luxurious, but full of interest and fun. Since she married Tony she's been slowly going downhill. She'll have been here three years shortly, and look what Queen's Lacy has done to her. Her health is not only a question of climate – it's psychological. She's downright neglected and unhappy.'

'Then she has no right to be,' said Julia, breathing hard and fast.

'You can't be the judge of that – you're not Christa. It might suit *you* to have a husband like Tony, but it doesn't suit Christa. Tony's so tied up with the farm and the family that he does nothing whatsoever about his wife; he just lets her fend for herself and thinks it's enough that he should go to bed under the same roof, eat the same food, and take her out occasionally to a picture, or help him play his damned Canasta. He knows she's fond of music. When does he ever take her to a concert? He knows she ought to go away now but he says he can't go because he's busy. He's too damn busy to remember that he's a married man – that's what's the matter with Tony and you encourage it.'

Dead silence. Richard had cooled down but he was shaking. He realized suddenly that he had said too much. He could see the astonishment and surprise in his mother's eyes. Then she said in an icy voice:

'Well, now I know! I must say I'm amazed. Tony's own brother runs him down – runs his mother down – and defends that stupid girl who is only an outsider.'

'Stupid is hardly the word I'd apply to Christa,' said Richard, stung once more to defence, although he knew that he was following a crazy course.

'Oh, I grant you she's intelligent in some ways, but what you've just said about Tony, *I* say about her. It's *she* who neglects her husband and does nothing whatsoever for *him*. *She's* wrapped up in herself and most ungrateful for all I've done for her and—' She broke off, for Richard had suddenly walked out of the room and shut the door behind him.

Julia drew breath and picked up her bag of tapestry work, the muscles of her face working. How abominably rude of Richard to go out like that in the middle of a conversation. She couldn't understand him defending Christa. It had never struck her that Richard was particularly fond of the girl; he rarely spoke to her.

Julia blamed Christa for all the trouble in this house. The girl had brought bad luck to Queen's Lacey. They were not the same happy united family that they used to be. It must be Christa's fault. Poor darling Tony was not to blame. It was monstrous of Richard to suggest it. In that moment Julia even disliked Richard for being the champion of Christa's cause. But then Richard had never meant to her what Tony and Pip had done – and she had her own innermost reasons for *that*. He, too, was ungrateful, and *he* had something to be sorry for. He had driven that poor girl, Susan Thornton, to wreck her life, and break her old father's heart.

Poor old Joe Thornton and Aunt Wyn lived alone at Hillside Farm nowadays, Susan had gone off with her Austrian farm labourer and actually married him. What a fool! Living in poverty in some remote village somewhere, they said. Nobody in the district had seen her. But everybody knew that she used to be in love with Richard. It was a terrible pity, reflected Mrs. Chalford, that her boys had ever had to reach the marriageable age, and conduct themselves so foolishly. Heaven grant that Pip fell in love with a suitable girl, or Julia would never have any grandchildren, at this rate.

Richard put on his duffle coat and walked out into the courtyard.

It was a bright clear March night with a keen wind blowing, but the stars were out. The long hard winter was over.

Once, Richard thought bitterly, I loved this place. Now I hate it and I almost hate my own family.

He had been shaken by the force of the words he had just spoken to his mother; but he was well aware that the tragedy of Christa and Tony's mis-mating was not as Mrs. Chalford asserted, Christa's fault. She had tried – God knows that she had tried – for Richard had watched, silently, and listened, too. At one time Tony used to be very pleasant to her. He would turn on the easy charm and hold her hand in public or tell her in front of the family that she looked pretty. He had carried her downstairs because she was so weak, after her last session in bed. Richard had come upon them once sitting in front of the fire, roasting chestnuts. He had been seized with a sensation of acute, bitter jealousy and marched out of the room again. Later, alone with his brother, he suggested that Christa needed a proper holiday and chance to convalesce.

'If you'd like to get away for a bit I'll hold the fort,' he said.

'Thanks, Rich, but I can't go at the moment,' Tony replied. 'There's too much on my plate. I'm having a hell of a lot of trouble with the income-tax consultants – you know the set-up – and I'm not going off until I've got it all straight. It means going through the books and accounts and making sure I haven't slipped up anywhere, and I don't want mother to worry about business matters. You know what Dr. Angus said.'

It had been on the tip of Richard's tongue to suggest that Dr. Angus had also said that Christa wasn't very well. But Tony had closed the conversation and it remained closed. But, at the time, Richard had thought: *God – what a chap! His blessed income-tax – saving the money – it all means more to him than his wife. He must be crazy!*

CHAPTER FOUR

RICHARD walked through the garden and down to the great barn. It was now almost empty of clover seed, waiting for the new crop. From a distant building came the plaintive lowing of a cow that had recently lost its calf, that sound which he knew was so abhorrent to Christa. Poor little thing, he thought, what a ghastly mistake she had made marrying into the Chalford family!

Then, suddenly, he heard a familiar sound; a dry, rasping, little cough. Christa's cough . . . he heard it far too often these days. She had not been able to get rid of it. Then he saw her. His muscles tautened and he braced himself as though for an ordeal. She, too, wore a short coat with the collar turned up, and a red woollen muffler tucked inside. Her fair hair glistened in the starlight. She stopped in front of him.

'Hullo!'

'You oughtn't to be out in this night air,' he said abruptly.

She laughed.

'Dear me, I'm not used to having such tender care taken of me. But I'm not "the Lady of the Camellias", neither am I dying of my "'acking corf".'

'Well, you look as though you're dying of something,' said Richard, dryly.

They stood facing each other by the door of the great barn. The night was luminous and they could see each other's faces plainly. Both those faces were defiant, secret, wary. Around them, the sighing of the wind through the trees, a rustle of bushes, that stirring of nature that was not to be silenced even though birds and animals slept.

Christa said:

'As a matter of fact I meant to have an early night and get rid of my headache, but I felt so restless, I put on a coat and came out for a walk. I suppose Tessa's with you? I couldn't find her.'

'No, she isn't with me, I think she's gone hunting. You're always very good to my Tessa. She likes you better than she does me nowadays.'

'That isn't at all true. There is no more faithful and devoted creature in the world than a spaniel, and after you went to Denmark she nearly died of melancholia. Will you ever go away again?' Chris asked the question in a low voice.

He avoided her gaze.

'Yes. I'm thinking of breaking the news to Mama tomorrow. I thought I could stick it here but I can't. I nearly told her tonight but we got led into another discussion.'

'What about?'

'You and Tony, if you want to know.'

'What did she say about us?'

'Oh never mind.'

'I know,' said Christa bitterly, 'she thinks our marriage is cracking up and that I'm to blame.'

162

'Well, you're not,' said Richard roughly.

'All the same, Tony and I are washed up,' she said.

His muscles tautened. He hardly dared look down at the white, tired, young face which when he had first seen it, had seemed the most beautiful in the world. He could hardly bear to look at this weary, disillusioned woman.

'Why, in God's name did you ever marry Tony, Christa?' he blurted out.

She began to tremble.

'Do you think we'd better discuss it?'

'Perhaps not.'

She whispered:

'You see, I daren't. I know I've been a fool. He isn't my type but I didn't seem to realize at the time. And he could be so attractive when he wanted.'

'It was always like that with old Tony.'

'But it was never me he needed,' she said, 'any sort of girl . . ; except me.'

'That's a nice thing.'

'Yes, isn't it nice? What do we do now?'

'*We?*'

'I mean *me*,' she said with a scorching blush.

He saw the blush even in that dim light and the shamed look that crept into her eyes. Tonight she was facing up to the truth – just as he faced it. She no longer had the strength left to pretend.

Richard wanted her. He wanted her so madly, and with such a fever of desire, that it destroyed reason and sent caution flying to the wind. Now their gaze met. They devoured each other, unable to tear their gaze away. Their breath was like vapour in the keen air. He caught the fragrance of her silvered hair. Her face looked cold and white. But when he suddenly snatched at her hands they felt hot and burning with a fever to match his own.

'Oh, God!' he said. 'Oh, God, what *hell* this is!'

She stood quiet, neither moving nor speaking. But it was as though her whole being surged upward in a rush of violent longing for his love and understanding; for all that her starved body and soul demanded. Then he said:

'It's no good. I can't see you and not love you.'

She whispered:

'That's how I feel about you. But since you came home from Denmark I thought you almost hated me.'

163

'I've tried to because I hate myself. You're such a menace to me, without meaning to be, poor darling,' he said.

Poor darling! The way he said those words tore at her heart. She was no longer capable of controlling herself. She was beyond it. He was her brother, he was her lover, he was the person whose image had haunted and worried her during all the long months that she had lived here without him at Queen's Lacey. He was the man whom she should have married instead of Tony.

'Oh!' she said in a small moaning voice. 'Oh, Richard, I need you so terribly.'

They were still standing apart. His fingers twined around hers in a convulsive and desperate way.

'I need you, too,' he said, torn between despair and joy.

She went on:

'You may not realize it, but lately you've half killed me by avoiding me. We've been like strangers,' she said.

' *"Strangers in Paradise . . ."* ' he repeated the familiar words with a harsh laugh, 'and what are those other words – *"Don't send me to dark despair, from all that I hunger for."* '

'I'm sure that's misquoting,' she said, and began to laugh helplessly.

'I never can remember verses,' he said, 'but the meaning's the same.'

She made a final effort to keep her head above the swirling waters that threatened to drown her.

'Let's go in, Richard. Let's not lose our heads again. We might regret it.'

'It's only what I haven't done or said so far, that I regret,' he said, and pulled her into his arms. He crushed her against him so fiercely that it made her gasp. Now it was too late. She was as incapable as himself of drawing back.

He went on speaking in a hard, demented voice:

'The way Tony treats you drives me mad. Like your un-happiness – I've watched that and that's driven me mad, too. All the time I was in Denmark I remembered your kisses. I can't stop remembering.'

He began to touch her hair, as he had yearned to do, smoothing it back from the small, beautiful bones of her forehead. He saw the shining gold of her long-lidded eyes, between the dark curtain of lashes; the sad young mouth that had so often roused a furious longing in him which out of loyalty to Tony, he had tried to smother. But tonight belonged to *them*. Tomorrow he would go from Queen's Lacey again and he would never come back. But this one moment was his and hers.

'Darling, darling,' he said, 'I want you so much that it's driving me insane.'

His lips touched her mouth, pressed deeper and stayed thus. Her unspoken protest was silenced as she reached up and clung to him. They exchanged a mad, almost terrible, kiss. And they both knew that they were not strong enough to carry out the renunciation.

Christa at last broke away – her slender limbs trembled violently like those of a startled colt. She kept saying under her breath:

'Dear God! . . .'

Richard said:

'That's done it . . .we can't take *that* back.'

'We can – we must. We agreed on it.'

'We did – but we failed. We are in love with each other. We must face it.'

'You're my brother-in-law,' she said in a gasping voice.

'*You* are my sister-in-law . . .,' he nodded and laughed. It made a harsh, unhappy sound in the quiet night. 'Dear God – *as* you say.'

'What are we going to do?'

'Nothing. There isn't a single thing we can do.'

'Because – I'm Tony's wife.'

'Yes.'

She nodded, trying to control that shuddering of her body.

'Richard, Richard, why did it have to happen?' she moaned. 'Why did you marry Tony?'

'We've been over all that – you know – it was just one of those things – a terrible mistake.'

'How soon did you find it out?'

'In Rome – on our honeymoon,' she said, her head drooping.

He looked with yearning at that bowed, lovely head.

'Poor darling.'

'Don't say that again – I can't bear it.'

'You've got to bear more than that and so have I.'

'It's been so terrible these last few months – it was worse after you came home on Boxing Day.'

'I know. Seeing you – and not seeing you. Not daring to speak – deliberately keeping out of your way – and watching them murder you by inches.'

'They didn't mean to ... your mother just can't understand or accept me. She never wanted Tony to marry me. She was right. Oh, Richard, she was right.'

'She's too damned often right, but it doesn't help any,' said Richard, and fumbled in his coat pocket for a packet of cigarettes. He took one out, his fingers unsteady, tried to light it but failed, and flung away the burnt matches one after the other. The wind was too strong for the tiny flame despite his cupped hands.

'Now it's all over,' he added. 'It's become impossible. I must clear out again.'

'I've reached breaking point, too. What shall I do?' She said the words more to herself than to him and hid her face in her hands.

'Christa, my love,' he said in a voice of anguish. 'You must face up to things and help me. I need your help.'

'I don't want you to leave me again.'

'Yes, you do, darling. You're loyal by nature. It's nearly three years since you first came to Queen's Lacey. You've done your damnedest for Tony.'

'Yes.' She admitted it.

'If I'd been outside this family – no relation of Tony's – I'd have asked you to go away with me. Tonight ... tomorrow ... long ago.'

She uncovered her face now. He could see tears – crystal drops shining on her lashes, and her pitiful mouth.

'Yes. And I'd have gone with you. I'm immoral enough to admit it.'

'You couldn't be immoral. It's just that you made a ghastly mistake and you're paying for it. Who could blame you for trying to get out of such a marriage? Up to now I've always respected my mother and although I never saw eye to eye with Tony, I used to get on with him – I never really crossed his path. Now I dislike my own mother for her abominable and heartless conduct towards you. As for Tony – I'm contemptuous of him – as I would be of any man who could throw away all the love and sweetness you brought to your marriage. He's just a fool.'

'Oh, Richard – I can't bear to feel it's through me all this has happened. Oh, why did I ever come to Queen's Lacey? I've brought nothing but trouble.'

'You didn't mean to, darling. Don't blame yourself. It's futile.'

'I do blame myself. I wish I could die,' she said, and suddenly turned and began to run away from him. But he caught her up and pulled her back into his arms. He covered her face with wild kisses, tasting the salt of her tears, feeling the quivering of her soft mouth and her deep hurt. Her response to his passion and tenderness was pitiably frank and revealing. He pitied her, yet adored her for it. She was so much his; and she could never belong to him. For another crazy, forbidden moment they clung to each other, their hands twining, their bodies straining, their eyes large and eloquent, concentrated upon each other's faces; white, blurred desperate faces in the shadowed night.

Then – gently – Richard put her away from him.

'I can't stand any more. Let me go, darling.'

She nodded speechlessly.

'I'd have cut off my right hand to save you from this misery,' he added. 'I'd have faced a scandal, a divorce, being chucked out of Queen's Lacey, disinherited, all the rest of it . . . if only you were not my brother's wife. But as things are I can't take you. That's final. You agree – don't you?'

'Yes,' she said.

'So I must clear out. I'll go back to Denmark or to Norway. I've some friends there.'

'My coming here has ruined everything,' she said in a voice of anguish.

'I keep telling you it wasn't your fault. It was partly Mama and partly because that fool Tony made no effort to keep your love.'

'Yes, that is true.'

'Then stop feeling guilty.'

'Yes,' she said, and gave the merest smile as she heard the rough command in his voice.

She looked up at him. He had never been more dear to her. She loved him with every breath of her body. It was some glimmer of consolation to her to know now, beyond doubt, that he loved her with equal passion and strength. But to lose him – that was terrible. The anticipation of further pain, when he was gone from her, was unbearable.

'I shan't stay at Queen's Lacey,' she said in a stifled voice. 'I am almost at the end, myself. I'll *have* to get a separation from Tony, go to London and find a job. I could always get one with some florist.'

'You must do what you think best. I refuse to be heroic and persuade you to stay with my brother,' he said sullenly.

'Oh, Richard.'

'Christa, I shall never stop loving you. That's one thing I once promised you and I promise it again.'

'I can swear the same.'

'Better go in,' he said in that changed voice made gruff by the aching necessity to preserve a balance, to control an almost uncontrollable desire for a woman forbidden to him.

Now she seized his hands, pressing them to her lips. He felt her tears sad and scalding, against them.

She whispered in French:

> 'Oh Richard, o mon roi
> l'univers t' abondonée
>   Sur la terre il n'est que moi qui s'intéresse de tes
> affaires!'

He pulled his hands away as though her tears stung him. He gave a shorty cynical laugh.

'It fits – doesn't it . . . my poor little troubadour . . . fancy you remembering Blondel's son. I'd forgotten it. He sang it to poor old Richard *Coeur-de-Lion* when the world had turned against him – didn't he? Yes, the universe abandons us both. My poor sweet Christa, good night, and good-bye.'

'Good-bye' – she echoed the words, desolately, pulling the collar of her coat closer around her neck, as the cold wind caught her.

Suddenly he took her in his arms again, holding her as though life itself depended on the warmth, the security that the temporary contact with her afforded him.

'My love, my dear love,' he said.

'O Richard, o mon roi,' she quoted the historic words again, sobbing, pressing her face to his shoulder.

'Try to be happy – or at least happier, even if you don't stay with Tony – I can't bear your unhappiness,' he said.

'I'll do my best,' she whispered.

It was at that moment that the two of them – engrossed in each other, in the anguish of their farewell – became conscious that they were no longer alone. The white beam of a strong torch flashed upon them. They sprang apart and faced Julia Chalford. In an old coat and the habitual beret, she stood looking at them, her eyes full of a bitter and horrified accusation.

CHAPTER FIVE

THE thing had come about because Julia Chalford, after the unsatisfactory row with Richard, had sat there in the sitting-room alone, brooding over what had been said to her.

The longer she thought about Tony and Christa, the more resentful she felt about the girl. She could not say with any sincerity that Christa had taken Tony away from her. On the contrary, she was quite sure that Tony now realized what a mistake he had made and appreciated his old mother more than ever. He was sweet to her. But Christa was a disturbing influence and the older woman wished she could rid of her. Intrinsically a religious worthy person, she had become painfully conscious of a malicious and wicked desire to see a divorce between those two. Divorce wasn't a pretty thing and at one time Julia would have been appalled at the possibility of it happening in her family. But now she believed that it might be the very best thing for Tony if he could get rid of this useless wife of his. A pity that there was no 'other man' . . . but Christa didn't seem interested in anybody else. As for Christa's ill-health – her cough and new delicacy – that all irritated Mrs. Chalford rather than roused her sympathy. She was just not going to allow Tony to be dragged off to the Continent at this moment, what with Pip away and so much going on at the farm.

She had been looking at a pamphlet that Tony had given her. They had just bought this machine – a Combine Harvester. She liked the look of it and must take a look at the machine when it arrived tomorrow, she thought. She wished that she felt her old strong self. She never used to get so tired. So far, she had defeated that old fool Dr. Angus – and the rest of them. She was not even troubling to diet now, but she couldn't say, sincerely, that she felt fit. She had had one or two dizzy fits again lately, and felt extra irritable and excitable; she wouldn't be surprised if the blood pressure wasn't going up again. But no more doctors for her, *or* stretches in bed, or letting that girl run Queen's Lacey!

Julia had had a row with Mitza last night. She accused the Austrian woman of being extravagant with cream and butter.

Mitza had wept and said she would leave immediately. It had been Christa who had persuaded her to remain. Mitza had tactlessly said so to Julia, and it had offended Mrs. Chalford. Sentimental fools, both the cook and Tony's wife. It always annoyed her to hear the two of them singing their German songs together. But even Tony had been unsympathetic when she had complained, and said that she hated German.

'Mitza is a good cook – and does more work than any English girl would do here – why not put up with her nationality?'

It had been Richard who had chimed in:

'Anyhow, I can't see your object in keeping up this anti-German spirit. In any case, Mitza is Austrian. What was the use in engaging a German-speaking woman and then objecting to her language? It's so prejudiced.'

Well, Julia Chalford thought to herself, compressing her lips as she folded her tapestry and prepared to walk up to her bedroom this evening, maybe she *was* prejudiced; and particularly against Christa, but she couldn't help it.

She decided to go over to the wing and have a little talk with Christa. She might try to persuade her to go away alone, in order to get rid of that irritating cough.

She might even say:

'I'm a little worried about the way you and Tony are getting on. But it's your fault, Christa. I don't think *you* are pulling your weight. . . .'

Richard, of course, would say that was interfering, well it wasn't his business. And Tony came first.

With a deliberate intent to stir up trouble, Julia made her way to Tony's and Christa's rooms. She was surprised to find the wing in darkness but soon became aware that it was not because Christa was in bed and asleep. The door was open and the bedroom empty.

Now where can she possibly be, Mrs. Chalford thought – and looked through all the rooms, noting with malicious pleasure that Tony still slept in the dressing-room. Certainly those two were not keen on each other these days, she reflected.

Once back in her own part of the house she stood in the hall pondering as to where Christa could have got to at this time of night. She couldn't be out in the car because Tony had taken his car and Christa never drove the big station wagon.

She might have gone out for a walk, of course; if so, what a fool, with that cough, and in this cold night air. Mrs. Chalford opened the front door.

'Christa, are you there?' she called out.

No answer – only the rustle of the wind in the trees and the *miaow* of a farm cat that darted out of the bushes, and began to rub its back in a friendly fashion against Mrs. Chalford's ankle. She prodded it away with the tip of her toe and shut the door with a little shiver. Then she thought suddenly:

'*I wonder if she's gone out with Richard.*'

It was just a thought ... the first time, in fact, that she had ever bracketed those two together in her mind. She had always believed that Richard was not too fond of his sister-in-law. However, the conversation tonight had been a bit of an eye-opener. Richard had so bluntly and ardently defended Christa. And now Julia remembered that those two had more than a bit in common; that it had irritated her to see them talking about books, or having their music sessions together (not that they had done that for some time). But she wasn't going to have Richard and Christa forming any sort of league against her, Julia, or darling Tony. Christa was wrong if she thought she could play on everybody's sympathy. Julia had put a stop to it the other day when even Pip had openly stated that Christa was the prettiest girl in the district.

'Handsome is as handsome does,' Mrs. Chalford had snapped, and when Pip scratched his head and asked for an explanation of these cryptic words, she had refused to give him one but added that she did not think Christa at all pretty; much too thin and, in her opinion, too affected.

Suddenly Mrs. Chalford decided to take a little walk and see what those two were up to, if they *had* gone out together. She didn't really know in her mind what she meant by the words '*up to*'. If she could have analysed them, it was that she imagined she might find them talking against her, or Tony.

So she had put on her coat and come out and looked first through the gardens, then gone a little way down the farm road. She had come round the back of the great barn very quietly and then, flashing her torch, illuminated those two figures in that close, all-revealing embrace.

At first she stared, her jaw dropping, her mind paralysed. She watched the couple spring apart. Then the sickness of all the evil that was in her subconscious mind, all her own repressions, her hatred of sex in any shape or form, flared up into a frenzy of indignation. Richard and Christa making love. *Richard and Christa.* Oh, how *abominable*!

Richard began:

'What on earth are you doing out here, Mama? You'll catch a chill.'

She left her torch full on, flashing it from his face to Christa's. The girl blinked in the strong light and turned away. She looked, Julia thought, the personification of shame.

'Mama—' began Richard again.

'You cad!' broke in Mrs. Chalford in a low trembling voice. 'You cad! Your own brother's wife.'

'Wait a minute—'

She cut him short, swinging now in her fury, upon Christa.

'As for you, you little *tart*. . . .'

She stopped, choking. That was a word she had never used before in her life. It spat like a bullet from a revolver. If she had had a weapon she might have shot her daughter-in-law. She was hysterical with hatred and bitterness. In all her days she never remembered so completely losing control. But the sight of Christa as she had seen her just now, wrapped in Richard's embrace – their lips clinging, had put the seal upon her loathing of Tony's wife. She could not or would not, stop to analyse the situation, to feel either sadness or pity or any form of understanding. She had never been one to excuse the frailty of human nature. And these two were beyond her understanding – or her pity. She only knew that she had come upon them doing something vile . . . making love to each other. And, perhaps, worse had happened before she arrived . . . how did she know?

Richard's anger rose now to met hers.

'You have no right to say such a thing. Christa is *not* a tart.'

'Yes, yes she is . . .' said Mrs. Chalford hysterically.

'Mama, calm yourself, please.'

'I'd better go,' said Christa in a strangled voice, but when she would have turned away, the older woman caught her by the arm:

'No, you won't, you'll stay here and hear what I've got to say.'

And again she flashed the torch on Christa's face, which was white and taut, streaked with tears. Richard caught the torch from his mother's fingers and switched it off.

'Give that back to me,' screamed Mrs. Chalford.

'Mother, do calm yourself, for heaven's sake.'

'You ask me to calm myself after what I've seen!'

'Oh, please—' began Christa, trying to get away from the woman's merciless fingers.

'You, Tony's wife, ' shouted Julia, 'meeting Richard down

here like a common bit carrying on some clandestine affair.'
Her breath was rapid and noisy. 'Well, I'm not surprised. I've
always guessed you were like that. I expect you've got boy
friends in London, too, admirers we none of us know about.
My poor Tony was mad ever to have married you and brought
you to Queen's Lacey.'

'Mother!' Richard thundered the word. 'For the love of
heaven, control yourself. You don't know what you're saying.
You're out of your mind.'

'And you,' she said, trying to peer up at him in the darkness,
'if you knew what I thought about *you*! And if you knew the
truth about yourself—' She broke off.

'I don't understand what you mean by that.'

'Never mind,' she said with a gasp.

He went on:

'It isn't as bad as you imagine. I admit that I was kissing
Christa, but it was for the last time. We were saying good-
bye.'

'A bit late. And how long have you been meeting Christa like
this, kissing her and deceiving Tony?'

'Never until tonight. Surely you must have noticed I've
hardly had anything to do with Christa while she's been at
Queen's Lacey, and that I had a reason for going to Denmark.
Christa was that reason. I wanted to get away from her.'

'That's what you say. I don't believe you and as for this one
...' she gave Christa a little shake, 'she's a deceitful liar. If
Tony could only have been here to see what I saw, he'd knock
you down, Richard, and be justified. But I'll make sure he does
know, and tells his wife to get out of Queen's Lacey, and stay
out.'

Now Christa shook herself free from her mother-in-law's
fingers. Driven beyond endurance, she said in a breathless voice:

'I want to go. I've wanted to for a long time. It's been mostly
your fault. You've made it hell for me here. And you've enjoyed encouraging Tony to neglect me; watching us grow apart.
I hate you as much as you hate me. I don't want to stay here, I
assure you.'

Mrs. Chalford opened her mouth to speak. No words came.
Her lips writhed and she swayed a little, feeling the starlit night
swirl suddenly around her. Her heart beat at such an alarming
rate that she could no longer control the pounding. She knew an
instant's terror that had nothing to do with Richard or Christa.
Then she said:

'*You've killed me! ...*'

And despite Richard's efforts to steady her, she slumped and fell down on the ground at his feet.

Across her prostrate body, Richard and Christa faced each other.

Then Richard said:

'Listen, Christa, I don't know what this means or how bad she is, but I'm horribly afraid it might be another stroke.'

'And we've done it ...' said Christa in a frightened small voice.

'*I've* done it, not you,' he said grimly.

He knelt down and touched his mother's cheek. Leaning close to her, he could just discern that the left side of her face was horribly twisted. He felt sick, and stood up again.

'It's my affair and not yours, Christa,' he said, 'I won't have you being blamed. Mother brought this on herself. She jumped to conclusions about us without even waiting to hear our side or knowing that we were intending to do the right thing.'

'I'll go and get help,' said Christa, shivering from head to foot.

'Say nothing, please, Go straight to your own rooms. *I'll* get help. I'll tell them that it was my fault. You're not to tell Tony anything, do you hear? There's no object in making things worse than they are.'

But now she was calm and fatalistic.

'I shall not let you take the blame,' she said. 'It's no use. I could never live with Tony again. I shall tell him the truth.'

Richard was too overwrought to argue. He knelt there chafing his mother's cold hands. He had ceased to love her but she was still his mother and no matter what his intentions, her terrible denunciation of him and of Christa, had left their mark. The breath of dishonour was upon him and the sickness of his own soul's guilt, even though it was rooted in no greater crime than a few desperate kisses.

'*He who committeth adultery in his heart ...*' thought Richard, as he knelt there in the cold night looking with despair upon his mother's prostrate form. What she had said could never be unsaid, and perhaps she was dying ... or even dead ... although he fancied he could still feel the faint flicker of her pulse. What had been done could never be undone, although he might wish to God it were not so, and that she had not left for him, the slime of a malicious hatred, a filthy suspicion, poisoning his boyhood memory of her.

174

He recalled those curious words that she had spoken in her fury:

'*If you knew the truth about yourself . . .*' she had said in that venomous voice. *What truth?* What had she meant? But, for the moment, he was not to know.

He took off his coat and pillowed his mother's head on it. He crouched there, holding her hand in a stupor, until the sound of footsteps roused him. Christa had come back with Mitza and two of the farm boys. They brought brandy, rugs, pillows. Mitza knelt down and looked at her mistress. She screamed:

'*Mein Gott, she is dead.*'

Julia was not dead but she was dying as they carried her back to the house. The tragic hulk of the woman who had given her life to this farm and to her sons, and spoiled the fine service of the years by letting the acid of her hatred and jealousy corrode her own soul. That final burst of fury had brought on the second and most serious stroke. When Dr. Angus arrived there was little he could do for her.

Christa stayed down in the sitting-room. The doctor stayed upstairs, talking to Richard, whilst Mitza, who, in her fashion had respected even if she had not liked her mistress, sat vigilant beside the bed. The only sound in that room was of Mitza's sobbing, otherwise a terrible stillness hung over the long gaunt figure under the eiderdown.

'She's still breathing,' said Dr. Angus, 'but she hasn't responded to the injection I gave her just now. She's in a coma. And I don't think she'll come out of it. That, perhaps, is a mercy for the poor lady as she would only be paralysed for life. Totally incapacitated.'

Richard said nothing. The elderly doctor thought that the young man looked pretty bad. He knew Richard well, but he had never before seen him like this. Under his rich tan the boy looked ghastly.

'What about coming downstairs and having a brandy, Richard?' said Angus. 'I'm afraid this has been a nasty shock for you.'

Richard looked towards the bed.

'You're sure there is nothing more to be done for her?'

'Sure.'

'How terrible,' said Richard.

'But it really is better than lingering on like some of them do with these seizures.'

'All the same it's more terrible than you realize.'

175

'You didn't tell me what brought the shock on,' said Dr. Angus curiously.

'No,' said Richard, drily.

'Mind you,' went on Angus, 'although she hasn't had me in lately, when I met her in Amersham the other day, I didn't think she looked too good. I imagined then that the blood pressure was going up. But she wouldn't admit it. She was a strong-minded woman, your mother.'

'*Was*,' thought Richard. Already they were speaking of her in the past. She was still a person – not yet a body . . . still breathing . . . but soon she would be forever silent, unable to speak, or to hear him tell her that he had not meant to do this thing to her. Poor Christa whom she had torn to pieces with her vituperous tongue – *she* had not meant to do it, either.

He hadn't spoken to Christa alone since they brought his mother in. But he knew what she would be feeling . . . he knew what *he* was feeling . . . yet they had done nothing; nothing at all But they were linked together like criminals, like the murderers of that woman on the bed.

'How ghastly and how unjust!' thought Richard.

'Well, whatever it was, don't blame yourself,' said Dr. Angus's voice, 'I'll be back in an hour or two. I've got to go because I was just on my way to an urgent case when your sister-in-law phoned. It's old Mrs. Gannell on the Common there. But I'll be back and I'll send in a nurse that I know I can get hold of. You'll want all the help you can get.'

'Yes,' said Richard.

'By the way, where's Tony? I know Pip's away.'

'I phoned Tony a few moments ago,' said Richard, in the same dull lifeless voice. 'I told him Mother had been taken very ill. He was dining at Forty Green, at the Corby's. He ought to be here any moment.'

Dr. Angus took a final look at his patient; issued a few further instructions to Mitza, and departed. Outside, the wind was getting up and the front door slammed as he left the house.

Richard walked into the drawing-room. Christa stood by the mantelpiece. He heard her coughing as he walked in. Her face was colourless and her eyes looked sunken. Trying to keep warm, she had switched on the electric fire. As he came into the room, she looked up at him, dully.

He answered her unspoken question.

'Not yet, but Angus doesn't think she can last.'

Christa shuddered uncontrollably.

'I shall always blame myself. Always.'

'For the love of God stop that,' said Richard harshly. 'You'll drive us both mad if you go on like that.'

She turned from him, some colour rising to her cheeks.

'I'm sorry.'

'Christa, it wasn't your fault and it wasn't really mine,' Richard said on a softer note, 'it was the devil's own luck that she saw us. And do try to remember that we were not just about to begin an illicit affair. We tried to put an *end* to the possibility of one ever taking place when I left Queen's Lacey a year ago. We were agreeing to separate again this evening.'

'I'll try to remember that,' said Christa, and added: 'but what has happened will make you dislike me now.'

He came close to her and looked her straight in the eyes.

'If I dislike anybody it's myself, but I love you, and I always will, with all my heart. This awful thing can't alter that fact. Neither can it alter my intention to go away and leave you. I want to stay and comfort you. But you know I can't. You must forgive me, that's all.'

'And you must forgive me,' said Christa, in a small pitiful voice.

Then they heard the car. They knew that Tony had come back. The wild blood tore to Christa's face. She put her hands to her throat.

'That's him.'

'Leave everything to me,' said Richard. 'I'll do the explaining.'

'Ought we to tell him what happened? Can we have it on our conscience? It isn't as though I meant to stay with him,' she said.

'Look,' said Richard angrily. 'I have no wish to get out of paying for my share of tonight's work, but there's been a lot of harm done already. Tony will be pretty cut up about Mother. I don't think we ought to face him with this other blow tonight.'

Christa hesitated.

'Perhaps not. Perhaps it would be better to tell him tomorrow – or when it's – all over. But nothing will make me agree to go on living with him any more, even though I never see *you* again.'

'Very well,' said Richard, 'but let him have one shock at a time. We'll tell him that we just found Mother – that's enough. I hate the falsehood ... especially as Mother is unconscious and can't speak for herself ... but it's necessary.'

'I hate it, too,' said Christa under her breath, 'but like you, I prefer to let Tony down lightly.'

And she felt a real pity for the man she had married, when finally he came hurrying into the room, looking very anxious, his fair hair tossed by the wind, and with some of his usual smugness and hauteur missing.

'Has Mother had another stroke?' he shot the question at them.

'Yes,' Richard answered.

'Worse than the other one?'

'You'll have to take it easy, Tony, but Dr. Angus says this time it's fatal.'

Tony blanched. He turned so white that Christa ran to him and put a hand on his arm.

'Poor Tony,' she said, 'let me get you a drink.' But he drew away from her hand almost as though he disliked her to touch him.

'What happened? Were *you* having another row with her or something?'

She flushed scarlet.

'So you want to think it was me—' she began.

'I want to know how it happened,' cut in Tony.

'She had a shock,' said Richard.

'What sort of shock?'

'She went out, down towards the farm,' began Richard, then stopped, clenching his hand.

Tony looked from him to Christa. She turned her gaze to Richard and shrugged her shoulders helplessly.

Tony opened his lips to question his brother again, but suddenly the door burst open, Mitza came hurrying in. Her round face was red and she panted.

'Please to kom kvick,' she said.

They asked no questions. Headed by Tony they ran upstairs. When they stood beside Mrs. Chalford's bed in the dimly lit bedroom they saw that she was already dead. She looked, Christa thought, not like Mummy had done, lovely and with an enigmatic smile that suggested that for her all life's problems had been answered, but as ugly, harsh and unbending as the living Julia had been. It seemed to Christa, also, that the dead woman's thin lips bore an expression of accusation directed towards her and Richard. She turned and ran out of the room.

Mitza followed her. It was into the arms of the kindly Austrian cook that Christa broke down, but the tears that she wept were not so much for Tony's mother as for the tragedy of death itself, for the hurt, the loss that would inevitably be felt by Julia Chalford's sons. As for Richard, Christa alone knew what *he* must be feeling in this hour. He looked stricken.

She did not see him again that night, but when Tony came into the bedroom where she was already undressed and in bed, he appeared less self-confident than usual and very tired. Taking off his coat he said, heavily:

'I think you should have stayed downstairs with us. I don't know why you ran off like that, Christa.'

As usual, she was rebuffed. The desire that had risen in her to try and comfort him a little, faded.

'I'm sorry,' she said, and wondered how many times she had had to say those apologetic words to him *and* to the remorseless woman who would never again be able to demand them.

Tony went on:

'I've had a ghastly shock, you know.'

Christa threw an arm up to shield her eyes from the lights that he had switched on.

Before she could even utter a word of sympathy, Tony continued to speak in a sulky, resentful voice as though determined to harbour his grief and pain against her.

'I can't help feeling that you and Richard didn't do much to help poor Mother, but there it is! Dr. Angus has just been back. He said it might have happened any time. Now I'll have to make all the arrangements for the funeral. Poor Mother! She was so marvellous to us boys, I think I was her favourite, don't you?'

Christa kept her eyes hidden. She felt utterly sick at heart. Any hope that might have existed of friendly contact between herself and this man vanished. He had always been pompous and egotistical. In this hour, even when he was facing real sorrow, he was the same, she thought cynically. He gloried in the fact that his mother had loved him best. He went meandering on about her and all that she had done for him, and how worried he was about Pip who would have no one to guide him now, until Christa dropped her arm and looked at Tony, stung into making a protest:

'You talk as though Pip was still a small boy, and as though even you, at your age, can't stand on your own feet. I *know* your mother was a marvellous manager but you can and will run Queen's Lacey without her. And it's high time Pip grew up, anyhow.'

Tony wrenched off first his tie, then his collar. He glared at the girl in the bed.

'Of course I know you didn't like my mother but *I* shall never get over her death.'

Christa exclaimed:

'When I first married you I *wanted* to love her – I tried—' then she flung herself back on the pillow, shaking the hair out of her eyes. 'Oh, don't let's start this, tonight of all nights. I'm desperately sorry for you, Tony. I know what I felt when my own mother died. But you are so horrid to me. Oh, don't, for heaven's sake, let us quarrel while her body is in the house.'

Tony hunched his shoulders:

'I must say I expected my wife to be of some help and comfort to me tonight, but I can see that you won't be. And you've shown pretty clearly for a long time that you hate Queen's Lacey. You have little consideration for me, or my work on the farm.'

Somehow she managed to keep her control.

'Anything more?' she asked in a low voice.

'No. I'm worn out and I'm going to bed. But I must say I feel both shaken and surprised, not only at the way *you've* behaved, but at Richard.'

Christa shut her eyes tightly. She felt exhausted. And the thought of the future terrified her. She who knew the truth, knew also that Richard who had tried so hard to do the right thing by his brother, would be cast into the outer darkness of his own remorse. After the funeral, he would leave Queen's Lacey and she would be left to *this*.

Her grief and her despair were too deep for tears. Long after Tony had muttered good night, she lay awake, dry-eyed, staring into the darkness.

CHAPTER SIX

FOR the last time Julia Chalford was conveyed along the familiar drive between the tall Dutch elms, followed by her three sons, her daughter-in-law, and most of the employees on the farm. A dismal procession of black-garbed people; whispering, one to another, that never had they seen such floral tributes. Hundreds of wreaths, crosses and sheafs of glorious flowers adorned the hearse. Julia was having a fine funeral.

To Christa the whole affair was a nightmare. An expensive, ostentatious, long-drawn-out ceremony, arranged, of course, by Tony.

Christa wore black from head to foot, because her husband wished it. He, himself, had taken on the imposing dignity of head of the household, thus stepping into his mother's shoes. He issued continual orders. Everything was done in a most methodical and correct fashion. Never, thought Christa, had she known such a case of heredity; it was as though Julia was there, herself, conducting her own funeral.

And it was such a lovely day, too. One of those late March mornings when the sun shone quite warmly from a pale blue sky and the young barley looked exquisitely green, shooting up from the rich ploughed earth, and they could hear the bleating of the new-born lambs.

The first daffodils were out. Queen's Lacey had never looked more pleasant or full of promise. But for Christa the promise lay buried under the darkness of her own private grief; her inevitable separation from the man she loved.

With a dogged obstinacy not really typical of her, she refused to feel any responsibility for Julia's passing. She, Christa, ought not to have fallen in love with Richard – that was true. She ought not to have kissed him on that fatal night; but the embrace that had caused Julia's hysterical outburst and subsequent death, had been an act of renunciation rather than of adulterous love. She *could not*, in all honesty, allow herself to feel that it was her fault. As for Richard – who was to know what *he* felt? He might have been carved from stone, sitting, silent and rigid, there in the car with her and his two brothers.

He carried out whatever orders Tony had flung at him in the house. Now he stared, woodenly, at the countryside, while they drove to Amersham, where Mrs. Chalford was to be buried. Only once he turned his gaze upon Christa. Then it was as though his heart melted. He thawed towards her, giving her a long look of indescribable tenderness. She looked so pitiably thin and forlorn in her mourning dress, and with that little black hat on her silver head. She returned his gaze dumbly. Then they both looked away again.

Pip, who had flown back from Spain, curtailing his holiday after receiving his brother's wire – looked ill-at-ease and wretched. His black tie was badly knotted and his sunburned chubby face bore a somewhat dazed expression. Tony kept snapping at him:

'For God's sake don't do *that*' ... or: 'For God's sake do this!'

Christa felt very sorry for Pip. Poor boy! Not much of a life awaited him, living on the farm alone with his eldest brother of whom he had always been rather afraid.

'I'll be gone – and Richard will be gone,' thought Christa. 'There will be a great change here for Pip!'

Just before they had left the house, she had made an effort for humanity's sake to console Tony.

'I do know what you're feeling – I'm so terribly sorry,' she had begun, putting her hands on his shoulders. But he had drawn away from her, stiffly.

'Later, not now, please,' he had said.

It was always '*later*' for Tony; now it was going to be too late. She would never make another effort to touch or to kiss him.

Somehow or other she had to bear the prolonged misery and awkwardness of that funeral. It was as though the ghost of Julia Chalford haunted her – sneering and jeering, while she stood beside Tony and shook hands with the relatives and friends who attended, and received their condolences.

The moment they got back to the house, Richard flung off his coat and announced that he was going to change. He wanted to get down to the farm, he said, and would be out until dark.

Tony tried to stop him.

'Let the men get on with the jobs today. You ought to come into the library with us, and see Mr. Parsons. . . .'

Parsons was the family solicitor. The will was to be read. But Richard made every excuse to escape. He had had as much as he could stand. He must get out of this house, away from the family, and into the fresh air. Working with the animals, or on a tractor, perhaps, he might regain some of his lost peace of mind.

He, and he alone, could sum up the measure of the agony he had felt all through that funeral service. He and Julia Chalford had never been close, but she *was* his mother. He could not drive away the ugly belief that he had helped to hasten her to her grave. Like Christa, he knew that it had all been a terrible mistake, and over-hasty conjecture on her part. But the result had been the same. It was difficult for him now to re-orientate

his feelings. The worst of the hell he suffered lay in the knowledge that he could do nothing to help or comfort Christa. He
must, in decency, keep away from her. But the look in her eyes
broke his heart.

It all seemed so useless – all this pain and grief – like the
tragedy of his mother's death.

When Tony began to nag at him, he turned so fiercely on him
that Tony flushed and shut his mouth. But as Richard flung
himself out of the house, Tony denounced him to Christa:

'Grief seems to have gone to Richard's head. He's behaving
in the most odd fashion.'

Christa started to shake from head to foot. She had felt very
cold, standing in the cemetery during the burial. She wondered
if she had a temperature again. She took it and found that she
had, and was glad of the excuse to crawl into bed. She let Mitza
come over to the wing and cherish her. Tony gave her a grudging word of sympathy but spoiled it by adding:

'It really is sickening, the one time you should be with us.
Now Pip and I will have to go through Mother's papers with
Mrs. Parsons. And, of course, that means I, alone. Pip's useless
at business.'

Christa turned her face from him and wondered wearily what
it must be like to have such a splendid opinion of oneself. She
envied Tony his conceit. But, after he had gone, she began to
cry very quietly. The tears ran down her cheeks. She whispered:
'O, Richard, o mon roi!'

All the universe had abandoned him, and her too, she
reflected. Why, why did she have to be his brother's wife? Why
couldn't she have put her hand in his and let him take her away
from this dark despair. She thought:

'I must give Tony a few days more and then tell him.'

Later that day, Tony came into her room and announced that
the will had been read by Mr. Parsons and, Tony said, with a
smug look on his face, although the money had been divided
equally, he, Anthony Chalford, had been left Queen's Lacey.

Christa sat up and looked at him, wide-eyed.

'You mean the whole farm?'

'Yes. I think Mother knew that it meant more to me than to
anybody.'

Christa flushed.

'It doesn't seem very fair. So much of the capital is locked up
in the farm and this house.'

'Oh, there are plenty of investments to be divided. Mother

183

was very rich in her own right, you know. All of us should get thirty thousand pounds apiece, even after death duties are paid.'

'But you will be the richest,' said Christa, looking at him through her lashes.

'Yes, I must say it sounds a bit tough on Richard and Pip,' he said, and spread out his hands and glanced at his nails. 'But I am glad I've got Queen's Lacey.'

'It's a case of gross favouritism,' was what Christa wanted to say, but had no intention of uttering one word against the dead woman. She did, however, ask what the other two boys had had to say.

'Oh, Pip doesn't mind,' said Tony. 'He knows Queen's Lacey will always be his home for as long as he wants it, and his job here is safe.'

'And Richard?'

'I told him when he came in. Strange to say, he didn't seem in the least interested. In fact he said something about going back to Denmark. And he said I could have as much as I wanted of his share of the money to put back in Queen's Lacey. I thought that quite decent of him. But he's a queer chap.'

'And is he – going?' Christa's heart beat violently as she asked the question.

'There'll be the hell of a row if he quits home again,' said Tony. 'I need him here.'

She broke out:

'Why do you always want to pin people down? Why don't you let Richard stay abroad if he wants to?'

'People can't do just what they want in this world,' said Tony in his most pompous voice.

Then, because he was in a good mood – delighted with his legacy – he sat down on the edge of Christa's bed and took one of her hands in his. She shrank back and lay very still. It was the first time that Tony had made this kind of gesture towards her for long months. Now the old charm was being switched on, she thought, cynically, and in silence she received his attempts to kiss her.

'What about me coming back to sleep in this room?' he whispered. 'Let's try and be more friendly. When things are settled up with old Parsons, I'll buy you some clips or something. And I believe Mother has quite a lot of jewellery locked away in the bank, which she never wore; it will come in for you.'

The blood beat in her temples and whipped the red into her

cheeks. She felt a sudden violent anger against him. Tearing her hand away she sprang out of bed. As she put on her dressing-gown, she trembled, tying the girdle around her waist.

'Why should you think that the promise of diamond clips and your mother's jewellery should alter anything between us,' she asked in a furious voice. 'I'm not the sort of woman who can be bought. For months you haven't kissed me or shown any real friendly interest in me. You haven't had time for me. And in the days when I *wanted* to be kissed by you, you yawned yourself to sleep. Why should you think that I can be just picked up when *you* want me? You're the most abominably egotistical man I've ever met in my whole life! I thought you were different when I married you, but I know now what you're really like. Your mother hated me, and I think you do, really. Oh, go away and leave me alone, *please*,' she broke off, choking.

He stared at her, open-mouthed. He had neither the wits nor sufficient understanding of a woman's psychology to delve into the reasons for her words and behaviour. He thought her attack upon him undeserved and was deeply injured by it. And because of her rejection he did, indeed, feel a kind of hatred for her; beautiful and desirable though she was. Poor Mother had been right. He had made a poor choice.

He got up, smoothing back his hair. His face was red and his eyes held the look of a man who had been unpardonably offended.

'Very well – if that's how you feel, good night.'

He walked into his dressing-room and shut the door.

For Christa, it was the end. She knew that she could not sleep under this roof another night. She could not go on acting the part of Tony's wife and Julia Chalford's bereaved daughter-in-law. She could not go on seeing Richard at meal-times, knowing that he was here, yet separated from her by such an impassable barrier.

She wandered downstairs feeling feverish and ill. After a while she took two aspirins and tried to sleep. Tomorrow she would telephone Judy, and ask if she could go down to Devonshire and stay with the Masters for a few days. She was worn out. She must have rest and peace before facing a final break with Tony. Even if she wanted it, she knew that it would be no use trying to be reconciled with him. They were as far apart in spirit and understanding as the North and South Pole. Mrs. Chalford's death had not made matters better. In death, as in life, her spirit triumphed over Queen's Lacey and Tony would abide by her laws, quote her, speak of her, unendingly. It would only drive Christa mad. Besides, nothing would induce her to live with him as his wife again after tonight. She could not belong to a man who imagined that she could be coaxed back into the connubial embrace by the promise of jewellery. She had not sunk as low as that. Besides, nothing could wipe out her love for Richard. That in itself raised an impenetrable wall between her and Tony.

Tony spared her a scene because he made no attempt to try and bridge the gulf the next morning. He marched through her room without even looking at her. He did not come up again after his breakfast. Mitza told Christa that Herr Chalford had shut himself in his mother's room and was going through her private bureau.

Christa, who felt far from well but had no temperature this morning, said to the Austrian in a low voice:

'I'm going away this morning, Mitza.'

'Goot!' said the woman, 'that vill be goot for you.'

'But not on a holiday, Mitza. I'm going for good. I'm never coming back.'

Mitza's short-sighted eyes blinked at the girl. Her face reddened.

'*Nein!* Not possible,' she exclaimed.

Christa told her briefly that she had decided to leave her husband and his home in which she had been so unhappy.

'I'm sorry but I must. Try to forgive me, Mitza. I shall never forget you because you've been so good to me always.'

Mitza began to cry. Christa went to her and put her thin young arms around the ample figure. For a moment she, too, wept.

Later, in broken words, Mitza made it plain to Christa that she was not surprised by this news; that she knew that her *liebchen* was not happy. She knew, too, the reason why.

'What are you thinking?' asked Christa.

The Austrian woman sniffed and nodded.

'It is Mr. Richard, *ach Gott*, yes, I know.'

Christa put a hand to her lips.

'No, you mustn't say it, Mitza.'

'But it is true. Mitza knows. Mitza has watched. You haf been very unhappy. He unhappy is too, poor boy.' And her tears flowed afresh.

Then Christa covered her face with her hands and moaned:

'Mitza, Mitza, there's nothing to be done. He is my husband's brother. There is nothing to be done. Nobody must ever know, ever guess.'

'*Ach Gott*, it is so terrible,' whispered the older woman. 'I vill go with you if you will take me. I vill come and look after my *liebchen*. Without you and Mr. Richard at Queen's Lacey, I vill not here a moment longer stay.'

'Mitza, you are sweet, but I can't take you. I have no home and I have no money. I shall forfeit everything when I go. *Much* as I would like to have you, dear, dear Mitza, I can't.'

Mitza sobbed openly now. She would wait until Christa had a home and then she would go to her, she declared.

Christa said:

'On your oath, Mitza, you must never say a word of what you think about me and *him*.'

'On my vord,' said Mitza sadly and solemnly, and went off to her kitchen still weeping.

Christa started to pack. She packed all her clothes and her own treasures, but everything that Tony had given her of value, including the Norwegian fox stole that had been her wedding present, she left behind; also, Mrs. Chalford's pearls. She wanted to forget that she had ever belonged to the Chalford family. She did not even feel that she would miss this beautiful home that she had made out of this wing. Only one person meant anything to her ... Richard ... and he, too, would soon be gone. He could not remain here with his memories.

As soon as she was well enough, she would try to get a job in London. Divorce was out of the question for the moment. Neither she nor Tony could accuse each other of infidelity. But after three years he could, if he wished, obtain a decree on the grounds of desertion.

'Then he'll probably marry Ursula Corby,' thought Christa wryly. 'Ursula will be sorry for him. The whole district will pity him and think I'm frightful. My name will be linked with that of poor little Susan. We will both be called deserters. But I don't care. The only thing I can hope for now is peace.'

She finished her packing and went downstairs. Now she must see Richard and they must agree on what Tony was to be told.

Tessa came bounding across the hall. Christa stopped and fondled the long silky ears.

'Poor Tessa, poor girl, you'll miss your walkies. I've no home to take you to.'

Then through the window she saw Richard walking up from

187

the farm beside Pip. As the brothers came into the house – it was nearing lunch-time – Christa approached Richard and said:

'Could I have a word with you?'

'Of course,' he answered in a formal voice, but looked at her in surprise.

He and Pip were both hot and untidy. They had been on the land the whole morning. Pip announced that he was going to wash his grubby paws and slouched off. Still wearing his muddy boots, thought Christa, and wondered if Mrs. Chalford's spirit did not enter the hall and deplore the fact that already her many hard and fast little rules and regulations were being ignored.

Richard smoothed back his unruly hair and followed Christa into the drawing-room. He gave her a quick, penetrating look.

She wore a grey suit and had put on more make-up than was usual except when she went up to London. He saw too that she carried a pair of gloves and a bag.

'You're going somewhere?' he asked.

'Up to Town, and later down to my cousin Judy,' she said.

'I see. Well, I'm making my own arrangements to get back to Denmark,' he said. 'I would have gone today, myself, but there's a bit of trouble with the men and I must get them settled before I push off.'

She stared around her. Mitza, with Continental feeling about funeral ceremonies and mourning, had drawn all the blinds again, so that the room was dim. It smelt of dying flowers.

Richard wrinkled his nose, drew the curtains and opened the windows.

'For heaven's sake let's have some fresh air in here,' he muttered.

Christa said:

'I'm telling Tony after lunch, I haven't felt I could before. I might have done last night, but we had a misunderstanding.'

'As usual,' said Richard with a harsh laugh.

She seated herself on the arm of a chair. She felt extra-ordinarily weak and tired these days. The skirt of this suit which she had not put on for six months, was so loose, she had had to wear a belt in order to keep it up.

Richard handed her a cigarette and lit one for himself. They smoked in silence for a moment. The sun was shining and out in the garden the blackbirds called and bickered with each other. Christa could see Tessa on the lawn, gnawing a bone which

Mitza had just flung through the kitchen window. Christa said:

'I shall never come back. For me this is good-bye to Queen's Lacey.'

'I'm beginning to loathe the place,' said Richard, in a low voice. 'Every time I pass that barn door I think of *her*.'

Christa's fingers shook as they carried the cigarette to her mouth.

'I think of her too, but we must both try not to.'

'Do we tell Tony the truth – or do we not tell him?'

'What do *you* want, Richard? I want to do what you think best,' she said.

He looked into the big sad eyes. They made him yearn to reach out a hand and touch her hair – show her one gesture of tenderness and sympathy. She looked so lost, so broken this morning, sitting there in that suit that no longer fitted her.

He said:

'I've thought over things a good deal, too, and it's been difficult for me to reach a conclusion. We're both guilty and yet not guilty. It is not our fault that we grew to love each other. We tried to do the right thing, but we had bad luck. It was the one moment that my mother chose to be suspicious. She *had* to come out and look for us!'

'Oh, Richard,' said Christa. 'I wish to God it hadn't happened, more for your sake than mine.'

'Not much good wishing. I might just as well say that I wish you were not my sister-in-law.'

'What are we going to tell Tony?' she asked in a whisper.

'Nothing,' said Richard; 'that's what I've begun to believe is the best thing. It's just damned useless to tell him what we feel about each other. We might enjoy what is known as the luxury of confession, and to what purpose? It can't bring Mother back, and it can't give us the right to go away together. I'm still Tony's brother. Confession, if we made it, would only make matters worse for him. You say that you intended to leave him long before Mama died – very well – do so. You can do no good by staying, feeling as you do. It could only mean hell for you both. Better for him to have his freedom and the chance to marry again.'

'That's how I feel, Richard.'

'But what's left?' he broke out, and his eyes were full of bitter pain as they looked at her. 'It's all so damnable for you. Poor darling. I'd give my soul to take you in my arms.'

'Don't,' she whispered.

'I won't,' he gave a brief laugh, 'don't worry.'

She smoked in silence for a moment, sick with the desire to feel his touch once more upon her hair and his lips upon her mouth. At last, with great difficulty, she said:

'So we are to keep the silence.'

'Yes,' he said, 'and you know it's not because I want to shirk owning up to my part in this wretched affair. I'm willing to take whatever blame is due to me, but for Tony and Pip's sake, and the general feeling down here – I think it's better we shouldn't talk about what happened the other night.'

Her head drooped.

'Very well.'

'I must go. Good-bye, Christa,' Richard said in that harsh, unhappy voice that cut her like a knife. She cried under her breath:

'Don't say good-bye, just go quickly and leave me. I won't come to lunch. I *couldn't*. I'll stay in my room. Mitza will bring me something to eat if I want it. Then I'll send into Amersham for a taxi.'

'I'd just like to know where you're going to be,' he said, painfully.

'Tonight, and perhaps for a day or two, in London with our old next-door neighbours in the mews, Dana and Bill Grant. I rang them up and they have one tiny room they can squeeze me into. They seemed delighted. I'd rather be with them than anybody because they knew my mother so well. I don't want to rush down to Devonshire straight away. Judy's only a very distant cousin and I hardly know her parents. I would have to pretend with them. They'll be going away this weekend, I'd rather be with Bill and Dana until then.'

'I see,' said Richard, then he hunched his shoulders as she had seen him do so many times in the past with that devil-may-care look on his face; a 'small-boy defiant look', pretending that he had not been hurt. 'Well, it won't matter to me really, I won't be able to see you,' and he added, 'I don't know why I asked.'

She bowed her head again. Her desolation filled him with an anguish that made him feel that he had paid for every possible shred of guilt that could ever be attributed to him. To leave her alone, without solace, was a torture he had to brace himself to stand.

'God bless you, darling. Take care of yourself,' he said, 'it will be better if we don't see each other any more, but you know that I'll remember you every day for as long as I live.'

When she lifted her head again he had gone. She was alone in the big sunlit drawing-room, and there was no sound save the drone of an aeroplane high over Queen's Lacey.

It seemed to her that she died there, just where he left her. She could neither move nor think. After a few moments she got up and went to her own wing.

Tony seemed neither to notice or care that she was not at the lunch-table. It was Mitza who let her know that immediately after lunch he got out his car and went into Aylesbury. He had gone into the kitchen and informed Mitza that he would be back for tea, after which he did not want to be disturbed because he was still busy going through his mother's private papers. There were two big black boxes, Mitza told Christa, that 'Herr Chalford' and Mr. Pip had carried down from the attic. The 'Herr' was in a bad temper because he could not find the right keys for one of them.

'Queen's Lacey vill not be the same without you,' she said to Christa, mournfully, as she watched her shut and lock her suit-cases.

'*I* will never be the same.' Christa said with a short cynical laugh, and wondered if the white-faced young woman with the red-rimmed eyes who stared at her from the mirror could possibly be the same as the gay enthusiastic bride who had come here not quite three years ago.

She waited till everybody was out of the house. Then she wrote a letter to Tony. She was going to be a coward and shirk a personal scene with him. He had chosen to go to Aylesbury without a good-bye or an inquiry as to how she was. It was his fault if she was not here when he got back. She wrote:

> Dear Tony,
> By the time you get this I shall be in London. I do not intend to return. We haven't been getting on at all well lately and I feel that your mother's death has only widened the gap between us. I myself am terribly unhappy and feel you must be dissatisfied so I have decided to break up our marriage. I am afraid I have done nothing to warrant a divorce but eventually you can get a divorce on the grounds of my desertion. Meanwhile if you want me please write to me care of my mother's solicitor, William Brownrigg, whose address I enclose.
> I do not expect you to support me nor do I want any

191

*money from you. You will find everything of value that you
or your mother have given me in the top drawer of my dressing chest. I'm sorry it's worked out like this. I did try but you
didn't seem to notice.*

*I feel you will be much happier without me. Forgive me
for any unhappiness I may have caused you.*

She signed it 'Christa' and dropped her wedding-ring into
the envelope with the note. That, she thought, made it very
final.

She could imagine his astonishment and chagrin when he
found the ring and read that note, but if her going should upset
him it would be only because of his injured pride; of that she
was certain. He did not love her. He did not know *how* to love.
She was quite sure that he would not grieve for her, nor even
make an effort to get her back.

The big house seemed very silent and empty when she left in
that March afternoon. The sun had gone in and the wind had
freshened. It no longer felt like spring but a continuation of the
long winter. As she stood in the hall with her suitcases, waiting
for the hired car from Amersham, she looked about her, shivering. The house had never received her with warmth or welcome.
It seemed now to watch her departure with the same cold
indifference. She had never been part of Queen's Lacey, and it
had never accepted her. She loved beauty and antiquity and at
first had seen both at Queen's Lacey. But later, under the
façade, she had found nothing but the loneliness and misery of
an unhappy marriage.

Like a sad star shining in the gloom, the memory of Richard's
love for her and hers for him, still shimmered. That love had
grown and flourished like a single flower among the weeds that
had finally choked her. Poor flower of love, she thought. A few
moments of shared passion and tenderness and now only the
emptiness of the lonely years ahead.

Well, it was all over and at least she would never again have
to live through one of those interminable winters at Queen's
Lacey.

There was only Mitza to see her off – a weeping sniffling
Mitza who reiterated her wish to join Christa should she ever
get another home of her own.

Before Christa got into the car, she kissed the Austrian on
both cheeks, and whispered:

'Remember to keep my secret, Mitza dear, and look after

192

him until he goes away, and don't forget Tessa's food. Be sure to fill her bowl with fresh water every evening.'

As she drove away from the house, she began to feel that she was not really alive, and she could almost envy Julia Chalford her quiet place in the tomb. She did not allow herself so much as a glance at the great barn as she passed the old building with its lichened roof and the great clump of winter jasmine that flowered close to the door. She dared not remember the starlit night near the barn – and herself in Richard's arms. But tears blinded her eyes as she looked towards the fields, for in the distance she saw two men walking across the paddock where Julia Chalford's old mare was grazing. She thought that she recognized one of the figures as being Richard's.

Good-bye to him – to a passionate love that had taken a long while to mature and must now be ruthlessly torn out and allowed to wither. She whispered:

'God be with you, my love. . . .'

As soon as she reached London she went straight to Brownrigg's office in Lincoln's Inn. She had not seen or heard from him for some months but she had telephoned from Queen's Lacey earlier this morning and made this appointment. She thought she would like his help and advice about a divorce from Tony. She also wanted him to look into her financial state. She still had a little of her own money – the income received from the original sale of The Greenhouse and the lease of Mummy's cottage – with the small dividends from investments left by her father. Then there was the couple of thousand Aunt Claire had left her, when she died.

She would not have much – but enough to live on in a quiet way. The sooner she got a job, the better, Christa told herself.

Mr. Brownrigg received his client kindly. He was an oldish man who had known Christa's parents well. When he heard her story he was discreetly sympathetic, but tried dutifully to talk her into giving her marriage another chance. But Christa was not to be influenced.

'There is absolutely no chance of a reconciliation,' she said quietly. 'My husband and I have never got on and it was a mistake from the start.'

'A pity,' said Mr. Brownrigg, and coughed. 'You're still both so young and when I met him I thought Chalford rather a nice fellow.'

'He has great charm when he likes to exert it,' said Christa in a bitter voice.

'Mind you, I know your dear mother never cared much for him,' added the lawyer.

'No,' said Christa in a low voice, 'she didn't. But people in love can be frightfully pig-headed, you know.'

'Well, well, let's take a look at our financial position,' said Mr. Brownrigg.

The end of the interview was unsatisfactory for the lawyer, because Christa was obstinate and refused to ask Tony for support even though she might be entitled to it. Even if he *offered it*, she said, which she did not think, in the circumstances, he would do. Her leaving him would cause a scandal in the district, and for that, alone, Tony would not forgive her.

She added to Mr. Brownrigg:

'If you don't intend to live with a man any more, you have no right to ask him to support you, have you?'

Mr. Brownrigg smiled at her over his spectacles and sighed.

'I wish *some* of the wives of my gentlemen clients thought as you do,' he said dryly.

When Christa left the office it was with the knowledge that she was at least a little better off financially than she had imagined. As soon as she was quite well and could think clearly, she would work.

Meanwhile, she was going to relax for a day or two in the company of that darling pair, Bill and Dana. She remembered how Tony had disapproved of them and called them 'arty-crafty' and 'scruffy'.

They welcomed her with open arms. Dana had tremendous news. *She was going to have a baby*. It would spoil her figure, she said, but she didn't care. And it would mean that eventually she and Bill would have to leave the mews and find something bigger, and perhaps not so attractive, but she did not care about that either.

'Bill's tickled to death at the idea of being a daddy,' she said. 'He's already started to compose songs to it. He's a scream. One night it's *my little boy is father's joy*! – and the next night, *my darling daughter who didn't oughter*, etc!'

'It's going to be the hell of a kid,' put in Bill, with a grin. 'Only we can't agree on names. However, now you've come back into our lives it's all settled. You shall be the godmother and if it's a girl we shall call her *Christa*.'

'I shouldn't if I were you,' said Christa, 'it's obviously not a lucky name. Although I'd adore to be the godmother, and I'll save up for a really lovely mug.'

194

Already – within an hour of being in that cottage, she began to feel relaxed. The tension eased. The pain and the horror of the last few days became less unbearable. It was almost as though she were next door, back with Mummy, in that free and easy atmosphere of good comradeship, of artistic appreciation.

Queen's Lacey ... gracious, beautiful old place in the most beautiful of grounds ... with all its wonderful pastureland ... and the splendid prosperous farm ... one would have thought it an enviable possession, and that in leaving-it, she was robbing herself of something worth keeping. Instead of which the mere memory of Queen's Lacey set her shuddering, and here in this uncomfortable, untidy funny little cottage with Bill sitting at his piano (sheets of music all over it) and Dana in slacks and jersey, coming in and out from the tiny kitchen, peeling a potato as she walked and making silly friendly remarks ... she was at home.

Through tear-filled eyes, Christa looked out of the window and craned her neck to see the next-door house that had once been her own home. It was changed. The window-boxes which had been Mummy's pride, once filled with pink geraniums and fuchsias, were sadly neglected and full of weeds. Instead of Mummy's pretty frilly curtains, she could see a sad choice of dreary cretonne.

When she went upstairs to unpack, Dana and Bill grimaced at each other.

'My God,' whispered Dana, 'did you ever see such a change in any human being? Poor angel, we must try to cheer her up.'

'Yes, I agree she certainly looks crushed,' said Bill, 'though I thought I saw a flicker of the old humour just now.'

'That's because she's with us. I gather she went through hell in the country.'

Bill sat down on his piano stool and ran his fingers over the keys.

'I'm not surprised. I thought that chap, Tony, the most ghastly pompous prig I've ever met. So did you.'

'He was very good looking. That's about all.'

'To hell with good looks if there's nothing more,' said Bill, and for some unfortunate reason best known to himself, began to play tunes from *Kismet*, which he and Dana had been to see last night, having been presented with stalls by a friend who was in the show. He was playing *Stranger in Paradise* very emotionally, when into the room came Christa, her face rather white, and her eyes large and tragic.

195

'Darling Bill – do you mind not playing *that* . . . just not that one . . . anything else you like. It may seem silly but I just don't want to hear *Stranger in Paradise*.'

'Okay, sweetie,' said Bill cheerfully, and switched into another melody.

'Idiotic of me,' said Christa, and with an apologetic smile at Dana went out of the room again.

Dana whispered in her husband's ear:

'Now I *know* . . . there's another man in her life . . . and he's connected with that tune. Mark my words, Bill, it isn't only that she didn't get on with Tony Chalford. There's *another* man.'

Bill touched his wife's cheek with a forefinger.

'My little psychologist! It's wonderful how women always smell a romance.'

Dana kissed the top of his head. She wrinkled her nose at him as she marched towards the kitchen.

'I must say it's ever so romantic being "preggers",' she called out, 'I can't get into my one and only suit. How will you like me in an ever-so-gay smock this winter?'

'I shall adore it, darling, just as I adore you,' he said, banged out two chords, and then began to scribble some notes on a blank sheet of manuscript on top of the piano.

Dana went into the kitchen muttering:

'Poor darling Christa. I expect she'll tell me all about it later on.'

But Dana was doomed to disappointment. Christa did not tell her. But she seemed quite peaceful and contented, sharing their supper, and afterwards listening to the music that Bill had composed for his unborn child. But there were two things that she refused to do; either to sing or to talk about herself. She seemed to be exceptionally tired. She went early to bed.

CHAPTER SEVEN

EARLY next morning when Bill had gone to Lime Grove and Christa was helping Dana wash up the breakfast things, the telephone rang. Dana answered and held out the receiver to her guest.

'It's for you, sweetie.'

'Who is it?'

Dana inquired, then made a funny face at Christa.

'*Monsieur votre mari*,' she said in a dramatic whisper and with a vile French accent.

Christa flushed. She had slept well last night because she had been so utterly exhausted. She felt calmer and better able to face life this morning. She had wondered whether Tony would try to get in touch with her and made up her mind that if he did, she wouldn't speak to him. But Tony insisted on her coming to the telephone.

Giggling under her breath, Dana passed the receiver over to Christa.

'His Highness says will you have the goodness to speak to him if only out of common courtesy.'

'How like him,' muttered Christa.

When she had awakened in the Grants' tiny guest-room this morning and heard the sound of a milk van rolling down the mews and all the familiar sounds of Chelsea, she had felt Queen's Lacey to be far away; almost as though she had never lived there. Now Tony's voice, ice cold, haughtier than usual, dragged her back.

'I guessed you might be with your friends in the mews,' he said. 'I didn't ring last night because I was much too upset.'

'I'm sorry,' said Christa.

'Of course you can't mean to leave me,' went on Tony, 'this is just a piece of childish nonsense.'

'But I *do* mean to leave you. I've *left*!' said Christa.

She heard him click his tongue against his teeth in the way his mother used to do when she was annoyed.

'Don't be ridiculous, Christa,' he snapped. 'Why *should* you want to leave me?'

Even now, after nearly three years with him, she was amazed by his lack of perception or understanding.

'I really can't go into a long discussion, Tony,' she said. 'I think you know. I summed it all up in the note I left you when I said we just don't get on.'

'That may be, but it's no excuse for divorce. No possible excuse.'

Then she said with difficulty:

'You may think so. I have other reasons.'

'There can't be another man in the picture,' he said, 'because you don't know any.'

Christa clenched her hands. Her face was white now.

'Very well, I don't know any, and there *isn't* a man in it. All the same, I'm not coming back to you. Nothing will make me change my mind, so don't waste your breath.'

He began to lose his temper. He shot a dozen questions at her. What had he ever done to deserve such treatment? How dared she think that she could walk out on him and her commitments just because she wasn't happy? What would the district think? Didn't she realize that there would be a ghastly scandal; that she was making a fool of *him* as well as herself, and that even if there wasn't another man in the picture people would say there was, and so on.

When he paused to draw breath, Christa said:

'I'm very sorry. Everything you say may be right but the fact remains that nothing will induce me to come back to Queen's Lacey. Not only do we disagree but you are completely wrapped up in the farm, and *your* life as you want to lead it. You have absolutely no time for me or my affairs, I've literally withered down there with you for three years, and I don't intend to wither any more.'

She added that she was going to get a job as soon as she could and lead her old existence.

'You won't get a penny from me ...' began Tony, furiously.

'I haven't asked you for money,' she broke in. 'But I'd be obliged if you'd send that list of my investments, and any other papers you have of mine, to Mr. Brownrigg. I left you his address.'

'Look here, Christa,' came Tony's voice, 'I give you one more chance. You either come back to Queen's Lacey this afternoon and put an end to this monstrous idiocy, or you *never* come back.'

'I'm sorry, Tony. Good-bye,' she said.

She hung up the receiver, shaking. The peace, the pleasure of being here with the Grants, had gone again. That short, sharp conversation with Tony had brought back all the mad irritation and bitterness of their marriage; of her hopeless efforts to please him.

'I can't go back,' she thought, 'I *can't*.'

It was quite obvious that if she did, it would be not to a kind, understanding, forgiving husband but to a tyrant who stood firmly in the shoes of his dead mother. And, of course, he didn't know the truth – that was the worst part of it all. He did not think there was 'a man in it'. She felt guilty about *that*. O, Richard, O mon roi, where are you, Richard? What are you *doing this morning? How do you feel? When are you going away?*

She tried hard not to think too much about Richard or Queen's Lacey. She spent the morning shopping – after lunch, she lay down and tried to sleep. At least, her cough was better. The air at Coleshill was too strong, too cold for her. It seemed a paradox but dear old foggy London suited her; always had done.

At four o'clock an unexpected visitor arrived. Astonished and a little perturbed, Christa opened the door of the cottage (Dana was in the bathroom) to find Pip standing at the door. She ushered her youngest brother-in-law into the cottage and instinctively raised her face for his kiss. Pip was the only one at Queen's Lacey who ever used to kiss her in his youthful friendly way.

'I'm very glad to see you,' she said, 'you're just in time for tea.'

'I can't stay – I mean, just for a few minutes,' he said awkwardly, and looked around the Grants' untidy room with his blue stare. Then he added:

'As a matter of fact I quit the farm and dashed up because I felt that I *had* to see you.'

'What is it, Pip?' she asked.

He balanced himself on the arm of the sofa and put his pipe between his teeth. He looked terribly embarrassed she thought pityingly. He was so immature. He had been for too long the willing slave and echo of his mother and elder brother. He asked:

'Is it true that you've left Tony, Chris?'

'Yes.'

'Oh, I say!' he exclaimed.

'I expect you're shocked. You think I'm an awful woman, but I just had to do it. Try to forgive me, Pip, I'm glad you've come to see me so that I can tell you how grateful I am for all your kindness. I didn't see a lot of you, but you were always sweet to me.'

He dragged off the muffler he was wearing. His ears were scarlet.

'I'm jolly sorry about it,' he said. 'I liked you awfully.'

'Did you, Pip?' Christa put a hand on his shoulder and felt the tears sting her eyelids. 'Thank you dear,' she added.

'I know it wasn't always easy for you with my mother, and Tony's damned difficult to get on with.'

'Never mind. It's over now.'

'But I say, it *will* be grim down at Queen's Lacey without you. And Mother dead, too.'

'Oh, Pip, I'm sorry,' she said, with a rush of genuine feeling for him. He looked so lonely and so out of place in this tiny cottage. If anybody was a born farmer it was Pip. He was much more in character in one of his tractors, smoking that pipe and with his curls blowing in the wind. He was like Tony in colouring, and yet so unlike ... so much more simple and genuine. He had none of Tony's arrogance.

'I hate to think of you being sad and lonely at Queen's Lacey,' she said, 'but what can I do? I can't stick it down there any more.'

'You see,' said Pip mournfully, 'even Rich is quitting again. It was rotten without him before. Now it's worse. Nothing's going to be the same.'

She had to brace herself not to show what she felt as she heard that name.

'How is – Richard?'

'Tony thinks he's gone peculiar, and so do I. He hasn't a word to say for himself. Sort of dug-in and dumb.'

Christa turned away. She stared out of the window. The March day was drawing to an end. Outside, it was cold and misty, with a drizzle of rain.

'When is he off?'

'Oh,' said Pip, 'so *you* know he's going away?'

'Yes.'

'Well, I think he means to get off next week. Tony's livid – biting everybody's head off. I'm afraid you haven't been very happy with us, Christa.'

'I dare say I'm to blame as well as Tony,' she said. 'I never should have married him. We weren't suited.'

'Well, if you'd been my wife I'd have tried to make you happy,' said Pip, very red in the face. 'I think old Tony is a B.F.'

'You're sweet,' said Christa, swallowing.

'I admire you awfully,' he stumbled on, 'and the place won't be the same without you. Mitza's been blubbing ever since you left.'

Christa thought:

'If only he had a message for me from Richard. If only he'd brought me some kind of contact. And soon I won't know where Richard is or how ... I'll be completely cut off from him. It hurts so terribly ... almost more than I can bear.'

200

'Well, I'd better be going,' sighed Pip. 'I really came up to ask you if you couldn't come back.'

'I'm sorry I can't.'

'I was afraid you wouldn't.' Pip picked up his muffler and fingered it miserably.

'As soon as you've got someone to replace Richard you must try and go away and take that holiday with your friends,' Christa said gently. 'You'll meet some nice girl and get married soon, I hope.'

'Well, if I do, I'll jolly well see that we have a home of our own,' muttered Pip.

'Very sensible of you,' said Christa, with a short laugh.

'I didn't tell Tony I was coming,' Pip added, 'but I told Richard.'

Her heart jolted:

'What did he say?'

'He said to leave you alone and mind my own business and that I'd only worry you. I think although he didn't show it much, that *he* admired you, too.'

The tears were blinding her now. She leaned up, kissed Pip on both cheeks and said:

'Better go home, Pip. Try not to be too upset. Try to forgive me. Remember me kindly.'

'Of course I will,' he said, and kissed her back; 'will you get a divorce or something?'

'Eventually, I expect.'

'Well, you're so jolly pretty, I bet you'll meet some chap and marry again.'

She turned away, blowing her nose, trying to dab the tears from her eyes.

'I shan't do that, Pip.'

'Any messages for them at home?' he asked from the doorway.

Silence. Then, with difficulty, she said:

'I don't think it will serve any useful purpose for you to tell Tony that you've been here, but you might give Richard my love, will you?'

'Okay,' said Pip.

'And, Pip, if you ever want a friend or I can do anything for you – do please let me know. You can phone or write here care of my friends, the Grants.'

'I know,' he said, 'Mitza gave me the address and I will keep in touch with you.'

'Give my love to Mitza and – Tess. Take Tess for a walk sometimes, will you?'

'Okay,' said Pip again, and went out, closing the front door behind him.

She heard him start the car. He had brought up the station wagon. She watched it from the window, shivering a little. It conjured up so many memories of unhappy drives with her late mother-in-law. Those awful dreary excursions into Slough or Aylesbury on market days; biting cold in the winter. And somewhere in the ploughed fields, or in and out of the farmhouse, the figure of Richard drawing her like a magnet; bringing her the deepest joy and the most searing pain. She was astonished how much the visit from Pip unnerved her.

It was about the same time on the next day that the unexpected and dramatic happened and once more altered the whole face of destiny for Christa.

Bill and Dana were out. Dana had gone to a clinic that she was visiting regularly these days.

Christa was cleaning up. She thought it high time somebody introduced a little law and order into the overcrowded and neglected sitting-room. Dana was sweet as honey and a wonderful cook, but no good at cleaning. Christa could put up with disorder, but cleanliness was to her an essential. Dust had settled over the records and music piled up in one corner. Cobwebs clung to the books. The carpet was moth-eaten in one corner. Christa was busy dusting a few volumes when that telephone call came through.

'Hullo,' she answered the call, flushed and breathless from her exertions.

'Christa, is that you?' said a man's deep voice.

Now she felt as though an electric shock passed through her being. Duster suspended in one slim hand, she whispered:

'Richard!'

'Yes.'

'Where are you?'

'In London!'

'London,' she repeated, dizzy with sudden joy and anguish.

'Yes, I want to see you at once.'

'Oh, no,' she began. 'No darling, we decided not to. We must try to stick to it. It'll only upset us both.'

'When we made that decision things were different. I've got the most incredible, stupendous news for you.'

'Oh – what?'

202

'I can't tell you on the phone. I must see you.'

'But what is it?' she repeated wildly. 'What can you possibly have to tell me that could alter the situation?'

'Meet me somewhere, and you'll soon know.'

She thought dazedly for a moment then said:

'You'd better come here. My friends are out. Dana has only just gone. We shall have an hour alone at any rate, if not more. Where are you?'

'At the Blue Star Garage in the King's Road. I stopped for petrol. You aren't far from here, are you?'

'No, just a couple of minutes down towards the Classic Cinema. You turn right there and you'll see Clarion Mews. On the left is a little red-bricked house with a yellow-painted door, next to a double garage that has yellow doors too. I'll be looking out for you.'

'Right,' he said, and hung up.

Christa sat down in a chair. Her legs refused to support her. A sweat had broken out over her. Her heart thumped madly. This was the last thing she had expected. Richard in Town, and he would be here in a few moments. *Oh, God, why?* What could possibly have happened to make him come up here today to see her? But at the mere thought of hearing his voice, touching his hand, a wild ecstasy shot through her. Forbidden ecstasy it might be, but not to be denied. Christa suddenly rushed upstairs. She washed hands and face, combed back her hair and put on some make-up. She finished by dabbing a little perfume behind each ear. The eternal female, she thought, wryly, out to seduce the male, but what woman did not want to look her best for the man she loved?

A few moments later she heard a car turn into the mews. She looked out of the tiny window and saw Richard's car. He was stepping out of it. He was hatless but wore an old tweed coat over a greyish check suit in which she had often seen him in the evenings at Queen's Lacey. As he turned towards the front door she saw his face now – that darkly tanned face that had grown so lean, so much older of late. The wind stirred a dark lock of hair that brought back a thousand memories of Richard and her desperate love for him.

She ran down the stairs, cheeks burning, and opened the front door.

CHAPTER EIGHT

THEY sat opposite each other in the Grants' studio. Richard was smoking. He was obviously nervous and strung up. There was an undercurrent of excitement about the way he spoke and moved his hands and so rapidly smoked that ciga-rette. It communicated itself to Christa and set her own pulses racing, just as the first sight of him had done. When they had met they had not so much as touched hands. She had just said:

'Hullo.'

And he looked long and deeply into her eyes and had answered:

'Hullo, Christa . . .' then followed her into the sitting-room.

Here he was now, telling her what had brought him here and why he had broken his pledge never to see her again.

What he had to say seemed out of the bounds of possibility, yet was real and possible. It held her speechless. She listened with tremendous interest, keeping her gaze upon him – savour-ing, weighing up every word.

It seemed that Tony had spent most of last night reading through papers and documents that he had found in those two deed boxes that had lain in that attic for years. None of the three boys had known of their existence. The secret that lay locked in one of them had been well kept. The thing that none of them could understand, Richard told Christa, was why Julia Chalford had ever preserved those papers, for they were evi-dence of a secret which she had rigorously kept from the world for more than twenty-six years. There could be only one excuse for her not having destroyed such evidence, Richard said – the woman who had appeared to remorselessly cold and logical, still had possessed certain feminine weaknesses. Women, more than men, seem reluctant to tear up letters no matter how dangerous or destructive.

This strange woman who had reared three boys, been wid-owed young, and run and organized their lives and her own with such machine-like efficiency, had had her 'skeleton in the cupboard' yet never destroyed the key of the locked door. Perhaps she had meant to do so before she died, but like many before her, took it for granted that she was not yet near the grave. Then sudden death had come early and defeated her purpose. *And now, Richard knew that he was not her son.* He was not even a Chalford. He had no right to that name, except by adoption. The woman whom he had called 'mother' was in fact, his aunt.

When Richard first broke this extraordinary news to Christa, she put her hands to her cheeks and gasped.

'It isn't true!'

'It is true,' he nodded and tapped his coat pocket. 'I have every proof of it here, if I wish to make use of it.'

'But how – why—?' Christa broke off as though she could not get out the words.

He told her.

Tony had sent for him late last night, tossed these documents into his lap and told him the truth, with a lack of kindliness or tact which might be called typical of Tony.

'He never cared how much he hurt other people. He didn't care what this thing would mean to me or how it would affect me,' said Richard grimly. 'The fact that it was no particular blow but very much the reverse, was coincidental. He could not guess that. He just said: "This is a very grave matter and it concerns you. I suppose my mother never intended that you should know, but I think she was wrong. I don't think she should have kept it from you. So – here it is." '

And 'it' was a collection of vital letters including a diary which had been kept at the crucial time by Julia's sister, Marianne. This contained vital information concerning Richard's birth.

Richard did not go to bed last night. Hour after hour he sat up sorting through the papers, piecing information together, devouring the pathetic diary.

'Kept by my Aunt Marianne who was in fact my mother – my poor little mother,' said Richard, and Christa saw his lips compress as though the mention of it pained him. She could see that he had been under a very great strain. There were deep lines under his eyes. He looked deadly tired. Yet there was that strange air of excitement about him – of discovery, which might, Christa thought, surround any man who stands upon the brink of a new adventure.

He went on talking.

'I'll tell you the story briefly although it is a long one, then you can see all these papers and read it for yourself, but I want you to hear from me as quickly as possible, what it is all about.'

He had always known (they had all known, of course) that
Julia Chalford had once had a sister, two years younger than
herself. They had also known that their aunt's name was Marianne which, the boys had thought, was rather attractive. She
had died (so Julia had told them) before Richard was born.
They none of them remembered ever having seen a photograph
of her. Then in the old deed box with the rusted padlock that
Tony forced – he had discovered surprising revelations and a
photograph which Richard now handed to Christa.

'Here's evidence for you,' he said with a short laugh, that held
a note of pleasure. 'Have you ever seen such a likeness? It
stands out even for me as though I see my own face in a
mirror.'

Christa looked at the pictured face. It was of a youngish girl
with short curly hair and eyes that were Richard's – those long-
lidded handsome eyes full of sparkle and gaiety. Richard had
her short, straight nose, too. It was a photograph taken perhaps
thirty years ago, but looked quite modern because Marianne
wore a silk dress with a floral pattern which might belong to any
period. She had a long slender neck and her chin rested on one
hand which was delicate with pointed finger-tips. She certainly
bore no resemblance to her sister, Julia, except perhaps for
those well-shaped hands.

'Julia was auburn-haired and had those freckles which spoilt
her. This girl – my little mother' – again he spoke those words
tenderly, 'doesn't look the freckled kind, does she?'

'No,' said Christa in a low voice, 'she must have been too
beautiful, and you are the image of her. But I don't understand.
What does it all mean?'

Richard continued. Twenty-seven years ago, Marianne, who
had still been living with her father in Kent – it was just before
he died – had had a love-affair. It was her first, with a young
officer, once in the R.A.F. In her little diary, she described him –
the man whom Richard now knew to be his father. He read a
few lines aloud to the amazed Christa.

*'I met my True Love today and knew that he was to be the
beginning and end of the world for me. His colouring is that
combination I have always admired, very blue eyes, very
black hair and a wonderful smile. He is a gay, wonderful person, full of vigour and sweetness, and with Irish blood in him.
His name is Tim Riley – he was Squadron-Leader Riley. He's*

*as brave as he is attractive. He is a test pilot now – attached to
some aeroplane factory. It would be awful to be in love with
such a man or to be married to him, and have to wonder
every time he took up a new plane whether he would ever
come back or not. The strain would be too terrible. . . .'*

Richard looked up at Christa.

'So now I know,' he said. 'I'm not the son of old Anthony
Chalford but of Tim Riley, afterwards described by Aunt Marianne – my mother – as an impoverished young man with no
background, poorish parents in Dublin and no money beyond
his pay.'

'I am not surprised,' said Christa softly, 'to hear that your
father was brave and gay like yourself.'

The rest of the diary, he told her, was the outpouring of a
romantic, tender girl, deeply in love with Tim Riley, whom she
had met at a local dance while staying with friends in the district. It described her father's displeasure. She must also have
received many disapproving, menacing letters from her sister,
Julia, who was at that time married and living at Queen's
Lacey. Her first baby, Tony, had been born.

Marianne's letters were in the deed box. Richard unfolded
and read one of them aloud to Christa.

*'Oh, Julia, why do you and Daddy dislike people just be-
cause they haven't any money. What makes you both so sure
that money and position are the only things that count in life!
Sometimes I don't really feel I am your sister. You're so hard
and mercenary. You and Daddy dislike Tim just because he
has nothing to offer me. But if I were of age I would marry
him now. I know Mummy would have been in sympathy with
me. She was like me – she cared much more for love than
£ s. d. But she's dead and I have no one. And Tim won't take
me away because Father is rich and prosperous and he has
nothing. You and Daddy have given him an inferiority complex and I'm not of age. I'm not surprised. . . .'*

Richard looked through half-shut eyes at Christa.

'You see how it all links up? It's so easy to imagine now. The
woman I called "mother" was hard – mad about money and
power even when she was a girl. But my poor little mother was
like grannie, and I've often heard *her* described as a silly old
fool. . . .'

'But, Richard,' broke in Christa, 'before you go any further, tell me why this was kept a secret from you.'

'I'm coming to that,' he said.

Tim Riley had continued to meet Marianne in secret. Her diary and letters were full of anguish, describing the many times they tried to say good-bye and could not. Marianne's vain appeals to her father to allow her to marry – and to Julia to help her – were all rejected. Then came the awful day when Tim met the death she had so often dreaded. He had crashed whilst testing a new aircraft. So she lost forever her first, her one and only love.

Now the letters and the diary grew deeply tragic. Just before the fatal crash Marianne and Tim had made up their minds to run away; to cast themselves on the mercy of a court if need be, and hope that the judge would take their side and grant them permission to marry. In an agonized effort to gain her freedom and her husband, poor Marianne had given herself entirely to her lover. She was going to have a child. She did not dare tell her father, but wrote to her sister Julia:

'I know you will despise me and call it weak and wicked, but I loved Tim and meant to marry him. For God's sake help me. You are my sister, all I have. I don't want to bring distress on the family name. Help me, do.'

That letter had been addressed to Queen's Lacey Farm. Then came others, grateful and relieved. Julia seemed to have shown herself human enough to listen to that desperate appeal. She had promised to help. Possibly, Richard told Christa, Julia's fear of scandal played a part in promoting the act of mercy which she extended to her unfortunate young sister.

Julia had confided only in her husband who was a weak man entirely under her thumb, ready to do anything that she deemed best. He agreed when Julia planned to take a trip by sea to Australia accompanied by Marianne. The visit was to be described to their father 'for health reasons'. What Julia intended to do about the coming child neither Richard nor anybody knew. The facts were not contained among the papers. But Marianne's scribbles gave him enough information to be able to piece the rest of the story together.

The child, a boy, *himself*, was born in a remote town fifty miles out of Melbourne. Marianne's diary contained a vivid description of that affair. Her anguished pleasure at the birth of

208

hers and Tim's son; the one remaining link with her dead lover. But it was a pleasure that turned to bitter pain because Julia, at once cool and practical and as unsympathetic as usual, informed Marianne that she could not be allowed to keep her baby. Julia had laid careful plans. She would return to England with the infant and announce that it was her own. Tony's father had his orders and had already announced to relatives and friends that Julia was expecting another child. She would take the little boy, whom they named Richard, back to England as her own, providing that Marianne disclaimed him entirely, and never told her father the truth. There was to be no scandal. She would bring Richard up with Tony.

There appeared to have been quite a bitter struggle between the sisters on this matter. Julia's first intention had been to leave the child behind them in Australia and wipe out all traces of him. But Marianne had held firm and said that unless Julia would give little Richard a chance in life and let him grow up as a Chalford – she would refuse to abandon him and she would let everybody know the facts. Richard was her flesh and blood – as well as Tim's. Their father's grandson. She could not have him left like a piece of driftwood, in a strange country. . . .

So Julia – reluctantly no doubt – consented to adopt him and the boy was christened in the name of Chalford. The voyage home commenced. Telegrams had, of course, been sent to Coleshill. Julia's friends expected her home after eight months' absence, with 'Anthony's little brother'. After this, whatever happened, Julia had no choice. She could not retract her promise.

'And after this,' Richard told Christa, 'it is more difficult to follow the story, because my poor little mother's diary broke off very suddenly.' She described her departure from Australia and her difficult, painful effort to regard Richard as a nephew instead of a son, and of getting used to seeing him in Julia Chalford's arms, and hearing people congratulate Julia on her 'fine new boy'. She did write that she had no doubts at least, that Richard would be well taken care of, because her sister made an excellent mother.

Richard could only guess at the tragic finale – the fact that his mother must have been taken ill and buried at sea, because among the papers he found a cable from the old father to Julia while still on board ship – expressing his sorrow at 'the shocking news of little Marianne's sudden death'. There were other relics such as formal notes expressing deep regret from relatives and friends at home. One which Julia had kept was from a neighbour near Queen's Lacey. It gave Richard a strong clue as to what had happened.

'It is always shocking' (she had written) *'when a young, beautiful person like your sister dies suddenly, and of an unsuspected heart condition. How terrible and mournful that funeral at sea must have been! I can imagine it all, but thank God you have your new dear little baby to comfort you....'*

Richard read this aloud to Christa, and gave a grim laugh. 'I was the comfort,' he said. 'Well, now you know all. I was never really a comfort to Mother (I must get out of the habit of calling her that, mustn't I?). She carried out her promise to my mother – she made little difference between me and Tony, and Pip who came afterwards. She even divided her money equally between us. According to her lights she was a good woman and one who kept her word. And, no doubt, my mother's death on board was a real and painful shock to her, and made her more than ever determined to do her best for her sister's flesh and blood. But it must have been even more painful to her in the years that followed, to watch me growing up so like her sister. And now I understand why there was no real link between us, and why she never gave me the real love and sympathy that she felt for her own two sons.'

Christa exclaimed:

'Good heavens, but it is a *fantastic* story!'

Richard tapped the documents on his lap.

'They say that truth is stranger than fiction. Here is the proof of that saying.'

'But wouldn't you have thought that Mrs. Chalford would have burned every letter, every document before leaving Melbourne?'

'We shall never know why she didn't,' said Richard. 'But she was obviously strangely reluctant to destroy the proofs of my true identity.'

'So you're not a Chalford at all—' began Christa.

'By adoption only,' he cut in. 'It was all done legally and with the thoroughness and precision one expected of Aunt Julia. As for my so-called grandfather, he died soon after our return from Australia. I never really knew him. But I have grown up as the brother of Tony and Pip. They are in fact, my cousins and I am illegitimate. All the same, it isn't disagreeable to me to know that my father was a test pilot, a man who was more human, if less virtuous, than the Chalfords. This accounts for so much, doesn't it, Christa? The *complete* difference between Tony and myself, for instance.'

Christa nodded.

'Yes, the more one thinks of it the more it explains a hundred and one little things. But I can't get used to the idea.'

'Imagine how *I* felt when Tony first enlightened me.'

Christa put a hand to her throat. She said:

'What did he say to you? How does he feel about it?'

'Tony,' said Richard, 'remained true to type. He was cold and polite but he began at once to treat me as though I was a distant cousin and not his brother. But do *you* understand the full implication of this?' Richard added, with a searching look at her.

Silence a moment. A van drove through the mews, hooting noisily. Christa's gaze rested upon Richard's brown face. What she saw in his eyes made her heart feel as though it leapt in her breast.

'Oh!' she said under her breath, and again, *'Oh!'*

He leaned forward and took both her hands, pressing them between his.

'Yes, my dear – I am not Tony's brother. I am only a half-cousin and you and I are no relation. I feel now also that I am nothing to Tony and that I owe him nothing.'

Under her breath, Christa whispered:

'Richard, *Richard.'*

He stood up, pulling her on to her feet. He took her in his arms.

'I am an outsider and not a Chalford,' he said. 'I have a right to ask you to go away with me, and I am going to ask it. My darling, it is quite impossible for me to feel any further allegiance to Tony. I have never liked him nor has he liked me. Because we thought we were brothers, and grew up together, we behaved as such, but underneath we have been enemies. It cannot be right to take away another man's wife and from that sin I will not try to exonerate myself. I only know that Tony is the wrong man for you, and that you have been bitterly unhappy. So I ask it. Will you come away with me now and let me try to make you happy? I do swear I will spend the rest of my life trying to do that thing.'

She could not speak. Emotion had got the better of her and

211

she was weeping. She clung to him, great sobs tearing her slight body. He kissed and comforted her, smoothing back the silver beauty of the hair that had always seemed to him so miraculous. He kept saying:

'Don't cry, my love. Don't cry, my darling love. I love you so much and it's such a *terrific* relief to me to know that I am no longer bound to Tony by the ties of brotherhood. Of course, the world will condemn us. We shall stand condemned in the eyes of all those who have ever known us. That I deplore for your sake. Will it matter to you very much?'

She raised her face.

'No, it won't matter at all. Nothing does now, except you. I broke my heart when I said good-bye to you. I had nothing to look forward to but loneliness and despair. To be divorced on your account won't seem a very great misery. It won't even seem wrong, because I believe that it is a greater wrong for two people who do not love each other, and are so fundamentally wrong for each other, as Tony and I are, to stay together. If I had had children I *would* have stayed. I do not think a woman has a right to leave her children, and make them pay for their parents' incompatibility. But, thank God, Tony and I have no family.'

Richard took her hand and kissed it.

'You're right. We have only ourselves to think of.'

She added with a deep sigh:

'If Tony wasn't so monstrously egotistical I'd be sorry for him. It won't be pleasant for him.'

'But you give me permission to tell him now?'

She answered without hesitance.

'Yes, of course. And I'm willing to take my share of the blame.'

'You're very beautiful,' he said, 'and very brave, too.'

'Oh, Richard,' she said, and pressed her eyes against his shoulder, because they were filling with hot tears again, 'how wonderful, how *wonderful* that this has happened!'

He stroked her hair tenderly.

'It does take the sting out of things, doesn't it? But we have much to regret. I shall never stop being sorry that poor Mother – poor Aunt Julia – died because of that night. . . .'

'Don't think of it,' broke in Christa, '*never* think of it. It was a terrible thing but we *were* intending to do our duty. *She* will know that now, if indeed it is true that those who die see and hear and understand all. *She* will surely know that we *did* want

212

to do what was right, and that we were not as bad as she imagined.'

Richard took his arms away from Christa. He found another cigarette. They were silent for a moment. Then Christa smoothed back her hair and said:

'I'll go and make you some coffee. You look so terribly tired, my darling.'

He blew a cloud of smoke through his nostrils.

'Yes, I'm just beginning to feel it. I'd love that coffee, and then I must get back to Queen's Lacey and tell Tony.'

'Tell him how sorry I am for my share in hurting him,' she said painfully. 'But I do know that it isn't only *me* he'll regret losing. It'll be the scandal he will object to.'

'Of course I shall give him his chance. He can tell everybody, if he wants to, that I'm *not* really his brother,' said Richard.

Christa looked at him sadly:

'Once you were so proud of your family name and of Queen's Lacey.'

He shrugged his shoulders.

'These things are transient. So perhaps are human emotions. Only I hope you understand I shall have little to offer you.'

'I want nothing but you,' she said.

He gave her his sudden, sweet smile.

'My angelic love! We *must* eat. But I will not touch a penny of the Chalford money.'

'I couldn't care less. We'll get a job together.'

'I shall write to old Jim,' he said. 'He's with his uncle in Winnipeg. I've had a letter from him to say that the farming out there is terrific. I don't see why we shouldn't emigrate. Would you like that?'

'Anything with you, Richard.'

'I don't know what I've done to deserve your love. I only know that I love *you* very much,' he said.

She had reached the doorway but she ran back to him again and he put aside his cigarette and took her in his arms. She whispered the well-remembered words against his lips:

'O, Richard, o mon roi.'

He whispered back:

'Yes – I shall be abandoned by the Universe and yet with you at my side I shall feel that I embrace a new and wonderful world.'

CHAPTER NINE

THE scene between Anthony Chalford and the man whom all his life he had believed to be his brother was short, sharp and singularly disagreeable to them both.

They faced each other in the study on the evening of that same day that Richard and Christa had made their vital decision. Until then, Tony had been out.

Richard told Tony that he had fallen in love with Christa and she with him; that the love had come gradually; that once it had developed he had left home. When he came back they knew that they felt the same and tried to avoid each other. But now he knew that he was no longer closely related to Tony, he did not see why they should go on sacrificing their love.

Tony reacted to this in much the same way that would have been expected of him. At first he was stunned and then became bitterly hostile and suspicious.

'I don't believe a word you say,' he announced to Richard. 'I am convinced you and Christa are guilty and have been carrying on behind my back without scruple. I dare say Mother knew it too, and that's what killed her.'

Richard did not flinch but he went dead white. It was so near the truth and yet untrue. But it was the thing he would have on his conscience for the rest of his life. Death had struck at Julia suddenly and violently before he could explain to her the true nature of that first – and last – embrace.

Tony started to walk up and down the room, insults pouring from his lips, not loudly but coldly and bitingly. He made no allowances for the lack of love and understanding he had given Christa; no allowances for the spiteful and deliberate way in which his mother had tried to break up the marriage. He had no sympathy for anybody but himself. He, alone, was the injured party. The sin, in his opinion, was less heinous than the gossip that would ensue.

'Look what everybody will say,' he kept repeating.

Richard, stony-faced and taut, eyed Tony with grim humour. He was certainly being true to type. Self-centred to the last. Richard had never really cared for this egotistical and pompous young man and now that he knew that Tony was not his brother, he even disliked him.

'Christa did her absolute best for you, and she hadn't a dog's chance. I repeat that she had no intention of giving way to her feelings for me, and that when she left you, she meant to face life alone and I, as you know, planned to go back to my friends in Denmark. Now it is different – I shall join Jimmy in Canada, and hope to take Christa with me.'

Tony went scarlet with anger. With a violence that he rarely showed, he snarled at Richard:

'I thank God that you are not really my brother.'

'I thank God for it, too,' said Richard, with irony.

Tony made a gesture of exasperation.

'How loathsome. I think it was so wonderful of Mother to leave you some of her money, knowing that you were only Aunt Marianne's bastard.'

In another moment Richard would have sprung at him. But only for an instant did he feel blind rage – then it cooled. This was the last time he would ever see Tony. The last night he would sleep under this roof. Already there had been too much harm done, why add an act of violence to it. A doom hung over Queen's Lacey, the very walls seemed impregnated with bitterness, as though the old farmhouse had been waiting ... waiting ... for this tragedy. For tragedy it was, and no one knew better than Richard. But he had only one burning ambition now – to spare Christa from further pain. The woman whom he had believed his mother lay sleeping quietly in the graveyard at Amersham. His own unhappy young mother had long since been consigned to the depths of the ocean. And in sixty or seventy years time they would all be dead and there would be an end of bitterness, of hatred, of tragic love. A new generation would live and love – or hate – at Queen's Lacey.

Richard sighed and said:

'This is scarcely the moment for a free fight, else I would have much pleasure in knocking you down. All I want to do is to tell you that I do not want my share of the money. I shall hand it over, legally, to the Chalford estate, and it can be divided between you and Pip.'

Tony cooled down. He felt slightly better as he heard those words. To know that this man who was no more than a cousin – an alien – was to have laid claim to a large share of the family's money had been almost more than he could bear. Now a grudging admiration came into the eyes. Tony turned upon Richard. He admired few qualities in a man other than being able to accumulate wealth – and keep it – or ride well to hounds.

'Oh, well,' he said, 'you're doing the decent thing there.'

'Believe it or not I have tried to do the decent thing all along,' said Richard. 'I'd like to say here and now that if Christa had shown the slightest desire to give your marriage with her a second chance, I'd have stepped aside. But it has been a total failure and I can't imagine even *you* wishing to carry on with it.'

'Quite so,' said Tony, 'and if you were anybody else I would have no hesitation in saying that I would divorce Christa and cite you, gladly. But *you* going off with my wife – that's pretty unsavoury!'

Richard said:

'I've thought of that. Christa and I both deplore the affair from that angle. I can only suggest that after we've gone, you tell your friends the truth. It all happened long ago, and you don't need to expose the full facts about my poor little mother. Just say that she married in Australia and died when I was born and that my Aunt Julia adopted me, but that it's the first we heard of it. To elope with the wife of a distant cousin won't, perhaps, seem so bad.

'It's all beastly,' muttered Tony. 'It defeats me how Aunt Marianne could have acted the way she did – with Mother's blood in her veins.'

'I don't think my mother could have had very much of Aunt Julia's blood in her veins,' said Richard dryly; 'they were singularly unalike.'

'It's all a bit tough on Pip, too,' added Tony.

Richard agreed with this.

'Yes, it's tough on Pip, but he's young and eventually he'll marry and find his own level. These disasters occur in families from time to time. They appear to be terrific in dimension to the people concerned for a little while. Then they're forgotten. The world moves on. Yesterday's news is of little interest today. It won't be long, my dear Tony, before Christa and I will be forgotten and you no doubt, will settle down and find a new wife. It's Christa's earnest wish as well as mine that you should find happiness.'

'Thanks,' said Tony, 'I don't want your good wishes.'

'That being so,' said Richard, 'I'll say good-bye. I'm packed and I'll clear out lock, stock and barrel, first thing in the morning, taking with me only my own possessions.'

Tony looked gloomily out of the window. The curtains were not drawn. It was a fine night. Moonlight silvered the walnut tree.

216

He thought of all the work there was to do on the farm – the jobs at which Richard was so useful. He, Tony, would have a hell of a lot to do until he could replace Richard permanently. Tony's mind teemed with the financial problems ahead despite the sudden and welcome addition of Richard's money to his own. Not once did he turn his thoughts to Christa. Richard, watching him, knew it. The fundamental coldness and self-seeking, the lack of real heart in Tony were things that sickened Richard. How could any man pity him? He had no pity for the young tender girl whom he had treated like all his possessions – without tenderness. And he was so self-righteous. Not once in the years ahead would Tony blame *himself* for having himself destroyed the eager love that Christa had brought to her marriage.

Richard looked around the untidy room with all the books; the big roll-top desk littered with papers and ledgers; the portrait of their grandfather which hung over the fireplace. Yes, even though Richard was no longer Tony's brother, this was still his grandfather. Father to both Julia and Marianne. And this was the last time that he, Richard, would ever talk to Tony in here where they had so often discussed the workings of the farm. This was the absolute end of Queen's Lacey for *him*.

At this moment Tessa nosed her way through the half-open door and bounded up to Richard. He gathered the warm, affectionate spaniel into his arms and began to fondle the silky ears. There were burrs clinging to them. She had been hunting. He murmured:

'Dear old Tessa, you shall come with me. I shan't leave you behind, old girl.'

He glanced over the dog's head at Tony who was lighting a cigarette, scowling at nothing.

'I'm sorry, Tony,' he said, 'I know it's damned unpleasant and awkward. But by all means let it be known to those who know us that you and I are not brothers. It will be a nine days' wonder, but people like Ursula Corby won't desert you. On the contrary she'll come and tell you what a bad fellow I am and how welcome you will always be in her house and everybody will be on your side.'

'Rightfully,' said Tony in his stiffest voice.

Richard gave a sardonic grin.

'It must be nice,' he said, 'to know that one is so right in all ways and at all times. Do human emotions never concern you? Do Christa's feelings, for instance, not concern you now?'

'Certainly not,' said Tony, 'she can go to hell as far as I am concerned, and you with her.'

Richard stood up. He gave another smile.

'Okay, if that's the way you want it, we'd be glad if you'd petition for a divorce as soon as you can. The thing is that there's no evidence at the moment because there are no guilty parties. But we'll let you have the evidence. There seems no other way out.'

'I'll see Mr. Parsons in the morning,' said Tony.

'I trust you won't put in a claim for damages,' added Richard, 'as I've handed all my money over to you.'

Tony suddenly realized that he was being made to feel a fool – and not a very nice one. For the first time he was conscious of his own guilt in this affair, remembering, uncomfortably, all that had transpired between himself and Christa over the last two years. His mother's share in it too. . . . If indeed Richard and Christa had felt 'like that' about each other, they had certainly put up a battle against it. He couldn't deny that. But he was furiously angry about the whole thing, mainly because he had made a mistake in marrying Christa and Tony did not like making mistakes.

'I've had enough of this conversation, I'm going to bed,' he said. 'I repeat that I'm thankful that you're not my brother.'

'Once more,' said Richard, 'I reciprocate your feelings.'

Tony walked out with a lack of dignity that he rarely showed, slamming the door after him. For a moment Richard stood still, automatically picking burrs out of Tessa's long ears. He must send a cable to Jimmy. Thank God he had saved a bit this last year and mde a few personal investments. He had enough capital that he could call his own and justifiably draw it from the bank before signing away the main capital over to Tony and Pip. He and Christa would need *something* before he got established in a new life – a new world.

Suddenly the door opened and Pip looked in. His fair hair was tousled as though he had just been out in the wind. His face reddened as he saw Richard.

'Oh, come in, Pip, I want to talk to you,' said Richard.

Pip walked in. He stared at Richard. Richard gave a brief laugh.

'Don't look at me like that, I'm not a waxwork in Madame Tussaud's.'

'I say!' exclaimed Pip, 'what in the name of fortune is this all about? I can't make head or tail of what Tony's been telling me.'

'Sit down and hear my version,' said Richard.

Pip seated himself. Richard looked with affection at Pip's untidy hair and fair, chubby face. If he regretted leaving any-body at Queen's Lacey it was Pip. *Cousin Pip*. This knowledge that he had no brothers now, wanted some getting used to. When he had finished telling Pip about Christa and himself and straightened out the whole strange story, Pip sucked in his breath.

'Good *God*!' he ejaculated.

'Yes,' said Richard, 'I dare say it's very surprising to you. It was a shock to me, as you can imagine.'

'It's absolutely *staggering*, Rich.'

'Nevertheless true. Mother – Aunt Julia to me – just didn't destroy the evidence and, of course, now I'm thankful she didn't. It means that I can at least take Christa with me when I go away. Before, I couldn't. It was too difficult.'

'I don't know what to say,' Pip said.

'I shouldn't say anything. It's much too involved. Just try to accept it and don't think too hardly of me. I've always been very attached to you, you know, and I always will be.'

Some of Pip's healthy colour faded now. He looked pathetic. He said:

'Well, it's damned awful. I wish Mother had destroyed the evidence. I shall never get used to thinking of you as a cousin. You were always the brother I liked best and I don't mind saying so, now.'

Richard's eyes softened.

'Thanks, Pip, it makes good hearing. Tony and I haven't had a very pleasant discussion and I admit I ought to be the perfect hero and walk out alone. But I can't. The rest of the world will say some very hard things about us. Christa needs me as much as I need her. I should like to think that you understand and won't feel too antagonistic towards us.'

After a pause, Pip said:

'I don't understand these things but I can imagine how you and Christa feel. Even Mother used to say that you and Christa were more suited than Christa and Tony. You never *were* like Tony or me. Now that I know, I'm not really surprised that you aren't our brother.'

'Well, Pip, I'm sorry to leave you to the unpleasantness, but as I said to Tony – it won't last long, and it's Christa I'm thinking about now. She deserves some kind of happiness. She's absolutely at the end. She can't take much more. I must look after her.'

'I'm glad about that,' said Pip, with an embarrassed cough. 'I really am. I always thought she had a hell of a time with Tony – and poor Mother.'

'She did,' said Richard grimly.

'I wish you weren't both going so far away,' said Pip miserably. 'Nothing's going to be the same at Queen's Lacey any more. Even Mitza says she will only stay here till you and Christa send for her. She wants to emigrate with you, she says.'

'We can't afford to take Mitza with us, but I hope *you'll* come and see us in Canada.'

'I jolly well will. I'll take all my holiday all at once and fly out to you.'

'In spite of all the things that will be said about us?'

'Yes,' said Pip.

Richard reddened slightly with an emotion that he tried not to show, but he held out a hand which the boy whom he still thought of as a young brother, took and shook fervently.

After that there was no more to be said. But as Richard went up to his room – he paused outside the door of the bedroom that had been Julia Chalford's. Suddenly on an impulse he opened it and looked into the empty room. It had a ghostly air. Bed and furniture were covered in dust sheets. Richard stared through the dimness at that bed in which he had so often seen *her* lying; he thought of the days when he had been a small boy and she had been kind to him; of her justness and her efficiency as well as her failings, and of the final hatred that had destroyed her. He said under his breath:

'Good-bye, Aunt Julia, thank you for all you did for me, but you know, now, don't you, that it was your hatred, not my wrong-doing that finished your life that ghastly night. Forgive me, as Christa and I forgive you.'

Then, as though a sudden chill struck him, he shivered, left the empty, silent room and hurriedly closed the door behind him. It was not only the closing of a door, he thought, but the farewell to the past. Tomorrow a new life would begin.

CHAPTER TEN

Two years later.

On a brisk October morning four people stood in the sitting-room of Hillside Farm, sipping a glass of sherry and chatting. An air of excitement sat upon them. Mr. Thornton, grown a little stouter and greyer, wore a morning coat that belonged to his grandfather and a waistcoat that was buttoned so tight it looked as though it might burst. Aunt Wyn wore the same dress that she had bought for Anthony Chalford's wedding to Christa Morley, five years ago. She was snow-white now, and her face looked more weather-beaten than ever but it held an expression of supreme satisfaction just now, because, eyes raised to the ceiling, she was listening to the crying of a baby. It was Susan's daughter, aged eighteen months, and Great Aunt Wyn worshipped her. A lovely little girl with the flaxen curls of her Austrian father and Susan's dark eyes. She had been christened after Susan's mother. At the moment she was in a temper because she did not want to be put down to sleep and the young daily girl who came to help out in the mornings was not as good with her as Susan. Susan, however, was waiting with the rest of them for the taxi that was to take them into Amersham to the wedding of Anthony Chalford to Ursula Corby.

Anton, Susan's husband, was also here. He had no morning clothes but wore a dark blue suit, with a carnation in his button-hole. He was a finely built man of genial countenance, with soft, kindly eyes. He and Susan seemed on the best of terms and, in Aunt Wyn's opinion, that marriage which had so shocked Joe and herself in the beginning, had turned out quite for the best.

Susan was a different person these days. A little plumper, a good deal better tempered. Anton was getting on well, too. He was head-man now on the farm on which he had been employed since he married Susan. They had a nice little cottage and the whole family had been reunited soon after Susan's baby was born. Neither her father nor her aunt had been able to resist that child. There was talk now of Joe Thornton retiring and of Anton and Susan returning to farm Hillside, which, eventually, Anton and Susan would inherit.

'Just fancy,' said Aunt Wyn, 'at this moment, we went to Tony's first wedding and now we are off to his second.'

'Well, let's hope he'll make a better go of this one than he did of the other,' put in Mr. Thornton.

Susan chimed in:

'I bet he will. He's such a snob. Now he's going to have a titled woman for his wife and be right in her set, he'll make a much bigger effort than he did for poor Christa.'

Anton said, with his slight, attractive accent:

'What was she like – the first Mrs. Anthony?'

'Perfectly beautiful, wasn't she, Aunt Wyn?' said Susan, turning to her aunt.

'She was smart and pretty and all that,' said Aunt Wyn, grudgingly, 'but I don't approve of what she did.'

'Well, I do,' said Susan. 'I've always hated Tony, but I used to have a frightful crush on Richard. I don't blame her for running away with him, once she found out he was only a cousin.'

The Austrian patted her shoulder.

'Anton knows that you were once in love with Mr. Chalford. But now you are my good little wife.'

'You're a good old thing, too,' said Susan, and pressed his arm.

'All the same,' put in Mr. Thornton, 'it was a scandalous affair. A man going off with his brother's wife.'

'Do remember what I've just said, Daddy. Tony was *not* his brother – he was only his cousin.'

Mr. Thornton drained his sherry glass.

'I've never understood that business. Never heard of such a thing. It is wrong, anyhow.'

'Well, anyhow, here we are,' said Susan, 'and Tony is bringing a new wife to Queen's Lacey. She's got him right under her thumb – everybody says so. One of my hunting friends dined at Forty Green the other night and said he'd become an absolute "yes man" to Ursula. She'll rule the roost at Queen's Lacey just like Mrs. Chalford did – you'll see.'

'It seems to me in these days that all the women are ruling the roost,' announced Mr. Thornton gloomily. 'But I reckon Anthony Chalford will be quite a match for My Lady.'

'Oh, I think they'll have a high old time,' said Susan, 'packets of dough between 'em and they'll give smashing parties and buy terrific horses and be the life and soul of the hunt.'

'Has anybody ever heard about those other two?' asked Aunt

Wyn suddenly. 'I've been trying to get news but no one in the district seems to know anything, except that they went to Winnipeg.'

'Well, *I* know,' said Susan, 'because I met Pip yesterday, and we had a long chat. Incidentally, he's not staying at Queen's Lacey.'

'You mean he doesn't relish playing second fiddle to the second wife?' asked her father.

'Quite so. He's going out to Canada, too.'

'Oh, I'm sorry to hear that,' said Aunt Wyn. 'I rather liked Pip.'

'Richard was always his favourite brother,' said Susan. 'He was bullied and nagged by Tony.'

'That taxi ought to be here,' said Mr. Thornton.

'Oh, dear, I wish I hadn't said we'd go,' said Aunt Wyn. 'It's going to be such a posh affair. I shall feel so shabby. They say that church at Amersham will be full to overflowing. Susan dear, you haven't told us yet what Pip said about Christa, and Richard.'

'Well, he'd had a long letter from Christa and she said that she and Richard have quite a nice farm and although they really prefer England, they are settling down and are divinely happy out in Canada. She sent Pip a cutting from a Winnipeg paper. I asked him to lend it to me – I shall give it back to him at the wedding, but I thought I *must* show you. It's given me quite a thrill.'

Aunt Wyn, filled with curiosity, grabbed the cutting, put on her spectacles and read aloud:

'CHALFORD, on September 2nd at the Queen Elizabeth Hospital for Women, Winnipeg, to Richard and Christa Chalford, a son – Stephen Richard.'

Aunt Wyn passed the cutting on to her brother and uttered an exclamation:

'I never! Well, that *is* news, fancy those two with a son. What *ever* relation is that child to Tony and Pip?'

'Cousin twice removed,' said Susan, and added, 'I can imagine how terribly happy Christa must be. I know I was happy when my little Greta was born. It just makes all the difference.'

'I *never!*' repeated Aunt Wyn.

Susan walked to the window. She looked through the trees at

the boundary line between her father's farm and Queen's Lacey. She thought of the days long ago when as a child she had run through the trees to meet the three Chalford boys and play with them. How afraid she had always been of Julia Chalford. How often Tony had made her cry, and what a hero Richard had seemed in her youthful eyes. She thought, too, of the later years when she had grown to love him and how her love had become a terrible burden of frustration and despair.

All that was past. She was at peace with herself. She loved Anton and their little daughter.

Richard was a farmer in Winnipeg. Christa of the silver hair and golden eyes was his wife. They had an infant son called Stephen. How strange – how very strange it all seemed! Yet how nice to know that what had started out as a tragedy was ending happily. It had all been for the best.

For the first year after those two had gone, Tony Chalford had undoubtedly suffered. He had loathed the divorce – the gossip – the whole affair. But now the bells in Amersham were about to ring out for his marriage to Ursula Corby. She had always wanted him and she would suit him much better than Christa had ever done.

Susan turned from the window and smiled at the family.

'I hear a taxi coming,' she said. 'Let's go and see old Tony getting tied up again.'

Her father handed her the cutting from the Winnipeg newspaper. Remembering what it was about, Susan gave a little secret smile. It was nice knowing about Richard and Christa and their baby. A nice beginning to the festive day.